Bantam Books by Louis L'Amour
ASK YOUR BOOKSELLER FOR THE BOOKS YOU HAVE MISSED.

NOVELS
Bendigo Shafter
Borden Chantry
Brionne
The Broken Gun
The Burning Hills
The Californios
Callaghen
Catlow
Chancy
The Cherokee Trail
Comstock Lode
Conagher
Crossfire Trail
Dark Canyon
Down the Long Hills
The Empty Land
Fair Blows the Wind
Fallon
The Ferguson Rifle
The First Fast Draw
Flint
Guns of the Timberlands
Hanging Woman Creek
The Haunted Mesa
Heller with a Gun
The High Graders
High Lonesome
Hondo
How the West Was Won
The Iron Marshal
The Key-Lock Man
Kid Rodelo
Kilkenny
Killoe
Kilrone
Kiowa Trail
Last of the Breed
Last Stand at Papago
 Wells
The Lonesome Gods
The Man Called Noon
The Man from Skibbereen
The Man from the
 Broken Hills
Matagorda
Milo Talon
The Mountain Valley
 War

North to the Rails
Over on the Dry Side
Passin' Through
The Proving Trail
The Quick and the Dead
Radigan
Reilly's Luck
The Rider of Lost
 Creek
Rivers West
The Shadow Riders
Shalako
Showdown at Yellow
 Butte
Silver Canyon
Sitka
Son of a Wanted Man
Taggart
The Tall Stranger
To Tame a Land
Tucker
Under the Sweetwater
 Rim
Utah Blaine
The Walking Drum
Westward the Tide
Where the Long Grass
 Blows

**SHORT STORY
COLLECTIONS**
Beyond the Great
 Snow Mountains
Bowdrie
Bowdrie's Law
Buckskin Run
Dutchman's Flat
End of the Drive
The Hills of Homicide
Law of the Desert Born
Long Ride Home
Lonigan
May There Be a Road
Monument Rock
Night over the Solomons
Off the Mangrove Coast
The Outlaws of Mesquite
The Rider of the Ruby
 Hills

Riding for the Brand
The Strong Shall Live
The Trail to Crazy Man
Valley of the Sun
War Party
West from Singapore
West of Dodge
With These Hands
Yondering

SACKETT TITLES
Sackett's Land
To the Far Blue Mountains
The Warrior's Path
Jubal Sackett
Ride the River
The Daybreakers
Sackett
Lando
Mojave Crossing
Mustang Man
The Lonely Men
Galloway
Treasure Mountain
Lonely on the Mountain
Ride the Dark Trail
The Sackett Brand
The Sky-Liners

**THE HOPALONG
CASSIDY NOVELS**
The Riders of High Rock
The Rustlers of West Fork
The Trail to Seven Pines
Trouble Shooter

NONFICTION
Education of a Wandering
 Man
Frontier
THE SACKETT COMPANION:
 A Personal Guide to
 the Sackett Novels
A TRAIL OF MEMORIES:
 The Quotations of Louis
 L'Amour, compiled by
 Angelique L'Amour

POETRY
Smoke from This Altar

WITH THESE HANDS

LOUIS L'AMOUR

BANTAM BOOKS

NEW YORK   TORONTO   LONDON   SYDNEY   AUCKLAND

WITH THESE HANDS
A Bantam Book

PUBLISHING HISTORY
Bantam hardcover edition published May 2002
Bantam mass market edition / May 2003

Published by Bantam Dell
A Division of Random House, Inc.
New York, New York

Library of Congress Catalog Card Number: 2001056730

Bantam Books and the rooster colophon are registered trade-
marks of Random House, Inc.

ISBN 0-553-58491-X

Manufactured in the United States of America
Published simultaneously in Canada

OPM   10 9 8 7 6 5 4

CONTENTS

WITH THESE
HANDS

FIGHTERS
DON'T DIVE

Nimbly "Flash" Moran parried a jab and went in fast with a left to the wind. Stepping back, he let Breen get a breath. Then he flicked out a couple of lefts, put over an inside right, and as Breen bobbed into a crouch and tried to get in close, he clinched and tied him up.

They broke, and Breen came in with a flurry of punches that slid off Moran's arms and shoulders. Then Moran's hip moved and a left hook that traveled no more than four inches snapped Breen up to his toes. Breen caught himself and staggered away.

The gong sounded, and Flash Moran paused . . . then he slapped Breen on the shoulder and trotted to his corner.

Two men were standing there with Dan Kelly. He knew them both by sight. Mike McKracken, an ex-wrestler turned gambler, and "Blackie" Marollo, small-time racketeer.

"You're lookin' good, kid," Kelly said. "This next one you should win."

"You might, but you won't stop him," Marollo said, looking up. "Nobody knocks Barnaby out."

McKracken studied Moran with cold eyes. "You got paper on him?" he asked Kelly.

"I don't need any," Kelly said. "We work together."

"Well, if you had it, I'd buy a piece," McKracken said. "I need a good middle. Money in that class now with Turner, Schmidt, and Demeray comin' up."

"I wouldn't sell," Kelly said. "We're friends."

"Yeah?" Marollo shot him a glance. "I'd hate to see somebody come along an' offer him a grand to sign up. You'd see how much friendship matters."

Flash Moran looked at Marollo, then dropped to the floor beside him.

"You've a rotten way of looking at things, Blackie," he said. "We aren't all dishonest, you know!"

"You're pretty free with that lip of yours, kid. Maybe somebody will button it up one day. For keeps."

Moran turned, pulled his robe around him, and started for the dressing room.

"That kid better get wise or he won't last," Marollo said. "You tell him, Kelly."

"You told him yourself," Kelly replied. "Didn't you?"

Dan Kelly turned and walked up the aisle after Flash. Behind him, he heard Marollo's voice.

"That punk. I'll fix him!"

"You won't do nothin' of the kind," he heard McKracken growl. "We got too much ridin' on this to risk trouble."

The voices faded out with the distance, and Kelly scowled.

In the dressing room the trainer spoke up. "Keep an eye on Marollo, kid, he's all bad."

"To the devil with him," Flash said. "I know his kind. He's tough as long as he has all the odds with him. When the chips are down, he'll turn yellow."

"Maybe. But you'll never see him when he doesn't have the difference." Kelly looked at him curiously. "Where you goin' tonight?"

"Out. Just lookin' around. Say, Dan, what do you suppose is bringing Marollo and McKracken around to the gym? One or the other's been down here five days in a row."

"Probably sizing you up, figurin' the odds." Kelly knotted his tie. "Well. I've got a date with the wife."

Shorty Kinsella was lining up a shot when Flash Moran walked into Brescia's Pool Room. He looked up.

"Hiya, champ! How's about a game? I'm just winding up this one."

He put the last ball in the corner and walked around, holding out his hand.

Moran took it, grinning. "Sure, I'll play."

"Better watch him." The man who Kinsella had played handed Shorty five dollars. "He's good!"

Moran racked the balls. "Say, what do you know about Blackie Marollo?"

Shorty's smile went out like a light. He broke, and ran up four, then looked at Flash thoughtfully.

"Nothing. You shouldn't know anything either."

Flash Moran watched Kinsella make a three-cushion shot. "The guy's got me wondering."

"Well, don't. Not if you want to stay healthy."

Flash Moran finished his game and went out. He paused on the corner and peeled the paper from a stick of chewing gum. If even Shorty Kinsella was afraid to talk about Marollo, there must be more behind Blackie than he'd thought.

Suddenly, there was a man standing beside him. He was almost as tall as Moran, though somewhat heavier. He lit a cigarette, and as the match flared, he looked up at Flash over his cupped hands.

"Listen, sonny," he said, "I heard you askin' a lot of questions about Marollo in there. Well, cut it out . . . get me?"

"Roll your hoop." Flash turned easily. "I'll ask what I want, when I want."

The man's hand flashed, and in that instant of time, Flash saw the blackjack. He threw up his left arm and blocked the blow by catching the man's forearm on his own. Then he struck. It was a right, short and wicked, into the man's wind.

Moran had unlimbered a hard blow, and the man was in no shape to take it. With a grunt he started to fall and then Moran slashed him across the face with the edge of his hand. He felt the man's nose crunch, and as the fellow dropped, Moran stepped over him and walked around the corner.

So, Blackie Marollo didn't like to be talked about? Just who was Blackie Marollo, anyway?

Up the street there was a Chinese joint, a place he knew. He went in, found an empty booth, and sat down. He was scowling, thoughtfully. There would be trouble. He had busted up one of Marollo's boys, and he imagined Blackie wouldn't like it. If a guy had to hire muscle, he had to keep their reputation. If it was learned they could be pushed around with impunity, everybody would be trying it.

Moran was eating a bowl of chicken and fried rice when the girl came in. She was slim, long-legged, and blond, and when she smiled her eyes twinkled merrily. She had another girl with her, a slender brunette.

She turned, glancing around the room, and their eyes met. Too late he tried to look indifferent, but his face burned and he knew his embarrassment had shown. She smiled and turned back to the other girl.

When the girls sat down, she was facing him. He cursed himself for a fool, a conceited fool to be thinking a girl of her quality would care to know anyone who earned his living in the ring.

Several times Moran's and the girl's eyes caught. Then Gow came into the room and saw him. Immediately, he hurried over, his face all smiles.

"Hiya, Flash! Long time no see!"

"I've been meaning to come in."

"How are you going to do with the Soldier?"

"Think I'll beat him. How're the odds?"

"Six to five. He's the favorite. Genzel was in, the fellow who runs that bar around the corner. He said it was a cinch to go the limit."

For an instant, Flash was jolted out of his thinking of the girl.

"Genzel? Isn't he one of Marollo's boys?"

"Yes. And Marollo usually knows . . . he doesn't know about this one, does he, Flash?"

"Hell no!" he paused a moment. "Gow," he said. "Take a note to that girl over there for me, will you?"

Hurriedly, Moran scribbled a few lines.

I'd like to talk to you. If the answer is yes, nod your head when you look at me. If it is no, the evening will still be lovely, even if not so exciting.

REILLY MORAN

Gow shrugged, took the note, and wandered across the room. Flash Moran felt himself turning crimson and looked down. When he looked up, his eyes met those of the girl, and she nodded, briefly.

He got up, straightened his coat, and walked across the room. As he came alongside the table, she looked up.

"I'm Ruth Connor," she said, smiling. "This is Hazel Dickens. Do you always eat alone?"

She moved over and made a place for him beside her in the booth.

"No," he said. "Usually with a friend."

"Girl?" Ruth asked, smiling at him.

"No. My business partner. We're back here from San Francisco."

"Are you?" she asked. "I lived there for a while. On Nob Hill."

"Oh." He grinned suddenly. "Not me. I came from the Mission District."

Ruth looked at him curiously.

"You did? Why, that's where all those tough Irish boys come from. You don't look like them!"

He looked at her again. "Well, maybe I don't," he said quietly. "You can come a long way from the Mission District without getting out of it, though. But probably that's just what I am . . . one of those tough Irish boys."

For a moment, their eyes held. He stared at her, confused and a little angry. She seemed to enjoy getting a rise out of him but she didn't seem to really be putting him down. So many times with girls this very thing happened, it was like a test but it was one he kept failing. Her friend stayed quiet and he was unsure of what to say or how to proceed.

The door opened then and three men came in. Flash grew cold all over.

"Sit still," he told the girls softly. "No matter what happens."

The men came over. Two of them had their hands in their coat pockets. They looked like Italians.

"Get up." The man who spoke was short, very dark, and his face was pockmarked. "Get up now."

Flash got to his feet slowly. His mind was working swiftly. If he'd been alone, in spite of it being Gow's place, he might have swung.

"Okay," Moran said, pleasantly. "I was expecting you."

The dark man looked at him. "You was expectin' us?"

"Yes," Flash said. "When I had to slug your friend, I expected there would be trouble. So I called the D.A.'s office."

"You did what?" There was consternation in the man's voice.

"He's bluffing, Rice," one of the men said. "It's a bluff."

"We'll see!" Rice's eyes gleamed with cunning. "Tell us what the D.A.'s number is."

Flash felt a sudden emptiness inside.

"It was . . ." He scowled, as if trying to remember . . . "It was seven . . . something."

"No," Ruth Connor said suddenly. "Seven was the second number. It was three-seven-four-four-seven."

Rice's eyes dropped to the girl, swept her figure with an appraising glance.

"Okay," he said, his eyes still on the girl. "Check it, Polack."

The man addressed, biggest of the three, turned to the phone book, and leafed through it quickly. He looked up.

"Hey, boss," he said triumphantly. "He's wrong, the number is different."

"It was his home phone," Ruth said, speaking up. "He called him at home. No one is in the office at this time of the night."

Rice stared at her. "You're buttin' in too much, babe," he said. "If I were you, I'd keep my trap shut."

The Polack came over, carrying the book.

"She's right, Rice. It's Gracie three-seven-four-four-seven!"

Rice stared at Moran, his eyes ugly. "We'll be waitin', see? I know your name is Reilly."

"My name is Reilly Moran," Flash said. "Just so you know where to look."

"Flash Moran?" Rice's eyes widened and his face went white. ". . . who fights Barnaby the day after tomorrow?"

"Right," Moran said, surprised at the effect of his name. Rice backed up hurriedly.

"Let's get out of here," he said.

Without another word, the three hoodlums turned and hurried out.

For a full minute, Moran stared after them. Now what was up? No man with a gun in his pocket is going to be afraid of a fighter. If they'd been afraid they wouldn't have come. They could tell by what he did to the first man that he was no pantywaist. Moran shook his head in bewilderment and sat down.

Ruth and the other girl were staring at Moran.

"Thanks," he said. "That was a bad spot. I had no idea what the district attorney's number was."

"So you're Flash Moran, the prizefighter?" Ruth Connor said slowly. There was a different expression in her eyes. "Why were those men so frightened when they heard your name?"

"They weren't," he said. "I can't understand why they acted that way." He stood up. "I guess I'd better be taking you home. It isn't safe now."

They stood up.

"Don't bother," Ruth Connor said, "I'm calling for my own car." She held out her hand. "It's been nice."

He looked into her eyes for a moment, then he felt something go out of him.

"All right," he said. "Good night."

He turned and walked swiftly outside.

. . .

Dan Kelly was sitting up in the armchair when Moran came into the apartment that they'd rented, his wife was already in bed. The old trainer looked up at him out of his shrewd blue eyes. He didn't have to look long.

"What's the matter?"

Briefly, Moran told him. At the end, Kelly whistled softly.

"Dixie Rice, was it? He's bad, son. All bad. I didn't know Rice was working for Blackie. Times have changed."

Moran looked at him. "I wonder who that girl was?" he mused. "She was beautiful! The loveliest girl I ever saw."

"She knew the D.A.'s number?" Dan scowled. "Might be a newspaper reporter."

"Well, what about tomorrow?"

"Tomorrow? You skip rope three rounds, shadowbox three rounds, and take some body exercise. That's all. Then rest all you can."

In the morning, Flash Moran slept late. It was unusual for him, but he forced himself to stay in bed and rest. Finally, he got up and shaved. It would be his last shave before the fight. He always went into the ring with a day's growth of beard.

He was putting away his shaving kit when there was a rap on the door. Dan Kelly had gone, and Moran was alone. He hesitated only an instant, remembering Blackie Marollo, then he stepped over and opened the door. It was hardly open before a man stepped in and closed it behind him.

"Well?" Moran said. "Who the hell are you?"

"I'm Soldier Barnaby, Flash." For an instant, Flash looked at him, noting the hard, capable face, the black hair and swarthy cheeks, the broad, powerful shoulders, and the big hands. The Soldier pulled a chair over and sat astride of it. "We got to have a talk."

"If you want to work it, don't talk to me. I don't play the game. I just fight."

The Soldier grinned. "I fight, too. I don't want a setup. Not exactly."

He was studying Moran coolly. "You know," he said. "You'll make a good champ—if you play it on the level." He hesitated a moment. "You know Blackie Marollo?"

Flash Moran's eyes hardened a little. "Sure. Why?"

"Marollo's got something on my wife." The Soldier leaned forward. "She's a square kid, but she slipped up once, and Blackie knows it. If I don't do what he says, he's going to squeal. It means my wife goes to the pen . . . I got two kids."

"And what does he want?"

"Marollo says I go down before the tenth round. He says I take it on the chin. Not an easy one, as he wants it to be the McCoy."

Flash Moran sat down suddenly. This explained a lot of things. It explained why Marollo was watching him. It explained why, when they found out who he was, the gangsters had backed out of beating him up.

"Well, why see me?" Moran asked. "What can I do?"

"One thing—don't stop me before the tenth, even if you get a chance."

"Not before the tenth? But I thought you said it was in the tank?"

"I talked it over with the wife. I told her I was going sooner or later anyway, that you were a good kid and would make a good champ, and that I'd sooner you had it than the others. I knew you were on the level, knew Dan was, too.

"But she said, nothing doing. She said that she'd take the rap rather than see this happen. That if I lose this fight for Blackie, he'll force me to do other things. Eventually, I'll have to kill him or become a crook.

"She told me to come and see you. She said that not only must I not take a dive, but there mustn't be any chance that he'd think I took it.

"Then she asked me if I could beat you." Barnaby looked at Flash Moran and grinned. "Well, you know how fighters are. I told her I could! Then she asked me if it was a cinch and I told her no, that the betting was wrong. It should be even money, or you a slight favorite. You're six years younger than me, and you are coming up. I'm not. That makes a lot of difference."

Flash Moran looked at the floor. He could see it all. This quiet, simple man, talking quietly with his wife over the breakfast table, and deciding to do the honest thing.

"Then you want me to ease up on you in case I have you on the spot?" he said slowly. "That's a lot to ask, Soldier. You aren't going to be easy, you know. You're tough. Lots of times it's easier to knock a man out in the first round than any other time in the fight. Get him before he's warmed up."

"That's right. But you ain't going to get me in the first, kid. You might tag me about eight or nine, though. That's what I want to prevent.

"You see, the thing that makes guys like Marollo dangerous is money. They got money to buy killers. Well, I happen to know that Marollo has his shirt on this fight. He figures it's a cinch. He knows I'm crazy about my wife. He doesn't know that she'd do anything rather than let me do something dishonest. One bad mark against the family is enough, she says. But if we can make Marollo lose, we got a chance."

Flash Moran nodded. "I see. Yes, you've got something, all right."

"I think I can beat you, Moran. I'm honest about that. If I can, I will. I came because I'm not so dumb as to believe I can't lose."

"Okay." Moran stood up. "Okay, it's a deal. They want you down before the tenth. I won't try to knock you out until the eleventh round. No matter how hard it is, I'll hold you up!"

The Soldier grinned. "Right, then it's every man for himself." He thrust out his hand. "Anyway, Flash, no matter who wins, Blackie Marollo loses. Okay?"

"Okay!"

When Barnaby was gone, Flash Moran sat down and pulled on his shoes. It might be a gag. It might be a stall to get him to lay off. It would be good, all right. They all knew he was a fast starter. They all knew his best chance would be quick.

Yet Barnaby's story fitted the situation too well. It was the only explanation for a lot of things. And, he remembered, both Marollo and McKracken had been talking the impossibility of a knockout. That would be right in line. They would do all they could to inspire confidence in the fight going the distance, and then bet that it wouldn't go ten rounds.

He took his final workout, and then left the gym. It was late afternoon, and he walked slowly down the street. He'd never worked a fight. It wasn't going to be easy, for all his life he had thrown his punches with purpose. Well, he thought ruefully, it would probably take him all of ten rounds to take the Soldier, anyway.

Suddenly, he remembered . . . the Soldier had made no such promise in return.

He turned a corner, and found himself face-to-face with Ruth Connor, walking alone.

Her eyes widened as she saw him, and she made as if to pass, but he stopped her.

"Hello," he said. "Weren't you going to speak?"

"Yes," she said. "I was going to speak, but I wasn't going to stop."

"You don't approve of fighters?" he asked, quizzically.

"I approve of honest ones!" she said and turned as if to go by. He put his hand on her sleeve.

"What do you mean? I'm an honest fighter, and always have been."

She looked at him.

"I'd like to believe that," she said sincerely, "I really would. But I've heard your fight tonight was fixed."

"Fixed? How was it supposed to go? What was to happen?"

"I don't know. I heard my uncle talking to some men in his office, and they were discussing this fight, and one of them said it was all framed up."

"You didn't hear anything else?" he asked.

"Yes, when I come to think of it, I did! They said you were to win by a knockout in the twelfth round."

"In the twelfth?" he asked, incredulous. "Why, that doesn't make sense."

She glanced at her watch.

"I must go," she said quickly. "It's very late. . . ."

"Ruth!"

"Yes?"

"Will you reserve your opinion for a few hours? A little while?"

Their eyes met, then she looked away.

"All right. I'll wait and see." She looked back at him again, then held out her hand. "In the meantime—good luck!"

Reilly Moran walked all the way back to the hotel and told Dan Kelly the whole story.

Kelly was puzzled.

"Gosh, kid! I can't figure it. The setup looks to me like a double double-cross anyway you look at it. Maybe the story about Barnaby's wife is all hokum. Maybe it ain't true. It sounds like Blackie Marollo all right. I don't know what to advise you. I'd go out and stop him quick, only we know you've got blamed small chance of that."

"Supposing the fight went the distance . . . all fifteen rounds?" Flash said thoughtfully. "Suppose I didn't stop him?"

"Then neither way would pay off and the average bettor would come out on top. That's not a bad idea, but hard, Flash, damned hard to pull off."

The preliminaries were over before Flash Moran walked into the coliseum. He went to his dressing room and began bandaging his hands. It was a job he always did for himself, and a job he liked doing. He could hear the dull roar of the crowd, smell the strong smell of wintergreen and the less strong, but just as prevalent, odor of sweat-soaked leather.

Dan Kelly worked over him quietly, tying on his gloves, and Sam Goss gathered up the bucket and the bottles.

Flash Moran never had felt like this about a fight before. When he climbed through the ropes, hearing the deep-throated roar of the crowd, he knew that something was wrong. It was, he was sure, stemming from his own uncertainty. All he'd ever had to do was to get in there and fight. There had been no other thought but to win. Tonight his mind was in turmoil. Was Soldier Barnaby on the level? Or was he double-crossing him as well as Marollo?

What if he threw over his bargain and stopped the Soldier quick? That would hit the customers who were betting against a quick knockout hard. It would make money for Blackie Marollo. On the other hand, he would be betraying his promise to Barnaby.

When they came together in the center of the ring, he stared at the floor. He could see Barnaby's feet, and the strong, brown muscular ankles and calves. Idly, he remembered what Dan Kelly had told him one day.

"Remember, kid, anytime you see two fighters meet in the center of the ring, and one of them looks at the other one, or tries to look him in the eye, bet on the other guy. The fellow who looks at his opponent is uncertain."

They wheeled and trotted back to their corners, and then the bell rang.

He went out fast and led with a left. It landed, lightly, and he stepped in and hooked. That landed solidly and he took a left himself before he tied the Soldier up. This preliminary sparring never meant anything. It was just one of those things you had to go through.

Barnaby was hard as nails, he could see that, and fast on his feet. . . . A blow exploded on Moran's chin and he felt himself reel, falling back against the ropes.

The Soldier was coming in briskly, and Moran rolled away, straightened up, and then stopped Barnaby's charge with a pistonlike left. He stepped in, took a hard punch, but slipped another and smashed a wicked right to the heart.

He was inside then and he rolled with the punch and hooked his left to the ribs, and then with his head outside the Soldier's right he whipped his own right to Barnaby's head.

It was fast, that first round, and both men were punching. No matter what happened later, Moran decided, he was still going to soften Barnaby up plenty.

When the bell rang for the second, Flash Moran ran out and missed a left then fell into a clinch. As they broke, he hooked twice to the Soldier's head, but the Soldier got inside with a right. Moran smashed both hands to the body and worked around. The Soldier fought oddly, carried himself in a peculiar manner.

It was midway through the third when Flash figured it out. The Soldier was a natural southpaw who had been taught to fight right-handed. His stance was still not quite what a natural right-hander's would be, but the training had left him a wicked two-handed puncher.

Soldier Barnaby was crowding the fight now and they met in mid-ring and started to swap it out.

Outside the ropes all was a confused roar. With the pounding of that noise in Moran's ears and the taste of blood in his mouth, he felt a wild, unholy exhilaration as they slugged for all they were worth.

The first seven rounds went by like a dream. It was, he knew, a great fight. Those first seven rounds had never given the crowd a chance to sit down, never a chance to stop cheering. It was almost time for the bell, time for the eighth.

He got up eager to be going, and suddenly, out

of the ringside seats, beyond the press benches, he saw Blackie Marollo. The gambler was sitting back in his seat, his eyes cold and bitter. Beside him was McKracken, his big face ugly in the dim light.

Before the tenth.

He remembered the Soldier's words. Would Barnaby weaken and take a dive? And if he got a chance, should Moran knock him out?

The bell sounded for the eighth and they both came out slower. Both men were ready, and they knew that this was a critical time in the fight. As Barnaby stepped forward, Flash looked him over coolly. The older fighter had a lump on his cheekbone. Otherwise, he was unmarked. That brown face seemed impervious, seemed granite-hard. How like the old Dempsey, Barnaby looked! The shock of dark curly hair, the swarthy, unshaven face, the cold eyes.

Moran circled warily. He didn't like the look of things. What if the Soldier stopped him before the tenth? How was Marollo's money bet, anyway? *Was* it bet on a knockout before the tenth? Or on Moran to stop Barnaby?

Barnaby came in fast, landed a hard left to the head, then a right. Moran started to sidestep, his foot caught and for an instant he was off balance. He saw the Soldier's left start and tried to duck but caught the blow on the corner of the jaw. It spun him halfway around. Then, as Barnaby, his eyes blasting with eagerness, closed in, he caught a left to the body and a right to the chin. He felt himself hit the ropes and slide along them. Something exploded in his face and he went down on his knees in his own corner.

Through a haze of roaring sound, he stared at the canvas, his head spinning. He got one foot on the floor, shook his head, and the mists cleared a little. At the same instant, his gaze fell upon Marollo. The racketeer's face was white. He was half out of his chair, screaming.

At the count of nine, something happened to his legs and they straightened him up. As the Soldier charged, Moran ducked a driving right and clinched desperately. The referee fought to get them free. When they broke, Moran stabbed the Soldier with a stiff left to the mouth that started a trickle of blood down his face, then crossed hard right to the chin and the startled Soldier took a step back.

But he slipped the next left and came in, slamming both hands to Moran's body. Smiling grimly, Moran stabbed three times to Barnaby's split lip, stepped in, and hooked high and low with the left.

Barnaby's eyes were wild now. He charged with a volley of hooks, swings, and uppercuts that drove Flash Moran back and back. Moran got on his bicycle, fled along the ropes, and circled into the center of the ring, where he feinted with a right. As Barnaby came in, Flash Moran crossed his right to the chin.

The blow caught the Soldier coming forward and knocked him back on his heels. Moran followed it up fast and staggered Barnaby with a left, then stabbed another left to the mouth and crossed a hard right which caught the Soldier high on the head.

Barnaby staggered and almost went down. Clinching, the Soldier hung on. At last he broke and tried a wild swing to the head. It missed, but the next caught Moran on the chin.

He went down—hard!

The bell sounded as Moran was getting up. Flash turned and walked back to his corner. He was dead tired, tired and mad clear through. Two knockdowns! It was the first time he had ever been off his feet!

"How's it, kid? Hurt?"

"No. Just mad."

Kelly grinned. "Don't worry. This round coming up will be yours. Lots of left hands now, and watch that left of his."

The gong sounded. They both came out fast and the Soldier bored in. Flash Moran needled Barnaby's mouth with a left jab, then put a left to the body and one to the head. He sidestepped quickly to the right and missed with a right hand.

Now Flash Moran got up on his toes and began to box. He boxed neatly and fast. He piled up points. He kept the Soldier off balance and rocked him with a couple of stiff right hands.

For two and a half minutes of the ninth round, he outboxed the Soldier and piled up points. Barnaby had taken the eighth by a clear margin. The two knockdowns had seen to that.

As for himself, Moran knew he had won the first round and the seventh, while the Soldier had taken the second, third, and fourth. The fifth and sixth were even. It left the Soldier with a margin toward the decision; those knockdowns would stick in the judges' minds.

Moran stabbed in with a left, crossed a right, and then suddenly spotted a beautiful shot for the chin.

He let it go—right down the groove!

And then something smashed against his jaw like the concussion of a six-inch shell. Again he went down, hard.

The first thing he heard was five. Someone was saying "five." No, it was six . . . seven . . . eight . . .

Moran did a push-up with his hands and lunged forward like the starter in a hundred-yard dash.

The Soldier was ready. He set himself, and Flash could see the fist coming. It had to miss, had to miss, had to—miss!

He brought up hard against the Soldier's body, tied him up, and smashed two solid rights to Barnaby's midsection as the round ended.

He wheeled, ran to his corner, and sat down. As he sat he saw a small, wiry man sitting next to McKracken get up and slip out along the aisle.

A moment later the little man was in the Soldier's corner.

Flash Moran sat up. He shook his head, felt the blast of the smelling salts under his nose and the coolness of the water on the back of his neck. Dan Kelly wasn't talking. He was looking at Moran. Then he spoke.

"All right, kid? Got enough?"

Moran grinned suddenly.

"I'm just getting started! I'm going to stop this lug!"

He went out fast at the bell, feinted a left and crossed a solid right to the head. He hooked a left, and the Soldier clinched.

"To the devil with it, kid!" Barnaby said in his ear. "I'm going into the tank. Marollo will kill me if I don't!"

Flash Moran fought bitterly, swapping punches in the clinch with the Soldier, then the referee broke them apart. Suddenly, Flash Moran knew what Barnaby had said couldn't be true. The Soldier was too good a man. What if Barnaby had tried to double-cross him? What if—he stabbed a left to the Soldier's mouth, smashed both hands to the body, and then went inside and clinched.

"You dive and I squeal the whole thing!" he muttered. "I won't let you dive! I'll talk right here, from the ring. If you go out during the round, I'll spill it right here."

"Marollo would kill you, too!" Barnaby snarled. They broke, sparred at long range, and Flash Moran let go with a right. Even as the punch started, he knew the Soldier was going to take it. The punch was partially blocked, and Barnaby began to wilt.

Like a streak Moran closed in and clinched, heaving him back against the ropes.

"I told you!" Moran muttered. "Fight, you yellow skunk! Real fighters don't dive!"

Barnaby broke loose, his eyes cold. He stabbed a left to the mouth, crossed a right, and Flash went inside with both hands to the body. He staggered Barnaby with a left, and knocked him into the ropes. As they rolled along the ropes, the Soldier tried to fall again, but Flash brought him up with a left just as the bell sounded. At this moment, Moran looked over the Soldier's shoulder right into Marollo's eyes.

Blackie Marollo was looking like a very sick man. McKracken, his big, swarthy face yellow, was also sagging. Instantly, Moran knew what had happened. They had overbet and they wouldn't be able to pay up!

The bell clanged again, and the referee broke the two fighters and they went to their corners.

The eleventh was quieter. Flash knew nothing would happen in the eleventh. Marollo had frightened the Soldier into trying to dive in the tenth, but the Soldier's money was bet on a dive in the twelfth round.

Flash Moran walked in and feinted to the head, then uppercut hard with a left to the liver. He stepped in a bit more and brought up his right under the Soldier's heart. He landed two more punches to the body in a clinch and they broke. Moran was body punching now. He slipped a left and rapped a right over Barnaby's heart, then hooked a left. He landed twice more to the body as the bell rang.

The twelfth opened fast. Both men walked to the center of the ring and Moran got in the first punch, a left that started the blood from the Soldier's mouth. As he slipped a left, they began to slug, fighting hard. They battered each other from corner to corner of the ring for two solid minutes. There was no letup. This was hard, bitter, slam-bang fighting. Suddenly, Barnaby caught a high right and started to fall.

Moran rushed him into the ropes before he could hit the canvas and smashed a right to the head. Angry, Barnaby jerked his head away from a second punch, and slugged Flash Moran in the wind. Moran's mouth fell open as he gasped for breath. As he staggered back, all the fighter in Barnaby came back with a rush. This was victory! He could win!

Seeing a big title fight just ahead of him, Barnaby came in slugging!

Half covered, Moran reeled under the storm of blows and went down. He staggered up at ten, and went down again. Just before the bell rang, he straightened up. They clinched.

"You played 'possum, blast you!" Barnaby snarled.

"Sure! I always liked a fight!" Moran said and let go with a left that narrowly missed the Soldier and slid by him, almost landing on the face of the referee. The referee jerked back like he'd been shot at, and glared at Moran.

"Naughty, naughty!" Barnaby said with a grin.

The bell rang.

When they came out for the thirteenth, they came out fast.

"All right!" Barnaby snapped. "You wanted a fight. Well you're gonna get one!"

He ducked a left and slammed a wicked right to Moran's middle. Moran gasped with pain and Barnaby crowded on in, driving Moran back into the ropes with a flurry of wicked punches. A steaming right caught Flash on the chin, but he set himself and smashed a right to the body, a left to the head, and a right to the body.

Slugging like a couple of madmen, they circled the ring. Flash hung the Soldier on the ropes and smashed a left to the chin. The Soldier came off the ropes, ran into a stiff left, and went to his knees. He came up slugging and, toe-to-toe, the two men slugged it out for a full thirty seconds. Then Moran threw a left to the Soldier's mouth and the blood started again.

Barnaby broke away from a clinch, hooked a high right to the head, and followed it up with a stiff left to the wind. They battered each other across the ring and Barnaby split Moran's lip with a left. The Soldier moved in and knocked Moran reeling with another left. Following it up, he dropped Moran to his knees.

There was a taste of blood in Moran's mouth and a wild buzzing in his head as he waited out the count. He could smell the rosin and the crowd and the familiar smell of sweat and the thick, sweetish taste of blood. Then he was up.

But now he had that smoky taste again and he knew he was going to win. The bell rang. Wheeling, they both trotted back to their corners and the whole arena was a bedlam of roaring sound.

The fourteenth round was three minutes of insanity, sheer madness on the part of two born fighters, wild with the lust of battle. Bloody and savage, they were each berserk with the desire to win.

Every one of the spectators was on his feet, screeching with excitement. Even the pale and staring Marollo sat as though entranced as he watched the two pugilists amid the standing figures around him.

The Soldier dropped, got up, and Moran went down. It was bloody, brutal, sickening yet splendid. All thought of money was gone. For Moran and Barnaby there was no crowd, no bets, no arena. They were just two men, fighting it out for the glory of the contest and of winning.

The fifteenth opened with the sound unabated. There was a continual roar now, as of breakers on a great reef. The two men came together and touched gloves and then, impelled by driving fury, Flash Moran waded in, slugging with both hands.

Barnaby lunged and Moran hit him with a right that shook him to his heels. The Soldier started a left and again Flash brushed it aside and brought up his own left into Barnaby's wind.

Then the Soldier backed off and jabbed twice. After the first jab, he dropped his left before jabbing again. Louis had done that in his first fight with Schmeling. He was tiring now and falling back on habits that were unconscious yet predictable.

Flash Moran backed off and waited. Then that left flickered out. Moran took the jab and it shook him to his heels. But he saw the left drop before the second jab. In that brief instant, he threw his right and he put the works on it.

He felt the wet and sodden glove smash into Barnaby's jaw and saw the Soldier's knees buckling. He went in with a left and a right to the head. The Soldier hit the canvas and rolled over on his face and was counted out.

It was over! Flash Moran turned and walked to his corner. In a blur of exhaustion, he felt the referee lift his right hand, and then he slumped on the stool.

They put his robe around him and he was half lifted from the stool and as he stepped down to the floor, he saw Ruth and with her was a tall, gray-haired man who was smiling.

"Great fight, son—a great fight. We'd heard Barnaby was to quit in the twelfth. Glad the rumor was wrong, it would have ruined fighting in this state."

Flash Moran smiled.

"He wouldn't quit, sir. Soldier Barnaby's a great fighter."

Moran turned his head then and saw the Soldier looking at him, a flicker of wry humor in his swollen eyes.

The older man was speaking again.

"My name is Rutgers, Moran," he said. "I'm the district attorney, you know. This is my niece, Ruth Connor. But then I believe you've met."

"That's right," Flash said. "And we'll meet again, tomorrow night? Can we do that, Ruth?"

"Of course," she said with a smile. "I'll be at Gow's place—waiting."

WITH
THESE HANDS

He sat bolt upright in his seat, hands clasped in his lap, eyes fixed in an unseeing stare upon the crushed shambles of the forward part of the plane. His mind without focus, fixed in the awful rigidity of shock.

Awareness returned slowly, and with it a consciousness of cold. Not a shivering cold, not even the icy edge of a cutting wind, but the immense and awful cold of a land of ice, of a land beyond the sun. Of frigid, unending miles lying numb and still under the dead hand of the Arctic.

No movement . . . no life. No sound of people, no hum of motors, no ticking of clocks; only silence and the long white miles where the lonely wind prowled and whispered to the snow.

He had survived. He alone had survived. That thought isolated itself in his consciousness and with it came the dread of living again, the dread of the necessity for struggle.

Yet he need not struggle. He could die. He need only sit still until the anesthesia of shock merged without pain into the anesthesia of death. He need only remain still. He need only wait . . . wait and let the cold creep in. Once he moved the icy spell would be broken and then he must move again.

He was alive. He tried to shut away the thought and find some quiet place in his brain where he could stuff his ears and wait for death. But the thought had seeped into consciousness, and with it, consciousness of cold.

It was a cold where nails break sharply off when struck with a hammer; a cold where breath freezes and crackles like miniature firecrackers; a cold that drove needles of ice into his nose and throat . . . there was no anesthesia, no quiet slipping away, this cold would be a flaying, torturing death.

Icy particles rattled against the hull of the plane; a wind sifted flakes across the hair of the sitting dead. Of them all, he alone had survived. Curtis who had believed so much in luck, Allen who had drilled for oil in the most inhospitable deserts and oceans of the world, of the seven men returning to Prudhoe Bay, he alone had survived.

He slumped in his seat.

That was it. He had moved. To live he must move again, he must act. What could he do? Where could he go? Outside lay the flat sweep of a snow-clad plain and beyond the dark edge of forest, black and sullen under a flat gray sky.

Movement had broken the rigidity of shock. With that break came the realization; there must be no panic, for panic was the little brother of death.

"Sit still," he said aloud, "you've got to think."

If he was to survive it must be by thinking. To think before he moved and then to waste no movement. This power had enabled men to survive. Reason, that ability to profit by experience and not only from their own meager experience, but from the experience of others. That was the secret of man's dominance, of his very survival, for he not only had learned how to control heat, flood, and wind, but how to transmit to future generations the knowledge of harsh experience.

This was an ancient enemy, this cold. Men had survived it, held it away with walls and fire, and if he, Drury Hill, oil company executive and once a citizen of the air-conditioned city of Dallas, Texas, was to survive, it must be by brains, ingenuity, and perhaps through those shared experiences.

He would need matches, he would need fuel. Shelter first, then fire. Fire here was out of the question. There would be spilled gasoline from ruptured tanks. And this plane was his lodestone for rescuers. His only beacon to the outside world. Very well, then, the forest. He had matches and a lighter, recently filled. He would need tools or a tool. He would need a blanket or another heavy coat.

Carefully, he straightened to his feet. He moved to the body of Curtis, avoiding looking at his face. He searched his pockets and found a lighter, more matches, and a nail file. One by one he searched those he could reach, but it was "Farmer" Peterson whom he blessed.

Peterson came from Minnesota and had trapped his way through college. An astute geologist, he was still a country boy at heart. His pockets yielded a waterproof matchbox filled with wooden matches and a large clasp knife of the type carried by sailors, the blade all of five inches long.

In the back of the plane he found several Army blankets and some cans of C rations. Making a bundle of one blanket, he then took along a roll of blueprints for the new tank and distribution complexes to use as tinder to start a fire.

Pausing to think, he remembered that he must not allow himself to perspire, for when activity ceased the perspiration would turn to ice and then his clothing would become a chilling hull in which death could come quickly.

He sorted through the debris where the lockers had broken open, finding a cup and several other useful utensils. He stuffed them into the blanket along with the food and Curtis's coat, and dropped down from the ruins of the plane.

The black battalions of the forest were a dark fringe where sky and snow had a meeting place. With curious reluctance, he stepped away from the plane and, leaving behind his last link with civilization, comfort, and tangible evidence of man, he walked off over the snow.

It was cold . . . his boots crunched on the snow . . . his breath crackled lightly. The all-pervading chill seemed to penetrate the thickest clothing. Yet the movement warmed him and he paused, glancing back. The distance to the plane frightened him, but he turned, and face down from the raw wind, he walked on.

He floundered into the black and white silence of the tree line. This was the ragged fringe of the forest and the growth was not tall . . . white snow, gray and barren sky, the spidery undergrowth and the solemn columns of the trees.

Then he saw, scarcely fifty feet into the trees, a deadfall. This had been a greater tree than most, uprooted and flung down, black earth clinging to the root mass and making a solid wall against the northeast.

Lowering his blanket pack into the hollow where the roots had been, he gathered four thick branches for a foundation, and then with some of the blueprint paper for tinder, he built a small pyre of twigs. The tiny flame leaped up, hissed spitefully at the cold, and then reached warily for the paper. It caught . . . edges of flame crept along the folds, then the flame began to eat hungrily into the tiny stack of fuel. He watched with triumph as the flames increased and twined their hot fingers about the cold pile of twigs.

He had achieved a fire . . . a minor victory won. Man's first companion against the cold and dark, his first step forward from the animal. It was a simple thing, but it was the first thing.

Yet as the flames sank their eager teeth into his small stack of fuel, he realized with quick fear that he could well become the slave of the fire, devoting all of his time to serving it. He must keep his fire small and remain close or all his strength would be required to feed the insatiable flame.

The root mass of the deadfall was more than seven

feet of solid wall with a web of extending roots. Taking his time, Hill gathered evergreen boughs for a thick bed against the very base of the protecting wall, which supplied him not only with a windbreak, but with a reflector for his fire. Through the straggling roots, which extended out and down from the root mass, he wove other evergreen boughs, and into the roots overhead he did the same thing. Soon he had a cuplike hollow with an open face toward the fire.

After gathering more fuel, he banked his fire, placed sticks close at hand, then rolled up in his blankets on the bed of spruce boughs. He slept almost at once, awakening from time to time to replenish the flames, warned by the searching fingers of increasing cold.

At daybreak, he awoke in pain. The muscles of his back and neck were a tightly knotted mass. He had been hurt in the crash, and he was just now realizing it. The night in the cold and his odd sleeping position on the ground seemed to have turned his entire body into an assortment of seized and overstretched muscles. He moved and it hurt, but that wasn't the worst part. It was the sense of fragility that scared him, the sense that if he was called upon to use his body, it would fail him.

He moved close to the fire and, slowly, carefully, began to stretch, trying to loosen his knotted muscles. In two hours he felt slightly better, he made hot, strong black tea, and while the wind moaned among the icy branches overhead he ate one of the boxes of rations, and listened to the cracking and complaining of the trees. Out across the open field, the wind lifted tiny ghosts of snow and floated them eerily along.

Each day he must think . . . he must plan. He must go farther afield for fuel, for later he might become weak and must depend upon that which was close by. He must add to his shelter and he must return to the plane to search for whatever else might be useful. And he must keep the plane clear of snow.

During that first day, he thought little beyond his work. He brought more blankets from the plane. He located two more deadfalls that he could draw upon for fuel. He built a framework of evergreens that could be shifted to whatever angle to protect him from the wind. He added more boughs to his bed.

By now they would know the plane was down . . . a search would have already begun. Drury Hill believed their ship had been off course when it crashed, and with the present overcast, there was small hope of immediate rescue.

That night, he took stock of his situation. With no more exertion than was needed to live, his food supply would last three days. From his experience flying from Fairbanks to Prudhoe and back, he knew three days was simply not enough. In the vast area they must search, he could not gamble on them finding him in less than a week.

He must find other sources of food. He was too far from the coast for seals. There were caribou, but he had no rifle nor had he yet seen their tracks. There were lichens that could be eaten. That was what he had read. Hovering over his fire in the darkness and cold, he strove to remember every iota of information culled from his reading, listening, and living.

On the second morning he awoke in a black depression. The pain was back in full force. He had slept fitfully through the awful cold and now he lay staring into the fire. It was no use. He was a fool to expect rescue. He was one man in all this vast waste. They would never find him. He stared at his grimy hands, felt the stubble on his jaws, and then stiffly, he pushed himself to a sitting position and stoked the fire.

His head ached and his mind was dull . . . was he becoming ill? Had he overworked? It had been twenty years since he had done anything like this . . . twenty good years of living and leisure and seeing all the world held.

This could be a miserable way to die . . . on the other hand, suppose he lived? A fire of optimism blazed up within him . . . it would be something . . . they had said he was past his prime . . . that he should take it easy. He cursed. He made tea and ate several crackers. He must find food.

With a stout stick cleaned of bark, he started out, keeping to crusty patches of snow or ground swept bare by wind. He found, growing on some damp soil, a patch of Idelana lichen and gathered a bundle of it to take along. He searched for berries, having heard that some low-growing bushes held their berries all winter long. His back hurt as he walked but soon he was standing straighter and as he warmed up he felt less and less like a crippled old man.

Twice Arctic hares bounded away over the snow and once he saw a herd of caribou in the distance.

Nothing moved in the forest when he started back. The trees were more scattered. He crossed two streams frozen hard by the subzero cold. The branches of trees creaked in the wind. He cupped a gloved hand over his nose and tried to breathe slowly, his exhalations warming the incoming breath.

Wind picked up the snow . . . he should improvise some snowshoes . . . a gust of wind whined in the trees . . . he glanced at the sky. A storm was blowing up.

Darkness came suddenly and he found himself floundering through soft drifts. Feeling his way back to solid ground, he started on, then caught a whiff of wood smoke and then saw the black blob of his shelter. He started toward it, collecting wood as he went. His fire was almost gone, and he nurtured it carefully back to life.

With some meat from a can and some of the lichen, which he soaked to remove the acid, he made a thick stew. Huddled in his shelter of boughs, Dru Hill of Dallas, Abu Dhabi, and Caracas . . . all places that were warm and populated . . . added fuel to his fire and slowly ate the stew. He ate, and found it good.

Around him the walls of his shelter became suddenly friendly and secure. The wind caught at his fire and flattened the flame. It would use a lot of fuel tonight. He grinned as he leaned back against the root mass. He had plenty of fuel. Here he was, a lone man in an uncharted wilderness, yet he had created this little bit of civilization, it was a long way from being a building, even a crude one, but it was shelter nonetheless. He thought of the buildings he had ordered built, the oil and gas wells he'd drilled, the tank complexes and pipelines. All had been a natural outgrowth of this same simple need. Shelter and fuel. At one end of the spectrum it demanded a wood fire and a windbreak, at the other cracking plants and parking lots. He saw in himself an extension of the natural order of things. Man against the elements. Man triumphant against the elements. The third night coming and he was still alive. He could win. He could beat this racket. Old Dru Hill wasn't dead yet.

Tomorrow he would make some snares and catch a few Arctic hares or snowshoe rabbits. Maybe he could make a net and trap some birds. He would have meat and there were more lichens. East through the woods, there might be berries. He might even improve his shelter.

At seven in the morning, he heard the throbbing motors of a plane. The sky was heavily overcast but he rushed out, shouting loudly, uselessly. He heard it overhead, heard it pass on . . . at least they were trying. Hope mounted, then died. He considered a dozen unreasonable doubts, worried over fifty objections. They might never return to this locality.

Yet he did not despair, for they would continue to search. He worked through the fourth day at his usual tasks, a man below medium height, inclined to be fat, but he hurt less . . . in some strange way his body seemed to be stronger. To the west he found a vast stretch of tundra broken by only occasional outcropping of rock and by the stalks of some plant. Intrigued, he dug into the snow and frozen ground and got out the fattish sulfur-yellow roots. They tasted sweet and starchy. He collected enough to fill his pockets.

No more planes came over . . . by nightfall he was dead tired and glad for sleep. On the fifth morning, two snowshoe rabbits were in his snares . . . on the sixth morning a third rabbit. He had no luck with the larger and more cautious Arctic hares. On that day, he ate nothing but food he had gathered himself, except for tea.

He had avoided the plane except to clean off the snow . . . only once after his first leaving had he entered, but the motionless bodies of his former companions had filled him with gloom. Instead he collected debris from the crash, pounding sheets of aluminum into a crude stove and reflector.

On the seventh morning, his snares were empty and for the first time he failed to add to his supply of food. On the eighth day, they were again empty . . . he struggled to the tundra for more of the yellow roots. Returning, he found a patch of black crowberries and, sitting there in the open, he ate all he could find.

Since that one time he had heard no planes . . . had the search been abandoned? Had it been a searching plane at all?

On the ninth morning, he found a small snowshoe rabbit in a snare and made a rich stew using lichen and the yellow roots. But still he heard no planes. He no longer listened for them nor looked for them. He went on about the business of survival . . . he gathered lichen and roots, he checked his snares . . . the rabbits were more cautious now . . . he added to his supply of fuel.

Returning to the plane, he found his bag, forgotten until now. Back at his fire, defying the cold and the loneliness, he shaved. Almost at once he felt better. The smooth feel of his cheeks under his hand was better than the scraggy beard. He concealed the bag under the trunk of the tree.

His clearing had taken on a lived-in look. The snow was trodden down, there was a huge stack of fuel, the lazy smoke of the fire. There were the skins of the rabbits he had staked out. He added fuel to his fire, including a chunk of birch, and walked away.

Alone on the edge of the tundra, he looked across the flat white sea of snow . . . what lay beyond? Just a vast space, or perhaps a settlement? A trapper's cabin? He was slogging along over the snow, head down, when he smelled smoke. A lot of smoke . . .

His head came up—then he broke into a clumsy run. From the site of his shelter rose a bright column of flame!

Heart pounding, he lunged across the snow. Twice he fell, plunging headlong, facedown in the snow. He had been almost a mile away . . . he stumbled into the clearing and stopped, blank with despair.

His shelter was gone. His blankets were gone. The other coat was gone. Only charred, useless masses remained. More than half his fuel was gone and the rest still burned.

In a panic, he tore at the pile of fuel, pulling the pieces back, rubbing the fire away in the snow. A spark blowing into the dry, resinous stuff of the shelter must have set it off. A low wind whined among the bare boughs overhead, moaned in the evergreens, stirring the blackened ashes of his fire, rattling the dead fingers of the birch, whispering out over the tundra, a lonely reminder of the cold and the night to come.

Soon it would be dark . . . it would be colder. Wind would come . . . his clothing would turn to ice now for he had perspired freely . . . his strength was burned out from the running and the work . . . he would die . . . he would freeze.

He stared around him . . . what to do? Where to begin again? Begin again? He was a fool to begin again. Begin again . . . ? He laughed hysterically. His little corner of civilization was gone. But what had it been? A pitiful shelter. An almost irreplaceable pile of wood. Some junk that he had used to survive. Before the crash he probably would never have recognized it as a camp, he might have thought it trash collected by the wind. Before the crash he never would have recognized what had burned as being the difference between life and death. He never realized how little it took, never realized how simple the things were . . . as long as they were the right things.

He had to do something. . . .

With his knife he made rawhide strips of the rabbit skins. It was growing dark, the wind was increasing. Another storm was coming. He must contrive something new . . . there was a patch of willows no more than two hundred feet away. He went there, scanned a thick clump a dozen feet around, and then going into the clump he broke off all the central trees, none of them in the center being over two inches in diameter, mostly less. Then he drew the tops of the outer ones down and tied them together with the rawhide strips. When he had several of them with their tops tied at the center, he went out and wove others among them, using some willows but mostly evergreens. As the dark closed in he was making a strong, hivelike shelter with a hole in the top for smoke to escape. A shelter strong because it was made of living trees.

Trampling down the snow, he dug a hole with his knife and built a small fire there. He carried boughs within and scattered them around, then made a bed near the fire. Outside he threw more evergreens on the house, then gathered fuel. One of the deadfalls was close by, and working until long after dark, he carried as much of it to the door as he could, and several armsful inside.

Finally he made a door of woven boughs and pulled it across the entrance. Outside the snow was falling, the wind was blowing with hurricane force. Inside his wigwam of willow and evergreen, its framework rooted in the ground, he was secure.

His blankets were gone and his food was gone . . . including the precious tea . . . but outside the snow fell and packed tighter and thicker about his shelter. Inside it grew warmer. A drop from overhead fell and hissed gently in the flames. Reclining on the boughs, he considered the situation again. This storm would end hope of rescue . . . everything would be shrouded in snow and he doubted if he would have the strength to uncover the plane . . . and for days he would not have the time. He must find food again, set snares, gather more fuel.

If he could only trap a caribou! Sitting up suddenly . . . there was that book about China . . . what had its name been? It had told how they trapped deer in the Altin Tagh . . . a hole about eight to twelve inches in diameter and a couple of feet deep . . . less could do . . . and a ring of sharp sticks, the sharp ends pointing toward the center. When the deer stepped into the hole, the sharp sticks would prevent it being withdrawn. Then he could rush in with his knife . . . he grinned at himself. What preposterous thing would he think of next?

Awakening in the dark, icy cold of morning, he rebuilt his fire and this time the shelter grew quickly warm, testifying to the thick outer covering of snow. He squatted beside the fire, dreading the outer cold but dreading more the cold his leaving would let into his shelter.

He must have food, and unless the snow had buried the snares completely, he might have something. There had been a few more stalks of the yellow root not too far away on the tundra. The idea of the previous night returned. If he could kill a larger animal his food problem would be solved for days on end . . . and if trapped, he might kill it with a sharp stick or his knife. Banking his fire carefully, he went out of the hut, closing the door and covering it with snow.

All was white and still, but with a strange difference. Suddenly, almost with shock, he realized why. The sky was clear!

Now, if ever, a plane might come. But were they still searching? Had they given up? Then he remembered . . . the crashed plane was shrouded in snow and would be invisible from the sky!

He started toward it, then stopped. The chance of rescue was a wild gamble and he needed food. In this country, one's strength need wane only a little for the cold to kill. Weakness and exhaustion were fatal. Turning, he walked toward the snares. Two were buried and useless . . . the third had been tripped and the rabbit had escaped. He reset them and went through the woods to the tundra and found two stalks of the yellow-rooted plant. The roots were pitifully small.

Circling back, he stopped suddenly. In the snow before him were the tracks of a herd of caribou. The tracks were fresh and the herd must have passed within a few minutes! He was following them when suddenly he heard the roar of a plane!

Wheeling around, he ran from under the trees and stared up at the sky . . . it was there, big and silver and beautiful! It was low enough to see him. But it was also low enough to be quickly out of sight. He sprang into the air, shouting hoarsely. It disappeared off over the trees to the north. Rushing toward his shelter, he could only think that the crashed plane had been covered with snow. He went past the shelter and finally got to the plane. He had no more than reached it when he heard the ship returning.

It was coming too fast . . . he could never make it. Desperately, he began trying to uncover some part, the silver of a wing, to the sunlight. But the snow was heavy and he was too late, the plane soared off to the south and its sound died rapidly away.

Glumly, he started to turn back and then went to work and cleaned the snow from the one undamaged wing and the fuselage. It was a slow, heavy task and noon had come and gone before he completed it. He was physically exhausted and ravenously hungry.

A plane had come, crossed over the area and gone. He must, he told himself, appreciate the significance of that. It meant his last chance for rescue was gone. They would not cover the same ground twice. As he prepared his meal, he considered that, using the two yellow roots and his prize . . . an Arctic hare found in a snare set that very morning.

All right then. No rescue. If he was to survive until spring and then walk out, he must do it on his own. Dru Hill was surprised to find that he did not view the situation with alarm. He could survive . . . he had proved that . . . and if he could trap a caribou, he would have a good supply of meat. He could trap two if he could trap one. He could dry or smoke the meat and so build supplies for spring. He could make a pair of snowshoes and, now that hope of rescue was abandoned, he could afford to go further afield for food, not needing to remain near the crashed ship.

He took a deep breath and thought of the miles of wilderness that surrounded him. He didn't have much but the woods could provide, they had shown him that. He no longer thought of this Arctic forest with fear. It was beautiful, the trees comforting, the vast expanse of tundra a wonder and a challenge. His hearing had become supernaturally acute, his sense of smell delicate. He could survive.

This was something he never could have imagined two weeks ago. A man needed lights, an automobile, the complex comforts of the modern world. He, in his chosen profession, had provided the electricity, the gasoline, and the plastics to provide those comforts.

He grinned to himself. Farther afield there might be better hunting grounds, berries, perhaps more game. He thought of something else . . . of the change in himself. Here he was, calmly and with confidence considering surviving the entire winter where a few days before he had doubted his ability to survive a few hours. But he was right. His doubts were gone, and justly so. This place was warm and could be made warmer. He could take some metal from the plane for heads for a spear and for arrows. He could . . . he heard voices.

He pushed aside the door and thrust his head out. Three men, two of them in Canadian Air Force uniforms, and the third was Bud Robinson, were slogging down the path.

He stood there and they stared at him, and then Robinson said, "By the Lord Harry! It's Dru Hill!"

Robinson looked around curiously. "We never dreamed anyone would be alive, but when we flew over this morning, Gene thought he saw a black spot on the snow. Only it was not on the snow, but where the snow had melted off the trees over your fire, here."

"We flew clear back to the post," Gene explained, "but it kept nagging me. There shouldn't be anything black after all that snow falling, so we took a chance and came back. It's lucky for you that we did."

Hours later the plane dropped down onto the runway of an airfield surrounded by warehouses and industrial buildings. Nearby a pipeline ran toward the distant sea. Dru Hill was hustled across the field and into a waiting ambulance. He insisted on sitting in front with the driver and at the hospital they gave him a clean bill of health, something he had not doubted.

They left him alone finally, the reporters, and doctors, company representatives, and police, in a brandnew motel room near the airfield. The walls and roof seemed strangely close. He paced the odd green carpeting far into the night. To Dru Hill the room smelled of cleansers and cigarettes and wallpaper glue. It was uncomfortably warm. He opened the window, letting in the cold night air and a small shard or two of ice. Beyond the parking lot was a line of scraggly pines obscuring a set of trash bins and the highway. The sound of engines and tires on the asphalt filled his ears. The air outside smelled like gasoline. Gasoline and garbage.

But then the wind blew and after a moment it carried away those smells, replacing them momentarily with the smell of the great Alaska beyond. Beyond the suburbs, the trailers, the gravel pits and oil wells.

He remembered how, as the plane lifted itself from the snow, he had looked back. The trees at the edge of the forest were only a dark line. The place where he had built his hut, staked his furs, and piled the wood for his fire could no longer be seen.

But he knew it was there.

CORPSE ON
THE CARPET

She was sitting just around the curve of the bar, a gorgeous package of a girl, all done up in a gray tailored suit. The hand that held the glass gave a blinding flash and when I could see again, I got a gander at an emerald-cut diamond that would have gone three carats in anybody's bargain basement. Yet when she turned toward me, I could see the pin she wore made the ring look cheap.

No babe with that much ice has any business dropping into a bar like the Casino. Not that I'm knocking it, for the Casino is a nice place where everybody knows everybody else and a lot of interesting people drop in. But those rocks were about three blocks too far south, if you get what I mean.

At the Biltmore, okay. At the Ambassador, all right. But once in a while some tough Joes drop in here. Guys that wouldn't be above lifting a girl's knick-knacks. Even from a fence there was a winter in Florida in those rocks.

It was then I noticed the big guy further along the bar. He had a neck that spread out from his ears and a wide, flat face. His hands were thick and powerful. And I could see he was keeping an eye on the babe with the ice, but without seeming to.

This was no pug, and no "wrassler." Once you've been in the trade, you can spot them a mile off. This guy was just big and powerful. In a brawl, he would be plenty mean and no average Joe had any business buying any chips when he was dealing.

"Babe," I said, to myself, "you're lined up at the wrong rail. You better get out of here—fast!"

She shows no signs of moving, so I am just about to move in—just to protect the ice, of course—when a slim, nice-looking lad beats me to it.

He's tall and good-looking, but strictly from the cradle, if you know what I mean. He's been wearing long pants for some twenty-odd years, but he's been living at home or going to school and while he figures he's a smart lad, he doesn't know what cooks. When I take a gander at Blubber Puss, which is how I'm beginning to think about the big guy, I can see where this boy is due to start learning, the hard way.

Me? I'm Kip Morgan, nobody in particular. I came into this bar because it was handy and because there was an Irish bartender with whom I talked fights and football. Like I say, I'm nobody in particular, but I've been around.

This nice lad who's moving in on the girl hasn't cut his teeth on the raw edges of life yet. The babe looks like the McCoy. She's got a shape to whistle at and a pair of eyes that would set Tiffany back on his heels. She's stiff with the boy at first, then she unbends. She won't let him buy her a drink, but she does talk to him. She's nervous, I can see that. She knows the big lug with the whale mouth is watching her.

All of a sudden, they get up and the boy helps her on with her coat, then slides into his own. They go out, and I am taking a swallow of bourbon when Blubber Puss slides off his stool and heads toward the door.

"Bud," I tell myself, "you're well out of this."

Then I figure, what the devil? That rabbit is no protection for a job like that, and Blubber Puss won't play pretty. Also, I have always had confidence in what my left can do to thick lips.

They walk about a block and take a cab. There's another one standing by, and the big Joe slides into it. I am just about to figure I'm out of it when another cab slides up. I crawl in.

"Follow those cabs, chum," I say to the cabbie.

He takes a gander at me. "What do you think this is—a movie?"

"If it was, you wouldn't be here," I tell him. "Stick with them and I'll make it worth your while."

We've gone about ten blocks when something funny happens. The cab the Blubber is in pulls up and passes the other one, going on over the rise ahead of us. While I am still tailing the babe and her guy, and trying to figure that one, I see his cab coming back, and Blubber isn't in it.

Then, we go over the rise ourselves and I see the girl's cab pulling up at the curb near a narrow street.

They get out, and we slide past and pull in at the curb. Their side of the street is light, mine is dark, so I know what to do.

The cabbie takes his payoff, and I slip him a two-dollar tip. He looks at it and sneers.

"I thought they always slipped you a five and said keep the change."

I look at him cold. I mean, I chill him. "What do you think this is—the movies?"

The cab slides away and I go around the corner into the same narrow street where the babe and her guy are going, but I'm still on the dark side and there is a row of parked cars along the curb.

It doesn't figure right. If Blubber goes on ahead, that can only mean he knows where the babe and her guy are going. If that is true, that figures Blubber and the girl are working it together. That means mama's boy is headed for the cleaners.

Only the doll doesn't fit. She doesn't look the type. There is more in this, as the guy said eating the grapefruit, than meets the eye.

The babe has pulled up in front of the side entrance of an apartment house and is trying to give her young Lothario the brush. He is polite, but insistent. Then the big lug steps from the shadows and moves up behind the kid.

When he starts moving, I start. The big guy has a blackjack and he lifts it.

I yell, "Look out!"

The kid wheels around, his mouth open, and Blubber Puss turns on me with a snarl. Get that? A snarl. The big ape will have it for days, I figure.

When he turned, I plastered it right into his teeth, then fired another into the big guy's digestion.

You know what happened?

Nothing.

It was like slugging the side of a building. That stomach, which I figured would be a soft touch, was hard as nails. I'd thrown my Sunday punch and all I got was rebound.

Now brother, if I nail them with my right and they don't go down, they do some funny things standing up—usually. This big guy took it standing and threw a left that shook me to my socks. Then, he moves in with the blackjack.

The kid starts for him then, but—accidentally, or otherwise—the girl's dainty ankle is there and the kid spills over it onto the sidewalk. I blocked the blackjack with my left forearm and then made a fist and chopped it down to the big lug's eye. I was wearing kid gloves, and they cut to the bone.

Before he can get himself set, I let him have them both in the digestion again. No sale. He tried the blackjack and we circled. I stabbed him with a left, then another. He ducked his head and lunged for me. I caught him by the hair and jerked his face down and my knee up.

When I let go, he staggered back, his nose so flat he had no more profile than a blank check. He was blood all over, and I never saw him look so good. I set myself then and let him have both barrels, right from the hip, and my right smashed his jaw back until his chin almost caught behind his collar-button.

He went down. I'd a good notion to put the boots

to him, but I always hate to kick a man in the face when there's a lady around. Doesn't seem gentlemanly, somehow.

I rolled him over on the pavement and he was colder than a pawnbroker's heart. I turned around. The kid is standing there, but the babe has taken a powder.

"Listen," he said, "thanks awfully. But where did she go?"

"Pal," I said, "why don't you let well enough alone? Don't you realize that the doll brought you here for a trimming?"

"Oh, no." He looked offended. "She wouldn't do that. She was a nice girl."

"Buddy, I tailed you and the girl out of the bar because I saw this big mug watching you. Until this guy passed your cab and went ahead, I figured he was after the girl's ice. But he came here, and that could only mean he knew where she was going."

"Oh, no. I don't believe that," he said. "Not for a minute."

"Okay," I answered. "Better scram out of here before the cops come nosing around."

He scrammed. Me, I am a curious guy. The big potato was still bye-bye, so I gave him a frisk. He was packing a gun, which he might have used if I'd given him time. It was a snub-nosed .38. I pocketed the weapon, then found what I wanted. It was a driver's license made out to Buckley Dozen.

Well, Buckley was coming out of his dozen, so I turned away. Then, I saw the diamond pin.

Somehow, the doll had dropped it. Probably when her ankle had tripped the kid. I lifted it off the pavement, went around the corner, and made a half block walking fast. A moment later a cab came streaking by, and Buckley Dozen was in it. But he didn't see me.

For a couple of days after that I was busy. Several times I looked at that ice. I figured no dame like that would be wearing anything nearly as good as this looked, so decided it must be glass, or paste. Then I dropped in at the Casino Bar and Emery, the bartender, motioned me over.

"Say, there was a guy in here looking for you. Nice lookin' kid."

His description fitted the youngster who'd been with the girl.

"Probably figured things out," I said, "and wants to buy me a drink."

"No, it wasn't that. He looked serious, and was awful anxious to see you. He left this address here."

I took the visiting card he handed me, noted the address at a nice apartment away up on Wilshire, and the name Randolph Seagram.

That made me think of the pin again, so on a hunch, I left the bar and started up the street. There was a fancy jewelry store in Beverly Hills, just west past Crescent Heights and Doheny but a million miles away. I went there first, taking a gander at the stuff in the window. Glass or not, this pin in my pocket made the rest of that stuff look like junk. Walking around to the door, I went in.

• • • •

The floor was so polished, I hated to walk on it and everything seemed to be glass and silver.

A clerk walked toward me who looked as if he might consider speaking to either the Rockefellers or the Vanderbilts and asked what he could do for me. I think he figured on taking a pair of tongs and dropping me outside.

"Just give me a quick take on this," I said, handing him the pin, "and tell me what it's worth."

He took a look and his eyes opened like he was looking at this great big beautiful world for the first time. Then, he screws a little business into his eye and looks the pin over.

When he looked up, dropping his glass into his hand, he was mingling extreme politeness and growing suspicion in about equal quantities.

"Roughly, twenty thousand dollars," he said.

The night before, I'd been in a poker game and my coat had hung on a hook alongside of a dozen others, with all that ice loose in my pocket! I took it standing.

"I'd like to speak to the manager," I said quickly.

The manager was a tall, cool specimen with gray hair along his temples and looked like he might at least be Count von Roughpants or something.

"Listen," I said, "and while I'm talking, take a gander at this." I dropped the ice on the table.

He looked at it, and when he looked up at me, I knew he was thinking of calling the cops.

"I'm not going to tell you how I got this," I said. "I think maybe the party that owns it may be in trouble. I don't have any way of finding out where the party to whom it belongs is—unless you can help me. Isn't it true that pins like this are scarce?"

He lifted an eyebrow. "I would say very rare. In fact, I believe this to be a special design, made to order for someone."

"All right. I want you to make some discreet inquiries. Find out the name of the person it belongs to and where they live. I don't want anybody to know why we're asking. This party may have some relatives or friends who would be worried. When I find out who, what, and why, then I'll know what to do."

"You have some idea to whom it belongs?" he asked.

"I think so. I hope to find out for sure. Meanwhile, do this for me. Take down an accurate description of this pin, then my name and description." I could see the suspicion fading from his eyes. "Then if anything goes haywire, I'll be in the clear."

"And the stone?" he asked.

"I'll see it gets to a safe place."

Leaving the store, I turned into a five-and-dime and after picking up a box several times larger than the pin would need, I wadded the pin in paper, stuffed it in the box, and then had the box wrapped by their wrapping service. Then I addressed it to myself and dropped it in a mailbox.

Emery, the Casino bartender, had said the kid was worried. He might have something.

I caught a cab and gave the address that was on the visiting card the kid had left for me.

None of this was my business. Yet I could not leave it alone. The girl had measured up to be the right sort, yet somehow she was tied up with Blubber Puss, who was a wrong G from any angle.

No girl wears jewelry like that when she's willingly working with a strong-arm guy. There was something that smelled in this deal, and I meant to find out what.

The kid lived in a swank apartment. I stopped at the desk and when the lad turned around I said, "Which apartment is Mr. Seagram in?"

He looked at me coolly. "He lives in C-three, but I don't believe he's in. His office has been calling and hasn't gotten an answer."

"His office?"

"Asiatic Importing and Development Company."

"Oh? Then if they are calling him maybe he didn't go to work this morning."

He frowned. "I'm sure nothing is wrong. Mr. Seagram is often out of town."

"I'll go up," I said.

He was watching me as I started for the elevator. I found C-3 around the corner of the hall, out of sight of the foyer.

There was no answer to my knock, and then I saw that the door wasn't quite closed. I pushed it open and stepped in.

Randolph Seagram lay on the floor near an overturned chair. He was dead, half of a knife sticking from his chest. The lights were on, although it was broad daylight and one whole side of the place was windows.

"Got him last night," I told myself. I took a quick gander around, then stepped to the phone. "Get me the police," I said.

In about a minute, the clerk downstairs is on the phone. I'm still looking the place over.

"What's the trouble?" the clerk asked. "We mustn't have the police."

"Listen, brother," I cut in quickly. "You've got to have the police. This guy is stone cold dead on the carpet. Get them on the phone, I'll do the talking."

When he got them, I asked for Homicide.

"Mooney talkin'," a voice said. "What's up?"

"There's a guy down here in apartment C-three of the Cranston Arms," I said, "who came out on the wrong end of an argument. He's lying here on the carpet with a knife in his ribs."

I heard his feet come off the desk with a thud. "Where's that again? Who are you?"

"My name is Morgan," I told him, "Kipling Morgan. Kipling as in Gunga Din."

"Don't let anybody leave," he said. "We'll be over."

Kneeling beside him, I gave the lad a hurried frisk. He didn't have any folding money, and his wallet was lying on the floor. They had nicked him for his dough, too. But it wasn't what I was looking for.

Knowing my own habits, I took a chance on his.

There were three addresses on a worn envelope, three addresses and a telephone number. I stuck the envelope in my pocket.

When the police came in, I was sitting in the chair by the telephone like I hadn't moved.

"Detective Lieutenant Mooney." The guy who said it was short and square-shouldered, but looked rugged enough for two men. He gave the body a quick looking over, picked up the empty wallet, then looked at me. "Where do you fit?" he asked.

"Acquaintance," I said. "Met the guy in a bar on Sixth Street. He left word that he wanted to see me. I came up, he was dead."

"When'd you last see him alive?" Mooney was watching me. He had an eye, this dick did.

"About three days ago." I hesitated then told him how I'd followed him from a bar, and what I'd seen. I didn't mention the diamonds.

"Well," he said, "there wasn't anybody around to help him the second time. Looks like they killed him when he made a fuss."

"I don't think so."

Mooney looked up at me. "Why?"

"Seagram thought the girl was on the level. I think maybe he found her again. If I'm any judge, he was going to try when he left me. Well, he must have found her. Either he learned something he wasn't supposed to know, or they tracked him home and knocked him off."

"Know his family?" Mooney asked.

"Nuh uh."

"Who are you? Your face looks familiar." Mooney was still studying me. I could see he wasn't sure I was in the clear. He was a tight-mouthed guy.

"I used to be a fighter."

"Yeah, I remember." He studied me. "Every once in a while you hear of a fighter turning crooked."

"Yeah? Every once in a while you hear of a banker turning crooked, too, or a cop."

"It doesn't sound right," he said. "You followed them home because you figured it was a heist job. Why didn't you call the police?"

"What world are you living in? You can't walk up to a cop and tell him you think somebody is going to stick up somebody else just because you feel it in here." I tapped myself on the chest. "I knew the signs, and I tailed along."

"You had a fight with the guy?" Mooney asked.

"Yeah." I nodded. "You might check your hospitals. The guy had a broken nose when he left me, and he lost a couple of teeth. He had at least three deep cuts, too."

"You work 'em over, huh?" Mooney turned. "Graham, get started on that."

Mooney took my address and I left. Me, I had an idea or two. The girl didn't fit. Somehow she had got mixed up with the wrong crowd, and she might be afraid to ask for help even if she got the chance because of her folks or husband or someone hearing about it; women are funny that way. Seagram might have seen her again, followed her, and tried to learn something. That was when he tried to get hold of me. Then, he went home and they got him.

Yet Blubber Puss didn't fit into the killing. He was a gun man or muscle man. He wouldn't use a shiv. Also, he must have his face well bandaged by now. He would be too easily remembered.

Back in my own place, I dug out a .380 Colt that I had and strapped it into a holster that fit around the inside of my thigh under my pants. This one I carried before, and it was ready to use. There was a zipper in the bottom of my right pants pocket, the gun butt just a little lower. I could take a frisk and it would never be found. On my hip, I stuck the rod I took off Blubber Puss.

By nine o'clock, I had eliminated two of the addresses on the envelope. The third and last one was my best bet. It turned out to be a big stone house in the hills above Hollywood. It was set back in some trees and shrubbery with a high wall all the way around.

The gate was closed and locked tight. I could see the shine of a big black car standing in front of the house, almost concealed by the intervening shrubbery. Turning, I walked along the dark street under the trees. About twenty yards farther along, I found what I sought—a big tree with limbs overhanging the wall.

With a quick glance both ways, I jumped and, catching the limb, pulled myself up. Then, I crawled along the limb until I was across the wall; I dropped to the lawn.

My idea of the thing was this: Seagram had run into the girl again. Maybe he had talked to her, probably not. But, mindful of what I'd told him, he might have been uncertain of her, and so maybe he had tailed her. Then, he had tried to come in here. Perhaps he had convinced himself she was okay, or he was planning a Galahad. But he had died for messing with something out of his league.

This setup still smelled wrong, though. The house was too big. The layout cost money. No fly-by-night hoodlums who might use a girl as a plant to pick up some change would have a place like this, or a girl with diamonds like she had.

I did an Indian act going through the trees. When I got close, I dropped my raincoat on the grass behind some shrubbery and laid down on it where I could watch the house.

There was a distant mutter of thunder, growing off among the clouds like a sleepy man you're trying to wake but who doesn't want to get up.

The house was big and the yard was beautiful. A drive made a big circle among the trees. Another drive went past the house to a four-car garage. One of the cars was in front of the house. Another one, facing out, stood beside it. The last car had a Chicago license—an Illinois plate with the town name-strip above it.

There were two lighted windows on the ground floor, and I could see another on the second floor, a window opposite a giant tree with a limb that leaned very, very near.

Suddenly, a match flared. It was so sudden I ducked. In the glow of the match, as the guy lighted his cigarette, I could see Blubber Puss. His nose was taped up, and there were two strips of adhesive tape on his cheekbones. His lips were swollen considerably beyond their normal size.

Blubber Puss was standing there in the darkness. He looked like he had been there quite a while.

Footsteps on the gravel made me turn my head. Another man, skinny and stooped, was walking idly along the drive. He stopped close to Blubber, and I could hear the low murmur of their voices without being able to distinguish a word.

After a minute, they parted and both began walking off in opposite directions. I waited, watching them go. I took a quick gander at the luminous dial of my wristwatch. After almost ten minutes, I saw Skinny come into sight ahead, his feet crunching along the gravel, and then Blubber Puss came into sight. This time they were closer to me when they met.

"This standin' watch is killin' me," Skinny growled. "What's the boss figure is goin' to happen anyway? We're not hot in this town."

"That's what you say." Blubber's mouth shaped the words poorly. "You suppose they won't have word out all over the country? Then knockin' off that kid was a tough break. Why'd he have to stick his nose into it?"

"That's what comes of not havin' any dough," Skinny said. "We had to make a raise. What easier way to do it?"

"Well," Blubber said, with satisfaction, "we'll get plenty out of this before we're done. Gettin' in here was a break, too. Nobody'd think to look here."

"We better keep movin'," Skinny suggested. "The boss might come out and see us loafin' on the job. Anyway, it's near time for our relief."

The two walked on, each in their respective ways. I stared after them trying to make sense from what I'd heard. One thing was sure. A relief for these two meant that at least two more men, aside from the mysterious boss, were inside. At the very least that made me one against five. It was too many, this late in the evening, especially when I hadn't eaten any dinner.

The ground-floor window looked tempting, but

I decided against it. I'd not have time for much of a look before Skinny and Blubber would be back around, and the chances of being seen were too great. I didn't care to start playing cops and robbers with real bullets until I knew what the setup was.

Picking up my coat, I slid back into the bushes and weaved my way toward that tall tree. A leafy branch should offer a way into one of the upper rooms. It didn't seem like so desperate a chance as going for the ground-floor window.

A few drops of rain began to fall, but this was no time to be thinking of that. I looped my raincoat through my belt and went up that tree. From a position near the bole, my feet on the big limb, I could see into a window.

There were two people in the room. One of them was the doll who wore the diamonds. The other was a younger girl, not over twelve years old. While I was looking, the door opened and a guy came in with a tray. He put it down, made some crack to the girl, and she just looked at him. I could see her eyes, and the warmth in their expression would have killed an Eskimo.

Maybe I'm dumb. Maybe you'd get the idea sooner than me. But only now was it beginning to make sense; the girls were prisoners in what was probably their own home.

The babe who wore the ice that night had been working as a plant. She may have been forced to do it while they held her sister here. Maybe there were others of the family in there too.

Who this bunch were and how they got here did

not matter now. The thing that mattered was to get those two girls out of there, and now. Once they were safe, then we could get to Mooney and spread the whole thing in his lap.

The trouble was I knew how these boys operated. Randolph Seagram, lying back there on the floor with a knife sticking out of him was evidence enough. They were playing for keeps, and they weren't pulling any punches. Nobody had rubber teeth in this setup.

Nevertheless, I seemed to be cutting myself in. And that was the big question. After all, I wasn't any private dick. There was no payoff if I was successful and at least one of those guys in that house had reason enough to hate my insides. I could get down out of this tree, go back over the wall, make a call to Mooney, and then go home and get a good night's sleep.

I had a good notion to do it. It was the smart thing to do. Except for one consideration.

This was a tough mob. Maybe they had left the doll alone up to now. It looked as if they had. But there was no reason why they should any longer. They might decide to blow and knock off the babes when they left. They might decide to do worse. And they might make that decision within the next ten minutes.

I am still thinking like that when I hear one of the boys down below running. He's heading toward the gate. Another car comes in and swings up under my tree. Two men get out, one of them carrying a briefcase.

"Something's going down," I tell myself, "something interesting." See? That explains it. I'm just a nosy guy. Curious.

There was a dark window a little to the left of the one to the girls' room. Working out on the limb . . . I was out on a limb in more ways than one. I swung down to the ledge of the dark window. It was a French window, opening on a little, imitation balcony.

With my knife blade, I got it open and stepped down in the room.

For a moment I hesitated, getting my bearings. Then I felt my way through the room to the door.

The hallway was dark, too, and I made my way along it to the stairs, then down. I could see light coming from the crack of a door that was not quite closed and could hear the low murmur of voices.

Four men were inside. That scared me. There were two men outside, and two who had just arrived. Counting the three whom I already knew to be inside and the two who had just arrived, there should now have been five in the room.

That meant that there was another guy loose in the house.

Crouching near the foot of the stairs, I peered into the room and listened. I could see three men. One of them was a hoodlum, or I don't know the type when I see one. The other two were the ones who had come in the car, and I got the shock of my life.

The nearer of the pair, sitting sideways to me, was Ford Hiesel, a famous criminal lawyer, a man who had freed more genuine murderers than any two living men. The man facing me across the table was another famous attorney, Tarrant Houston, elderly, brilliant, and a man who had for a time been a judge and was now director of some of the biggest corporations on the Coast. The fourth man, the one I couldn't see, was speaking.

"You have no choice, Mr. Houston. If you attempt to notify the police, the girls will be killed. Their safety lies in your doing just what you are told.

"As the family's lawyer you are in the perfect position to help us. We know Dwight Harley and his wife are in Bermuda. They've left here one hundred and fifty thousand dollars in negotiable securities. If we took them, we'd get maybe thirty thousand dollars from a fence. But you can get their full value.

"You take these bonds, turn them into cash, and bring it here; I want you to work fast. I may add, that you'll be watched."

"What assurance do I have," Houston demanded, "that you will release the girls after you get the money?"

"Because we have no reason to add murder to this. If we get the money, we leave, and the girls remain here."

"All right." Houston stood up. "Since I have no choice in the matter. I can handle the bonds. But I wish you'd allow me to communicate with Harley."

"Nothing doing." The reply was sharp. "You can handle this. I'm sure you've done transactions for him before."

Crouched there by the steps, I stiffened slightly. That voice. I knew it from somewhere.

What Houston didn't know was that murder was already tied in with this deal, and what I knew was that those thugs would never leave the girls alive when they left.

Nor, the chances were, would Houston make it either.

"What's your part in this, Hiesel?" Houston demanded, as he rose from the table.

The criminal lawyer shrugged. "The same as yours, Houston. These men knew of me. They simply got me to contact you. I don't know the girls. Nor do I know Harley, but I've no desire to see the girls or Harley killed over a few paltry dollars."

"And some of those paltry dollars," Houston replied sharply, "will no doubt find their way into your pockets."

He turned and walked to a door to the outside, and Hiesel followed him.

As they reached the door, I glanced back through the archway into the library where they had talked.

A man was standing there, and he was looking right at me.

The gun in his hand was very large, and I knew his face as well as I knew my own.

It was a round, moonlike face, pink and healthy. There were almost no eyebrows, and the mouth was peculiarly flat. When he smiled, he looked cherubic and pleasant. When his mouth closed and his eyes hardened, he looked merciless and brutal.

He was an underworld character known as Candy Chuck Marvin.

"So," he said, "we've a guest." And he added, as I got up and walked out into the open, "Long time no see, Morgan."

"Yeah," I said. "It has been a long time. I haven't

seen you since the Redden mob was wiped out. As I remember, you took a powder at just about that time."

"That's right." He gestured me into the library. The fourth man, the hoodlum in the gray plaid suit, had a gun too. "And where are the boys who wiped out the Redden mob now?"

It took me a minute to get it. "Where are they? Why, let's see." I scowled, trying to recall. "Salter was killed by a hit-and-run driver. Pete Maron hung himself, or something. Lew Fischer and Joey Spats got into an argument over a card game and shot it out, both killed. I guess they are all dead."

"That's right. They are." Candy Chuck smiled at me. "Odd coincidence, isn't it? Fortunately, Pete Maron was light. That hook held his weight. I wasn't sure that it would when I first hung the rope over it. Salter was easy. It's simple enough to run a man down. And it's not too difficult a matter to fake a 'gun battle.' I pay my debts, Morgan."

I smiled at him. Candy Chuck Marvin was cunning, without any mercy, and killing meant nothing to him.

He had been convicted once, when a boy. After that, nobody ever found any witnesses.

"But this time there's going to be a change," I said. "You're turning those girls loose."

He laughed. "Am I?" He sat down on the corner of the desk and looked at me. "Morgan, I've found one of those setups I used to dream about. The boys pulled the Madison Tool payroll job, and they were on the lam. They came to me for a place to hole up. Then I got to talking with the little Harley girl on a train. It was perfect, see? Her parents gone, all the servants on vacations. The two girls were going to Atlanta—on a surprise visit. All we had to do was take them off the train at the next stop, return here and move in, a safe hideout for at least thirty days."

"Looked good, didn't it?" I said. "Until Blubber Puss followed the girl out of that bar."

His eyes hardened. "Was that you who beat up on Buckley? I might have known it." Then he nodded. "Yes," he said ruefully, "that was the bad part. We've got the sixty grand the boys lifted on the pay-roll, but it's hot money. Using it would be a dead giveaway. There was a little money on the girls, but my boys eat. So I sent the babe out with Buckley in order to pick up some cash."

"Winding up," I said dryly, "by knocking off Seagram."

"You know about that?" He looked at me thoughtfully. "You know too much."

Right then I wouldn't have sold my chances of getting out of this mess for a plugged nickel.

I wasn't kidding myself any about Candy Chuck. Take the wiping out of those killers back East. Nobody had ever tumbled that those killings weren't just like they looked—accident, suicide, and gunfight. Candy Chuck knew all the answers.

"There's no end to it," I told him. "You got in a bind and let Seagram learn too much. So you knocked him off. That got the police stirred up. Now you've got me on your hands. Are you going to knock me off too? Don't you see? It just leads from one to another. You got sixty grand in hot money, and for all the good it does you now, you might as well have none. You've got a lawyer with a lot of bonds, but you haven't any cash to work with. The trouble with you, Marvin, is that you figure it all your way. Just like when you were so sure I'd throw that Williams fight because you threatened me."

Candy Chuck Marvin's eyes narrowed and his mouth tightened. "You'd have been smart to let me forget that," he said. "I dropped ten grand on that fight."

"You're not the kind of guy who forgets anything," I said. "And you're in the spot, not me."

This hoodlum with the rod is standing by taking it all in. Most of my talk has been as much for his benefit as for Candy Chuck's. I knew Marvin liked to hear himself tell how smart he was. I knew he would keep on talking. The longer he talked, the better chance I had for a break. One was all I wanted, brother, just one!

The hoodlum was beginning to shift his feet in a worried fashion. He was getting ideas. After all, he and his pals were right in the middle of a strange city, the cops were on their trail, they didn't have any money, and they were trusting to Marvin to pull rabbits out of a hat.

Marvin was good. He had hostages. He was living in one of the biggest, finest homes in the city, the last place anybody would look. Tarrant Houston wouldn't peep for fear of getting the girls killed. Nobody was around to interfere, and soon Houston would be cashing in a lot of bonds.

"Think of your men, Marvin," I said. I turned to the hood. "What do you think will happen to you guys if the cops move in? You guys get sold down the river. You take the rap, and the smart boy here has his pretty lawyer to get him out of it. If you ask me, you guys are just losing time from your getaway to let Marvin use you for a fast take—if it works."

"Shut up." Marvin was on his feet.

"Y'know, the guy's got somethin'."

The voice was a new one and we all turned. I jumped inside my skin. Whit Dyer had a rep like Dillinger's. He was no smart Joe, but he had a nickel's worth of brains, a fast gun hand, and courage enough for three.

"I never did like this setup," Dyer went on.

"Don't pay any attention!" Marvin snapped. "Where would you be, Dyer, if I hadn't brought you here?"

"Search me." Dyer admitted. "But not being here might be good. After all, there's just one way in and out of this yard, as you know. One way in, one way out. If they block those, we're stuck."

Then I saw something. Little things jump to your mind in a spot like that. There was a side window and the gate that led to the street looked right on it. A car was coming along that street. If it turned the corner this way, the lights would—

"Look out!" I shouted.

The car turned and the lights flashed in the window. Nerves were tense and my yell and the sudden flash did it. I hit the floor and snaked out that snub-nosed .38.

Whit Dyer took a quick step back and tripped on the rug. Somebody yelled and I saw a leg and let go a shot at it. Then I rolled over and hit my feet, running.

I made the stairs two at a time and was halfway up before Marvin made the door. They still hadn't figured out where that sudden flash of light had come from and for all they knew the place was alive with coppers.

Dyer rolled over and tried a quick shot at me, but I snapped one back and put a hole in the floor an inch from his head. Candy Chuck steadied himself and I knew if he ever got me in his sights, I was a dead pigeon. I jumped upward and somehow got hold of the railing at the top of the stairs. I threw myself out of the way just as his bullet whipped by. Then I was running.

I had to get the girls out of there. Skating to a stop, I grabbed the knob on their door, but it was locked. One look at the door told me there wasn't time to bust it, so I fired at an angle against the lock and then with a heave the door came open.

"Quick!" I said. "This way!"

The Harley girls caught on fast. They didn't waste any time. I shoved them into the room through which I'd entered.

"Get out onto that tree," I whispered. "You've got to! If you can get down without being seen, hide in the shrubbery."

Dyer and Greer were coming up the steps. They were careful. I had that gun and they didn't know how much ammo I had. Actually, it was half empty, but I also had the .380, which was a better gun, and two extra clips for it.

Backing around the corner of the hall, I caught a glimpse of movement on the stairs and fired. Greer fell and started rolling downstairs. In the suddenly silent house, you could hear his body thump, thump, thump from step to step.

Could the shots be heard on the street? I didn't know. But I did know the house probably had walls a foot thick.

The back stairs. The idea hit me like an axe. There would be another way up, it was that kind of house. But by this time, Blubber Dozen and his skinny friend had been relieved of their guard duty and were coming inside. So that way was cut off.

I was on a long interior balcony from which rooms opened on two sides. The main stairway came up one side, but the railings partially cut off my view of it. I knew I had to get away somehow, but fast, before Dozen and his friend found me.

The hallway was hung with paintings and there were a lot of queer ornaments and art objects standing around. Down beyond me was an old chest of heavy wood and against the wall an Egyptian mummy case.

You didn't need to slug me with a ball bat. I grabbed the lid of that upright mummy case and pulled it open. It was empty, and I stepped in and pulled the lid as near shut as I could and still breathe. Inside the case smelled like a dead Egyptian or something; maybe this one had been embalmed in garlic.

Someone called, "Look out, Ed! He's in the hall!"

Then Blubber Puss answered, "Must've ducked into a room. He ain't in sight."

Heavy footsteps came along, and I saw a dark shadow pass the crack I was keeping open. That was Dozen. But it was Whit Dyer's voice I heard now.

"I don't like this," Dyer muttered. "He got Greer."

"He did?" Dozen's voice spoke back. "Whit, I don't like this either. This place will be hotter than a firecracker. Let's take the geetus and blow!"

"Maybe that's the smart thing. I was thinkin', though, if Marvin gets his dough from that mouth-piece of Harley's, he figures on keeping it. I'm for knocking Marvin off and taking the jack."

Honor among thieves? Not so's you'd notice it!

They moved off and I opened the lid just a little wider. And I stepped right into Skinny.

His jaw dropped open so far you could have put a bottle of Pepsi-Cola in edgewise, and he backed up, gulping. I guess he figured the dead was coming to life. He was so startled that I slapped his gun arm away with my left and lowered the boom on his chin with my right.

He went down like he'd been dropped off the Chrysler Tower, but his finger tightened on the trigger and a shot went off.

Somebody yelled down the line and I heard feet beating up the stairs. Those feet were coming toward me.

Grabbing up Skinny's gun, I opened up. I wasn't shooting at anything, just making the boys nervous. I let them have four rounds and then started off down the hall running full tilt. I was almost at its end when the roof seemed to fall in. I took about three steps and then passed out cold.

When I came out of it, I was lying on the floor in the library and Candy Chuck was sitting over me with a rod. I tried to move, but he had tied my hands behind me and wrapped me up with a couple of yards of clothesline. By craning my neck, I could see that Dyer, Skinny, and Dozen were also in the room.

"Don't squirm," Candy Chuck said politely. "Just rest easy." Then his face tightened and he leaned over and began slapping me. When he stopped, his face was a snarl.

"Where's the babes?" he said.

"What babes?" I asked innocently. "I thought you had 'em."

"Don't give me that," he said. "You hid them someplace. Now give, or I'm going to see how long it'll take to burn your foot off."

He would, too.

"Don't do it," I say. "I can't stand the smell of burning flesh. Reminds me of a guy I saw get it in the hot seat, once. You should be interested in that. It won't—"

He booted me in the ribs, and it hurt.

I stopped. I had no yen to get kicked around, and there was a chance he hadn't found my .380. No normal frisk would turn it up. Yet he might kick it, and then he would find it. Those ropes weren't bothering me. I had an idea that given a few minutes alone, I could shed them like last year's blonde.

"Listen, sport," I said, and I was addressing Dyer,

Skinny, and Dozen, as well as Candy Chuck. Skinny I noticed had a knot on his head where he had hit the deck, and his jaw was swollen. "Why don't you boys play it smart and drag it out of here with the dough you got?"

"Shut up," Marvin said.

His rosy plan didn't look so good now. He was sore, and he was also uneasy. The girls were gone. With the guards and all he probably figured they hadn't left the grounds but without the girls he wouldn't get the money from Houston.

"I'd take it on the lam," I repeated. Then I added, as an afterthought, "This place is filthy with telephones."

He jumped. Then he jerked erect. "Dozen, you and Palo get busy and hunt those babes! Don't stop until you find 'em. You, too, Dyer."

Dyer didn't move. "Look who's giving orders," he said. "I'm stayin'. This guy on the floor makes sense. I like to listen."

Candy Chuck looked up, and if I had been Dyer, I wouldn't have felt good.

"All right," Candy Chuck said, "stay."

Candy Chuck Marvin was big time. You couldn't dodge that. He had been the brain behind many big jobs, and he had stayed in the clear a long time. Also, he had friends. Whit Dyer was merely a guy with a gat, a guy who would and could kill. And he was only about half smart. When Candy Chuck softened up, I knew that Dyer didn't have long to live.

Candy Chuck Marvin had been a big operator around Chicago, St. Paul, and New York. He had connections. Back in the days when I was slinging leather, I'd seen a lot of him. From all I knew, I figured I was the only guy who ever failed to play ball with him and got away alive. He'd ordered me to throw a fight, and I hadn't done it. Then again, I hadn't been easy to find in those days.

Marvin got up and walked over to the fireplace. There was a little kindling there, and he arranged it on the andirons. Then he calmly broke up a chair and added it to the fuel. He lit a crumpled newspaper and stuck it under the wood. Then he picked up the poker and laid it in the fire. When he put the poker there, he looked at me and grinned.

Me, I was sweating. Not because it was hot, but because I was wondering how I'd take it. You may read about people being tortured, but you never know how you'll react to getting your feet burned until it happens.

The fire was really heating things up when suddenly, I heard the door close, the sound of footsteps, and there was Hiesel, the runt lawyer. He looked at me, then at Marvin.

"Who's this, Chuck?" he said.

"A nosy guy named Morgan. He got the girls out an' hid 'em someplace." He grinned. "I'm going to warm his feet until he talks."

Hiesel's smooth, polished face tightened. He looked down at me.

"This is the man they have the call out for, Chuck. A police call out for him. You'd better get rid of him."

My eyes went to Hiesel. Get rid of me? Just like that? Brother, I said to myself, if I get out of this I'm going to come around and ask you about that!

"And Chuck—Tarrant Houston's gone to work getting those bonds sold. He's working fast, too. He's afraid for the girls."

"He should be," Marvin answered and smiled. "We'll take care of the girls as soon as he shows with the money. And him, too."

He licked his lips. "That older girl, Eleanor. I'd like to talk with her, in private, before anything is done."

Candy Chuck Marvin looked up. He laughed coarsely. "Talk? I see what you mean. I'd like a private talk with her myself."

That poker was hot by now. Candy Chuck pulled it out of the fire and Ford Hiesel's face turned slightly pale. He left the room and Candy Chuck laughed, and began untying my shoe.

"I wouldn't do that," I said. "I haven't changed my socks since I started chasing you guys."

"Smart guy, huh?"

Candy Chuck's eyes were gleaming. He started to pull off my shoes when a calm, low voice interrupted.

"I wouldn't do that."

We both looked around. Eleanor Harley, her face a bit drawn, but as beautiful as that first day I'd seen her in the bar, was standing in the doorway. Candy Chuck lunged to his feet.

"Come here!" he demanded. But she turned suddenly and ducked out of sight. He ran after her.

It was my chance, and I took it. Kicking my tied feet around, I got the ropes that bound my ankles across the red-hot poker, then struggled to a sitting position and began working at my hands. The knots weren't a good job, and lying there on the floor, I had managed to get them a bit looser.

That clothesline burned nicely, and I could hear Candy Chuck Marvin banging around in a room nearby when the first rope came apart.

I kicked and squirmed, getting the other ropes loose, then managed to struggle to my feet.

Forcing my wrists as low as I could get them, I backed my hips through the circle of my arms. Then falling on my back, I got my hands in front of me by pulling my knees against my chest and shoving my feet down through my arms. Then I went to work on the knots with my teeth.

Then I heard somebody coming and looked around to see Blubber Puss. He opened his mouth to yell and I dove at him, driving my head for his stomach. He no more than had his mouth open before I hit him head down and with everything I had behind it.

He went back through the door with an *oof*, hitting the floor hard. Still fighting those ropes, I kept moving. They came loose as I was rounding into the passage to the back of the house, but suddenly I got an idea and my gun, out. I raced for the library again.

Grabbing up a couple of carpets, I stuffed them onto the fire. They caught hold and began to burn. Then I took another carpet and, spilling a pitcher of water they'd had for mixing drinks over it, I put it on the fire. All that smoke would make people very, very curious.

Somewhere out in the back regions of the house, I heard a girl scream. I wheeled around, and saw Whit Dyer looking at me. He had a gun in his hands and you could see the killing lust in his eyes.

My gun was ready, and I've had lots of practice with it. Dyer jerked his up and I let go from where mine was, just squeezing the shot off. The sound of that .380 and his .45 made a concussion like a charge of dynamite in that closed-in room.

I heard his bullet hit the wall behind me and saw a queer look in his face. Then, looking at the spot over his belt buckle, I squeezed off the rest of the magazine. He grabbed his middle like he'd been eating green apples and went over on the carpet, and I went out the door and into the hall.

Somewhere outside, there was a crash and then a sound of shots. I didn't know what it meant, but I was heading toward that scream I'd heard.

Candy Chuck Marvin had caught Eleanor in the kitchen. She was fighting, but there wasn't much fight left in her. I grabbed Candy Chuck by the scruff of the neck and jerked him back. His gun was lying on the table and I caught it up and heaved it out the window, right through the glass.

Then I tossed my empty gun on the floor under the range. There was a wicked gleam in Candy Chuck's eyes. He was panting and staring at me. He was bigger than me by twenty pounds and he'd been raised in a rough school.

He lunged, throwing a wallop that would have ripped my jaw off. But I slipped it and smashed one into his wind that jerked his mouth open. I hooked my left into his wind and he backed off. I followed him, stabbing a left into his mouth. He didn't have blubber lips but they bled.

I hooked a short, sharp left to the eye, and smashed him back against the sink. He grabbed a pitcher and lunged for me, but I went under it and knocked it out of his hand.

Eleanor Harley was standing there, her dress torn, her eyes wide, staring at us. Then the door opened and Mooney stepped in, two cops right behind him, and Tarrant Houston following them.

Mooney took in the scene with one swift look. Then he leaned nonchalantly against the drain board.

"Don't mind me," he said. "Go right ahead."

Candy Chuck Marvin caught me with a right that knocked me into the range. I weaved under a left and hooked both hands short and hard to the body, then I shoved him away and jabbed a left to his face. Again, and then again. Three more times I hit him with the left, keeping his head bobbing like a cork in a millstream and then I pulled the trigger on my Sunday punch. It went right down the groove for home plate and exploded on his chin. His knees turned to rubber, then melted under him and he went down.

Me, I staggered back against the drain board and stood there, panting like a dowager at a Gregory Peck movie.

Mooney looked Candy Chuck Marvin over with professional interest, then glanced at me approvingly.

"Nice job," he said. "I couldn't do as good with a set of knucks and a razor. Is he who I think he is?"

"Yeah," I said, "Candy Chuck Marvin, and this time you've got enough on him to hang him."

Ford Hiesel shoved into the room. "Got them, did you?" he said. "Good work!"

Then he saw me, and his face turned sick. He started to back away and you could see the rat in him hunting a way out.

"This guy," I said, "advised Candy Chuck to get rid of me, and told him it would be a good idea to get rid of the girls and Houston—to make a clean sweep!"

Eleanor lifted her head. "I heard him say it!" she put in. "We hid in the closet behind the mirror in the hall."

Ford Hiesel started to protest, but there had been enough talk. I shoved him against the drain board, and when I was between him and the rest of the room, I whipped my right up into his solar plexus. The wind went out of him like a pricked balloon and he began gasping for breath. I turned back to the others, gestured at him.

"Asthma," I said. "Bad, too."

"What about the diamonds?" Mooney asked suddenly. "Why didn't they fence them?"

Eleanor turned toward the detective.

"They talked about it," she said. "But the only man who would have handled the diamonds here was picked up by the police, and Marvin was hoping he could arrange things, meanwhile, to keep them for himself."

Then I told her about the pin, and she came over

to me as Mooney commented, "I know about that. A clerk named Davis, at the jewelry store, got in touch with me when they checked and found out the pin belonged to Eleanor Harley. That and the smoke tipped us off to this place."

She was looking up at me with those eyes, almost too beautiful to believe.

"I can't thank you enough for what you've done," she said.

"Sure you can," I said, grinning. "Let's go down to the Casino and talk to a couple of bartenders while we have some drinks. Then, I can tell you all about it."

Ain't I the cad, though?

SIX-GUN
STAMPEDE

It's no use, Tom," Ginnie Rollins said. "Dad just won't listen. He says you're no good. That you've no sense of responsibility. He says you haven't anything and you never will have."

"Do you think that, Ginnie?" Tom Brandon asked. "Do you?"

"You know I don't, Tom. You shouldn't even ask. But you can't blame Dad. He only wants what is best for me, and every time I mention you, he brings up the fact that you are always racing horses and fighting. He says he'll have no saloon brawler for a son-in-law."

"It isn't only that," Tom said, discouragement heavy in his voice, "it's that herd I lost. Every time I try to get a job, they bring that up. I reckon half of 'em think I was plumb careless an' the other half think I'm a thief." They both sat silent. Despite the cold wind neither felt like moving. It was not often anymore that they had a chance to talk, and this meeting had been an accident—but an accident each of them had been hoping would happen.

Whether they would see each other again was doubtful. Jim Rollins was a hard-bitten old cattleman with one of the biggest ranches in the country, and he had refused Tom Brandon the right to come on his spread. Not only refused him the premises, but had ordered his hands to enforce it. Though several of them were old friends of Tom's, the foreman was Lon Huffman, with whom Tom had two disastrous fistfights, both of which Huffman had won.

Lon was a good deal the bigger man, and skilled in rough-and-tumble fighting, but each time he had a bad time in beating Brandon, who was tough, willing, and wiry. His dislike for Tom was no secret, and it extended to his particular cronies, Eason and Bensch.

"I'll always think somebody deliberately stampeded that herd on me," Brandon said. "The whole thing was too pat. There it was, the herd close to the border an' well bedded down. All of a sudden, they busted loose an' started to run—right over into Mexico. An' when I started after 'em, there was the Rurales lined up on the border sayin' no. It looked like a rigged deal."

"But who would do such a thing, Tom?" Ginnie protested. "I know you've said that, but Dad claims it's just an excuse. Who would do anything of the sort? There's no rustling here, and there haven't been any bandits for years."

"Just the same," Tom insisted, "if a man made a

deal with old Juan Morales over at Los Molinos, he could get a good price for those cattle. Those Rurales were too much Johnny-on-the-spot."

Finally, they said a hopeless good-bye and Tom Brandon turned his grulla and started for Animas. He was broke, out of a job, and had nothing in sight. The wind was blowing cold from the north, but it seemed to be falling off a little. If the weather got warmer it would help some. It began to look like he would be camping out all winter, he reflected grimly, or riding the chuck line.

Animas was a quiet town. There had been but one killing all year, and that because of a misguided attempt by a half-breed to draw a gun on Lon Huffman. What had started the altercation was not known aside from what Huffman himself had said and Eason had verified. The half-breed, a man with a reputation as a hard character in Sonora, had come into town hunting Huffman. He had found him, there had been angry words, and Huffman had killed the breed. "Just a trouble hunter," Huffman said gruffly. "Came into town aimin' to kill somebody, an' picked me."

There were four general stores in Animas and but three saloons. The only gambling done was a few games of draw or stud between friends or casual acquaintances.

Tom Brandon swung down from his grulla and led the horse into the stable. Old Man Hubbell looked up at him. "Sorry to bother you, Tom, but

you better have some money soon. The boss is gettin' riled."

"Sure, Hub. An' thanks." He turned and walked
toward the Animas Saloon, reflecting grimly that if
he had any friends left, they would be there. It was
remarkable how a man's friends fell away when he
was out of a job and broke. Luckily, he had always
been considerate to old Hub, which was more than
most of the riders were. Hub remembered, and his
brother, Neil Hubbell, who owned the Animas, was
also friendly.

It was warm inside and the potbellied stove was
glowing with heat. Neil nodded from a table as he
came in, and indicated a bottle that stood on the bar.
"Help yourself, Tom. I'm about to take some money
away from Jim."

Jim Rollins glanced up briefly, his hard old eyes
showing his disapproval, but he said nothing. Lon
Huffman, who was sitting by the stove, tipped back
in his chair and grinned maliciously. "You goin' to
be that good to me if I become a pauper, Neil?"

The room was suddenly dead still and Tom
Brandon jerked his hand away from the bottle as if
stung. He turned slowly, his face white. Why he said
it, he would never know, but somehow the words
just came of their own free will. "I'd rather be an
honest pauper," he said, "than a rich thief."

Lon Huffman's face turned dark and his chair legs
slammed down. "I reckon," he said, getting to his
feet, "I'm goin' to have to beat some more sense into
that thick skull o' your'n."

"That's good because I'm not wearin' a gun, Lon,"

Brandon said coolly, "so you've no excuse to murder me."

Rollins turned sharply. "Brandon, that's uncalled for!" he declared angrily. "You got no cause to call Lon a murderer because some breed hunted him for trouble!"

Tom Brandon was raging inside. He had nothing on which to base his accusation but suspicion, and that, he admitted to himself, might stem from his own dislike of Huffman, but he spoke again regardless. "Nobody knows he came huntin' for trouble. Lon says so. Eason says so. But when didn't Eason say what Lon wanted him to?"

Lon Huffman's mouth was an ugly line. He was a big, hard man but he moved fast. Also, this talk was not doing him any good. The sooner it was stopped, the better. "You said enough," he said. "You done called me a liar! You called Eason a liar." He grabbed at Tom, and Brandon stepped back and hit him.

The punch caught Lon on the chin but lacked force, as Tom was stepping back. Huffman ducked his head a little and struck swiftly. The first punch caught Tom on the jaw and smashed his head back. The second hit him on the temple and he started to fall. Huffman lunged close, trying with his knee, but Tom grabbed both hands around the underside of the knee and jerked up. Lon Huffman lost balance and fell hard. Tom stepped back, wiping blood from his lips. He was still stunned by those first blows.

Huffman got up, then rushed. Tom struck out wickedly and the two fought savagely while the men in the room sat silent, watching.

Most of them had seen the other two fights and there was no doubt about what would happen now. And inevitably, it did happen. They had been fighting several minutes when Huffman's superior weight and strength began to tell. Tom fought back gamely but he was beaten to the floor. He struggled up, was knocked down again, and fell over against the bar. Huffman was only stopped from putting the boots to him by the other men in the room.

Bloody and battered, Tom Brandon staggered from the room. Outside the wind was cold and his face was left numb. Grimly he looked at his battered hands, and then he turned and half walked and half staggered to the livery stable, where he crawled into the hay and wrapped himself in his blanket.

Before daybreak he was in the saddle and heading out of town. He was through here, of that there could be no question now. He was being kicked around by everybody, and just a few months before he had been liked and respected. It had started with his first fight with Huffman, then the loss of the herd and the talk about it. After that, things had unraveled rapidly. There was nothing to do but drift.

By noon he was miles to the east and riding huddled in the saddle, cold and hungry. Suddenly, he saw several cattle drifting sullenly along the trail toward him. As he came up to them, he saw they wore a Rafter H brand. The Rafter H, he recalled, was a small spread some seven or eight miles further east. These cattle were rapidly drifting away and might never get home in this cold. Turning them, he started them back toward their home ranch, and through the next hour and a half, he kept them moving. When he sighted the cabin and the gate, he hallooed loudly.

The door opened and a stocky, powerful man stepped to the door and at Brandon's hail, opened the gate. Brandon herded the cattle inside and drew up.

"Thanks." The cattleman strode toward him. "Where'd you find 'em?"

Brandon explained, and the man looked at his face, then said, "My name's Jeff Hardin. Get down and come in, you look about beat. Anyway, I'm just fixin' supper."

Hours later they sat together in front of the fireplace. Hardin had proved an interested listener, and Brandon had been warmed by coffee and companionship into telling his troubles. Hardin chuckled softly. "Friend," he said, "you've had it rough. What you doin' now? Lightin' a shuck?"

"What else can I do? Nobody would give me a job there, an' I can't lick Huffman. He's whipped me three times runnin' an' a man ought to know when he's whipped."

Hardin shrugged. "How do you feel about it? Do you feel like you'd been licked?"

Brandon looked rueful. "That's the worst of it," he said. "I don't. I'd like to tackle him again, but he's just too all-fired big for me."

Hardin got to his feet and stretched. "Well, if you ain't headed anywhere in particular, why not spend a month or so here? I could use the help, an' she gets mighty lonesome by myself. I'm a good cook," he added, "but a feller don't feel like it much when he's by himself."

For three days, Brandon worked cattle, cut wood, and fed stock and then one morning, Jeff Hardin came from the house carrying a set of boxing gloves.

"Ever have these on?" he asked.

"Never saw any before," Tom admitted, "although I heard somebody invented something of the kind. What's the idea?"

"Why," Hardin said quietly, "I figure any man who will tackle a bigger, stronger man three times in a row an' is still willin' to try it again should have his chance. Now I used to take beef to New Orleans an' Kansas City, an' I used to know a few prizefighters. They taught me some things. I also know some Cornish-style wrestlin'. I figure you should go back to Animas in a couple of months and whip the socks off Huffman. You want to try learnin'?"

Tom Brandon grinned. "You've got yourself a pupil!" he said. "Let's have those mitts."

A month later, Hardin ended a hot session with Tom and grinned as he wiped sweat off of his forehead. "You're good, Tom," he admitted, "an' a sight younger than I am. You've got a good left an' you've got that short right to the body in good shape. I reckon you'll be ready in a little while."

Several weeks passed and the weather settled down into day after day of cold. "You know," Hardin said one evening, "this here breed you were sayin' was killed by that Lon Huffman—he reminds me of a feller used to ride with Juan Morales."

That brought Tom up straight. "Are you sure?"

"Sounds like him. One time I was way down south an' I seen someone who looked like that. Folks said he was mixed up in some shady cattle deals with Morales, and how he buys ever' stolen cow he can get." He puffed for a few minutes on his pipe. "Tom, d'you s'pose that Huffman could have suddenly decided to drive off that herd o' yours?"

Tom Brandon was dubious. "I practically accused him of it when we had that last fight," he admitted, "but it was temper talkin'. I never should have said it. Only something about that killin' didn't smell right."

"Pay you to look into it," Hardin advised, "when I get back."

"Back?" Brandon looked up in surprise. "Where you goin'?"

"Got a letter," he said, carelessly. "I'll have to leave you here alone. Look after the place, will you? I want to buy some stock. I'll be back in a couple of weeks."

Alone on the place, it surprised Brandon that he could find so much to keep him busy. There was the stable door that needed fixing, a couple of water holes that needed cleaning out, then a dam to stop a wash that had started. Day after day he was up with the sun, riding over the range, working, losing himself in the many tasks to be done. In all that time, he never went near town. He thought of far-away Animas, but that was behind him. Only at times, when he thought of Ginnie Rollins, it was almost all he could do not to saddle up and start back.

There was no word from Jeff for almost a month, and then a letter did come, from El Paso.

Been busy. Just returned from Mexico. Will see you next month. Met a mighty pretty girl.

Tom read the note and grinned. Met a pretty girl! At his age! He chuckled, and returned to work. That was the good thing about a ranch, he reflected, a man was never out of work. He could always find something to do. He branded a few strays, moved some of the younger stock down nearer the ranch, hunted down a cougar who had been giving them trouble, and killed two wolves, both with his Winchester at more than three hundred yards.

The days drifted into weeks, and alone on the ranch, Tom Brandon worked hard. Jeff Hardin had been a friend to him when he needed a friend, and he wanted to surprise him, but it was a pleasure just to do what he knew needed to be done. He broke horses, built and repaired fence, cleaned up a patch for a garden, and when Jeff had been gone two months, the place had changed beyond belief.

Then, suddenly, a package was delivered to him at the gate. Ripping it open, he found a letter from Jeff on top. Beneath the letter were several legal-looking papers.

These will explain the delay in returning. When you get this stuff, better high-tail it for Animas.

Stunned, he stared at the papers. On top was a statement, sworn to before a notary, that the signer had seen Juan Morales pay money to Lon Huffman for cattle. The second was a statement by a Mexican, that Morales had given him orders to be at the border to receive a bunch of stampeding cattle, and that the letter informing Morales about the cattle had been in English. The Mexican also testified that Lon Huffman had been with the stampeding cattle, which had all worn the Rollins R brand.

Staying only long enough to get an old man who lived nearby to feed the stock, Brandon threw a saddle on his horse and headed back for Animas.

Months had gone by since he had seen the town, and he came up the street at a canter and drew up before the saloon. Swinging down, he pushed through the doors and walked at once to the bar.

Neil Hubbell broke into a smile when he saw him, then glanced hastily at the door. "Tom, you be careful! Lon Huffman's been sayin' he drove you out of town an' that if you ever show your face around, he'll kill you."

"Neil," Tom requested, "come around here and search me. I'm not heeled except with this gun that I'm leavin' with you." He stripped off his pistol and belt, handing them over the bar. "I want to see Lon, but I want to fight him bare-handed."

"Ain't you had enough of that?" Hubbell demanded. "Tom, I think—" He broke off as the door opened and Lon Huffman came in with Eason and

Bensch. Huffman stopped abruptly when he saw Tom.

"You?" he said. "Well, I ran you off once an' I'll do it again!" He spread his hands over his guns.

"Hold it, Lon!" Hubbell's voice was stern. "Brandon just turned his gun over to me. He ain't heeled."

"Then give it back to him!"

Tom Brandon took an easy step forward, his heart pounding and his mouth dry. Here it was, the fourth time—would this be another beating? Or were the things that Jeff had taught him the answer? "Unless you're dead set on gettin' killed, Lon," he said quietly, "I'd like to beat your ears in with my fists."

Huffman stared, then he took a fast step forward and swung.

Tom's move was automatic, and it was so easy that it astonished him. He threw up his left forearm to catch the swing, then smashed his own right fist to the ribs. Huffman stopped in his tracks, jolted to the heels. Before he could get set, Tom chopped a short left to the cheek that cut deep and started blood coming down Huffman's face.

Huffman lunged close, swinging with both hands, and Tom stepped inside of a left and, grabbing the sleeve of Huffman's right arm with his own left, he threw his hip into Huffman and jerked hard on the left. Huffman hit the floor hard, and his face went dark with blood. With a lunge, he came off the floor, and Tom Brandon waited for him. This was easy, almost too easy!

Tom stiffened his left into Lon's face, then hit him with a short right to the wind. Huffman backed up, looking sick, and Tom closed in, then struck twice, left and right to the face. Blood was over Huffman's eye and cheek now, and he was staggering.

Brandon moved in, feinted, then whipped that right to the wind. Huffman stopped in his tracks and Tom hit him with a left three times before Huffman could get sorted out. He lunged forward and Brandon stepped in with a short right that dropped Huffman to his knees, his nose welling blood.

He looked up then and was amazed to see Jeff Hardin standing in the door with Jim and Ginnie Rollins beside him.

"Nice work, boy!" Hardin stepped forward grinning. "Very nice work!" Then his face became stern. "Have you got those papers?"

Tom Brandon reached into his shirt for the papers and Hardin handed them to the older man. As Rollins looked at them, his face became hard and cold. Lon Huffman was on his feet, helped there by Bensch.

"An' I trusted you!" Jim Rollins growled. "You dirty . . . no-good . . ."

Huffman wiped blood from his face and stared at them sullenly. "What's the matter?" he demanded. "You gone crazy?"

"Just a matter of a stampeded herd, Lon," Brandon said quietly. "Just a matter of a herd stampeded over the border so Juan could get his brother-in-law up there with the Rurales and prevent our recovering them. They call that stealing, Lon."

Huffman tried to bluff it through. "Didn't do no such thing!" he said. "An' there ain't nobody can say I did!"

Brandon smiled. "Those papers Jim has say so. We've got proof. Even Juan Morales hasn't any respect for a man who would double-cross his employer—or shoot a rider of his because he was afraid the fellow would talk too much while he was drunk!"

Awareness cleared Huffman's brain. He hesitated, then half-turned, throwing a meaningful glance at Eason. He was trapped.

He ran a hand over his face. "Guess there ain't nothin' but to give up—"

Eason had edged to the door and now he suddenly whipped it open, and at the same instant, Huffman went for his gun. Bensch plunged out the door, hit the saddle, and shucked his Winchester, but as Huffman's gun came up, both Rollins and Hardin fired. Struck with two bullets, Lon pitched over on his face.

Eason had frozen where he was, his fingers pulling away from the gun butt.

Bensch took one look, then wheeled his horse. Rollins lifted his gun, but Hardin brushed it aside. "Let him go. He won't do us any harm."

Hardin smiled then. "This here's that pretty girl I spoke of meetin', son. You told me so much about her an' about all that happened here that it decided me. I used to be a Pinkerton man. Well, you were in a bad position and it seemed to me the right man might get you out of it. It was small pay for the way you were fixin' up my ranch. Actually, I've been settin' around too long. Needed a vacation."

"You got here just in time," Tom admitted, smiling.

"Tom," Rollins thrust out a hand, "I reckon I'm an old fool. I'm sorry."

Tom took the hand and when he released it he took Ginnie's arm. "Why don't you two go get yourselves a drink? Because Ginnie and I have things to talk about."

PIRATES
OF THE SKY

Turk Madden came in toward the coast of Eromanger at an elevation of about three thousand feet. The Grumman amphibian handled nicely, and flying in the warm sunshine over the Coral Sea was enough to put anyone in a good mood. Especially when Tony Yorke and Angela waited at the end of the trip in the bungalow by Polenia Bay. A night of good company, especially Angela's, would take his worries away. The war in Asia was expanding. Someday soon America would be involved, and all this—the express freight and passenger business he had worked so hard to build—would be no more.

Curiously, Turk's eyes swung to the interior. The island was only about twenty-five miles long, and perhaps ten wide, yet it was almost unknown except for a few isolated spots along either coast. Several times, he had considered taking time out to fly over the island and down its backbone.

Madden shrugged. Flying freight, even when you were working for yourself, didn't leave much time or gas for exploring. When he saw Traitor's Head looming up before him, he banked slightly, and put the ship into a steep glide that carried it into Polenia Bay. Deftly, he banked again, swinging into the cove, and trimmed the Grumman for a landing. It was then he saw the body.

The ship skimmed the water, slapped slightly, and ran in toward the wharf, but Turk Madden's eyes were narrowed and thoughtful. Violence in the New Hebrides was bad medicine and there, floating on the waters of the cove, almost in the bay now, was the body of a native with his head half blown away.

None of Yorke's boys came running to meet him. Instead, a white man in soiled white trousers and a blue shirt came walking down to the wharf. He was a big man, and he wore a heavy automatic in a shoulder holster.

Turk cut the motor, and tossed the man a line, then dropped his anchor. He was thinking rapidly. But when he stepped up on the wharf, his manner was casual.

"Hello," he said. "I don't believe I've met you before. Where's Yorke?"

"Yorke?" The big man's eyes were challenging. He lit a cigarette before he answered, then snapped the match into the water with studied insolence. "He sold out. He sold this place to me. He left two weeks ago."

"Sold out?" Madden was incredulous. "Where'd he go? Sydney?"

"No," the man said slowly. "He bought passage on a trading schooner. He was going to loaf around the islands awhile, then wind up in Suva or Pago Pago."

"That's funny," Madden said, rubbing his jaw. "He ordered some stuff from me. Told me to fly it in for him. Some books, medicine, food supplies, and clothes."

"Yeah," the big man nodded. "My name is Karchel. He told me he had some stuff coming in. My price included that."

"You made a nice buy," Turk said. "Well, maybe I can do some business with you once in a while."

"Yeah," Karchel said. "Maybe you can." His eyes turned to the plane. "Nice ship you got there. Those Grumman amphibs do about two hundred, don't they?"

"Most of them," Madden said shortly. "This was an experimental job. Too expensive, so they didn't make any more. But she's a honey. She'll do two forty at top speed."

"Well," Karchel said, "you might as well come up and have a drink. No use unloading that boat right now. An hour will do. I expect you want to get away before sundown."

He turned and strolled carelessly up the path toward the bungalow, and Turk Madden followed. His face was expressionless, but his mind was teeming. If there was one thing that wouldn't happen, it would be Tony Yorke selling out.

Tony and Angela, he was sure, loved their little home on Polenia Bay. If they had told him that once, they had told him fifty times.

Now this man, Karchel, something about his face was vaguely familiar, but Turk couldn't recall where he had seen it before.

"You don't sound Dutch," Karchel said suddenly. "You're an American, aren't you?"

"Sure," Turk said. "My name is Madden. Turk Madden."

Instantly, he realized he had made a mistake. The man's eyes came up slowly, and involuntarily they glanced quickly at the brush behind Turk. Another guy, behind me, Turk thought. But Karchel smiled.

"I heard that name," he said. "Weren't you the guy who made all that trouble for Johnny Puccini back in Philly?"

Sure, Turk thought. That would be it. How the devil could he ever have forgotten the name of Steve Karchel? Shot his way out of the pen once, stuck up the Tudor Trust Company for $70,000, the right-hand man of Harry Wissler.

"If you want to call it that," Turk said. He stepped up beside Karchel. "Johnny was a tough cookie, but he wanted to organize all the mail pilots. I was working for Uncle Sam, and nobody tells me where to get off."

Karchel dropped his cigarette in the gravel path.

"No?" he said. "Nobody tells you, huh?"

Two men had come out of the brush with Thompson submachine guns. They looked tough. Covered all the time, Turk thought. Those guys had it on me. I must be slipping. Aloud, he said:

"You boys got a nice place here." He looked around. "A right nice place."

"Yeah," Karchel chuckled coldly. "Lucky Yorke was ready to sell." He motioned up the steps. "But come on in. Big Harry will be wanting to see the guy who thumbed his nose at the Puccini mob."

Turk walked up the steps and then the mosquito netting flopped from the door, and a man stepped out. He was a slim, wiry man with a narrow face. His eyes were almost white, his hair lank and blond. He was neatly dressed in a suit of white silk, and there was a gun stuck in his waistband.

"Who's this punk?" he snapped. "Didn't I tell you if you found any more to cool 'em off?"

"This guy's different, Chief," Karchel said. "He's a flyer. Just flew in here with some stuff for Yorke. I told him how we bought the place, and the stuff would come to us."

"Oh?" Big Harry Wissler sneered. "You did, did you?" He stepped up to Madden, his white eyes narrowed with ugliness. "Well, he lied. We wanted this spot, so we just moved in. Some of these damned niggers got in the way, so we wiped 'em out."

"What about Yorke?" Turk said. "And Angela?"

Wissler's eyes gleamed. "What? What did you say? Who's this Angela?"

Madden could have kicked himself for a fool. Somehow then, Angela Yorke had managed to get away.

"What d'you mean?" Wissler snapped. "Speak up, you damn fool! Was there a woman here? We heard she'd left!"

"She had," Madden said quickly. "I didn't think."

"Oh? You didn't think!" Wissler sneered. Then he wheeled, his eyes blazing. "You idiots get out an' find that woman! Find her if you tear the place apart. The one who finds her gets a grand. If you don't have her by night, somebody gets killed, see?"

The man was raging, his white face flushed crimson, and his small eyes glowed like white-hot bits of steel.

"Take this punk away. Put him somewhere. I'll take care of him later."

Karchel's hand was shaking when he took Turk's gun. The two men with tommy guns covered him so he was powerless. Then, they hurried him from the veranda and down to a big copra shed.

"The chief's got the willies," Karchel said. "We better watch our step."

"Why stick with him?" Turk said. "You'll get it in the neck yourselves, if you aren't careful."

"You shut your trap," Karchel snapped abruptly. "I would've burned if he hadn't helped me out of the pen. You couldn't leave him, anyway. He's got eight or ten million hid away. He'd follow you till the last dime was gone. He'd get you. Nobody ever hated like that guy."

Behind the copra shed a steep cliff reared up from the jungle growth, lifting a broken, ugly escarpment of rock at least two hundred feet. Here and there vines covered the side of the precipice, and from the rear of the shed to the foot of the cliff was a dense tangle. Once, three months ago, Turk had helped Yorke find an injured dog back in that tangle.

A sudden thought came to him with that memory. "Damn! My plane's sinking!" he shouted.

Karchel stopped abruptly, staring. Madden swung, and his big fist caught the gunman on the angle of the jaw, then he leaped around the corner of the copra shed and ran!

Behind him rose a shout of anger, then one of the men who had been with Karchel sprang past the corner and jerked up his submachine gun. Turk hit the ground rolling, heard bullets buzzing around him like angry bees, one kicking mud into his face. Then he was around the corner and into the brush. He dropped to his hands and knees and crawled between the spidery roots of a huge mangrove, wormed his way around the bole of the tree, and then on through another.

He halted, breathing hard, and began to work his way along more carefully. This was the way the dog had come, trying to find a place to die in peace. Almost before he realized it, he found himself at the foot of the cliff.

Again he halted, pulled aside a drapery of vines. He stepped quickly into a crack in the rock and found himself in a chimney of granite, its walls jagged and broken. It led straight up for over two hundred feet. Carefully, taking his time, he began to climb.

It was nearly a half hour later that he came out on top, and without waiting to look back, walked quickly into the jungle and started for the top of Traitor's Head.

He had been climbing for some time when he heard the movement. Instantly, he dropped flat on his face and rolled over into the grass beside the trail. The movement came to him again, and he edged along in the brush, peered out.

A girl was coming down the trail, moving carefully. In one hand she gripped a sharpened stick, a crude weapon, but it could be a dangerous one.

"Angela!" he gasped.

"Turk!" Her eyes brightened and she ran toward him. "I saw you flying in, tried to warn you, but you didn't see me. I was on the summit of the Head."

"Where'd they come from?" he asked. "How long have they been here?"

"They came in about three days ago. They've got a steam yacht hidden, with a lot of gunmen aboard. They've two planes, too. They killed Salo, our foreman. Tony came running down the beach and knocked one of the men down. They grabbed him then, and started beating him. I knew I couldn't help him by going down there, so I hid."

"A good thing you did," he said. "That blondheaded man? He's Harry Wissler, a gangster from the States, and as crazy and dangerous as they come. The big man is Steve Karchel, he's almost as bad."

"I heard them say they were going to hijack some ships," she told him. "They have a fast motorboat and two planes. They want to use this for a base, and loot ships going to and from Australia."

"That's absurd!" he said. "They couldn't get away—" He hesitated. "They might, at that. They wouldn't leave any survivors, and they'd sink the ships. There's a war on now, that might make the difference."

"What are we going to do, Turk?" Angela said. Her gray eyes were wide, serious. "We've got to do something! Tony's down there—they may kill him any time. And then some ship will come along . . . it would be awful!"

"Yeah," he replied, nodding slowly. "Where's their yacht?"

"In Cook Bay. But they won't leave it there long. It is too exposed."

"So's Polenia, as far as that goes. But the cove is okay. That is sheltered enough. Did you hear them mention any particular ship?"

"The *Erradaka*. I remember her very well because I once went from Noumea to Sydney on her. But they expect to get her before she reaches Noumea."

The *Erradaka* was a passenger liner of some fifteen thousand tons, running from San Francisco to Sydney. She passed within a comparatively short distance of the island.

"Our problem now is to hide," he told her. "They've got orders to find us—or else."

"We'll go where I've been." She walked faster, and he was glad to step out and keep moving. "It's in a place they'd never discover in years!"

They reached the round top of Traitor's Head, and she walked straight forward to the very edge of the precipice. Then she stepped carefully over the edge!

He gasped and jumped to catch her arm, but she laughed at him.

"Come on over!" she said. "See! There's a ledge, a few steps, and a cave!"

An instant his eyes strayed out over the edge. It was a long drop to the sea, and yet a more secure hiding place couldn't be found. The cave was invisible from above, and one had to dare that narrow, foot-wide ledge before they could see the black opening. Inside it was dry and cool, and somewhere he heard water running.

"How in the world did you ever find this?" he demanded, incredulous.

"I climbed the Head one day, just to be doing it, and saw a rat go over here. I hurried up to see why a rat should commit suicide and saw him disappear in the rock. I decided to investigate, and found this. Even Tony doesn't know it's here!"

Turk Madden looked around the bare, rock-floored cave. A perfect hideout if ever there was one. Their greatest danger was to be seen from the sea when coming or going. A boat or plane might see them, as it was coming through the entrance to Polenia. Otherwise, with food and water, they could remain indefinitely.

He stepped toward the opening, then stopped dead still. A low murmur of voices came to him, and Turk tiptoed to the cave entrance, motioning to Angela for silence. Above on the cliff edge, two men were talking.

"They aren't up here, wherever they are," one man

growled. "The chief's in a sweat about the dame; it's a waste of time, if you ask me."

"There's worse ways of wasting time, Chino," a second man said. "I'd like to find her. A grand is a lot of dough."

"What d'you think about goin' after these ships?" Chino asked. "I don't know a damn thing about ships."

"It's a steal. A war goin' on, lots of ships missin' anyway, an' if we don't leave anybody to sing, what can go wrong? Durin' the last war, a German tramp freighter did it for a couple of years. If they did it, why can't we? It's like Harry says. When everybody is fightin' there's always a chance for a wise guy to pick up a few grand."

"Well," Chino said. "I'm going back down in that jungle. I want to see if I can't find something. Coming?"

"I'll stick around," the man said, slowly. "I'm fed up crawlin' through the brush."

Turk Madden tiptoed back to Angela.

"One of them's leaving," he whispered. "There may be a chance!"

He picked up the stick Angela had carried. Then he turned and slipped back to the cave entrance. Stopping, he felt on the rocky floor to find a loose fragment of stone. Suddenly, there was a gasp behind him and he looked up.

A burly, flat-faced man was standing in the cave entrance, his eyes gleaming with triumph.

"Hold it, buddy," he said softly. "I don't want to

take no dead meat back to the chief. All you got to do is come quiet."

"How'd you find this place?" Turk demanded.

The man chuckled wisely. "I seen your tracks back a ways. I said nothing to Chino, because I want that grand for myself. Me, I done some huntin' as a kid, so I figured the lay. I seen half a heel print from a woman's shoe right on the rim where there was a little dust."

"That's clever, plenty clever." Turk took a firm grip on the stick. Half concealed by the darkness of the cave, he had inched himself forward to striking distance. Suddenly, like a striking adder's head, the sharp stick leaped forward, the point tearing a jagged gash through the gunman's wrist!

Involuntarily, the man's hand jerked up and his fingers opened wide. He dropped the gun and stepped back with a cry of pain. And in that split second, Turk Madden stepped in.

Slugging the man in the belly with a bludgeoning right, he knocked every bit of breath from his body. Then a short, vicious left hook slammed the man on the chin and drove his head against the jagged rock beside the cave entrance. The man staggered and then fell clear. Where the leering gunman had stood an instant before, now the cave entrance was empty and behind the falling man a cry trailed up through the still air.

Quickly, Turk stepped outside and up the narrow ledge. It was the work of an instant to brush out the tracks, then he retreated as swiftly as he had come forth, picking up the heavy automatic as he returned to the cave.

"That was close," he whispered.

For three hours, they waited in the cave, hearing the sounds of the searchers above. The gunman's cry had obviously carried far enough for Chino to hear, yet when they came searching, there was nothing. The men came and went, then darkness began to gather, and finally Chino spoke up.

"To hell with it!" he snarled. "I must've been dreamin'! Buck probably went off huntin' in the brush."

"No tracks left here," Karchel insisted. "Where could he have got to?"

"If you ask me," one of the men said abruptly, "I don't like it. No guy as tough as Buck vanishes into thin air. If he ain't here he went somewhere, didn't he? Well, I don't like it!"

"Afraid of ghosts?" Karchel sneered.

"Maybe I am," the man said doggedly. "Funny things happen in these islands! I been hearin' plenty!"

"Oh, shut up!" Karchel snapped, disgusted.

They left. "You know, Angela," Turk said softly, "we've got something there. Those guys may not think they are superstitious, but all of us are a little. And maybe—"

"Maybe what?" Angela asked anxiously.

"I'm going out," he said. "I'm going out to get Tony. And I'm going to throw a scare into those guys they'll never forget!"

It was two hours before he slipped through the brush near the house, and paused on the edge of the jungle, studying the layout thoughtfully. Yorke might be imprisoned in the copra shed, and he might be held in the bungalow itself.

Several windows were lighted, and Turk could see men moving about, apparently getting ready to leave. One of the men came out and stood near the roots of a giant ficus tree. Madden glimpsed his face in the faint glow of a lighted match as the man touched it to a cigarette.

With a quick slice of his pocketknife, Turk cut a strip of liana from a long vine hanging near him. Then, soundlessly, he made a careful way over the damp earth to the giant tree. Like a ghost he slipped into the blackness among the roots. Before him, he saw the man stir a little, saw the faint gleam of light on the metal of a gun. He stepped closer.

He made a crude running noose in the end of the liana, and with a quick motion, dropped it over the man's head, jerking it tight! With a strangled cry, scarcely loud enough to be heard a dozen feet, the man grabbed at his throat. Then, Turk stepped in quickly, and slugged him in the stomach. Without a sound the man tumbled over, facedown in the mud.

Taking his gun and cartridges, Turk slipped off the crude noose and slipped back among the roots. Working swiftly, he had almost completed a semi-circle around the house when he heard the man cry out.

Someone ran past him swearing, and Turk saw lights go out suddenly in the house. In the darkness, he could distinguish a stream of shadowy figures, starlight gleaming on their guns, as they poured from the house.

"What the hell's wrong now?" Wissler was demanding.

"It was Gyp Davis," Karchel said, with disgust. "Something jumped on him in the dark, or that's what he says. Some slimy thing got him by the throat, he says, then kicked him in the belly."

Wissler made an ugly sound, half a snarl.

"These yellow-bellied tramps!" he sneered. "Gettin' scared of the dark! You tell Gyp and Brownie to get those ships ready. We're taking off before daybreak. See that there's plenty of shells in those crates. And a half dozen of those bombs the Doc makes. We won't have any time to waste on this job!"

Suddenly, there was a burst of excited voices, and stepping forward in the brush, Turk Madden saw a cluster of figures coming toward the house. One of them was dressed in white, and his heart sank.

"Got her, Chief!" Chino exclaimed, eagerly. "We found the dame. She was in the brush up on Traitor's Head. Do I get the grand?"

Wissler stepped toward the girl, and grabbed her roughly by the arm, pulling her toward him. Then he stepped back again and let the flashlight travel over her from head to foot.

"Yeah," his voice was thick. "You get the grand. You take her up to the house and lock her up. Make sure she's there to stay."

Turk wet his lips. Well, here it was. There was only one answer now. He slipped both guns from his waistband and clicked off the safety catches. Go out there shooting, get Wissler and Karchel, anyway.

He took a step, then stopped dead still, feeling the cold chill of steel against his neck.

"Hold it, buddy!" a harsh voice said. "And don't get funny with that gun."

The man reached out from behind with his left hand to get the right-hand pistol. Then Turk dropped the other gun into the brush, speaking quickly to distract the man's attention so he wouldn't hear the sound of its fall.

"Okay," he said. "You got me. Now what?"

The man prodded him into the open and marched him across the small clearing to where Wissler and Karchel were standing.

"Got the guy, Chief. That Madden fellow."

Wissler stepped toward Turk. "Tough guy, are you?" He slapped Madden across the face with one hand, then with the other. But Turk stood immovable. A wrong move now, and they'd kill him. If they did, then Angela and Tony were done for, to say nothing of the hundreds of innocent people on the *Erradaka*.

Wissler laughed coldly. "All right, tie him up an' lock him up. I'll tend to this guy and that dame when we come back."

Somewhere down the beach, the motor of a plane broke into a coughing roar. It wasn't the Grumman. Probably one of the aircraft they were going to use for the attack on the *Erradaka*.

Three of the men hustled him away to the copra shed. He was hurriedly bound, then thrown on the floor. The three men left, and it was only a few minutes until Madden heard two planes roar away toward the sea. It would be dawn soon, and the *Erradaka* with several hundred passengers would be steaming toward a day of horror and bloodshed.

He rolled over, trying to get to the wall. Reaching it, he forced himself into a sitting position and managed to get to his knees. This done, his fingers could just reach the knot behind his ankles.

It seemed that it took him hours to loosen the knot, although as he realized afterward, it could only have been a few minutes. When the ropes fell loose, he staggered to his feet. It was growing light outside and it was gray in the shed. He moved the length of the building, searching for something he could use to free his hands.

In a corner of the shed, he found an old wood saw. By wedging it into the crack in the end-boards of a worktable, he managed to place the saw teeth in the right position. Then he went to work. Finally, a strand of the rope fell apart and he hastily jerked the loosened ropes from his wrists, rubbed them violently. Now—

"Pretty smart, guy," a voice sneered.

He turned slowly, his blood suddenly hot with hatred. Chino stood in the door laughing at him, a gun in his hand. Turk Madden's brain went hot with rage. Now, after all this struggle, to be deprived of escape? Chino was coming toward him, chuckling with contempt.

With one sweeping movement of hand and arm, Turk grabbed the saw and hurled it flat at Chino's face. Chino leaped back with an oath, and the gun roared. Turk felt the bullet blast by his face and then he sprang. The gun roared again, but Madden was beyond all fear. Chino's face was bleeding from a ragged scratch of the saw, and he lifted the gun to take aim for a killing shot when Turk dove headlong in a flying tackle. They hit the ground rolling, and Turk came out on top, swinging both hands at Chino's face.

The gun blasted again, and he felt the searing pain of a powder burn, then he knocked the gun from Chino's hand and sprang to his feet. The gunman scrambled up, his face livid with rage. Turk threw a punch, short and hard, to the chin. The gunman went down. Turk swept up his gun and started running for the door.

A man loomed in the doorway, and Turk fired twice. The man staggered back, tumbling to the ground. And another stepped up behind him, taking careful aim with a pistol, but Turk fired from the hip, and the man staggered, his bullet clipping a notch in a beam over Madden's head. Then Turk fired again, hurled his now empty automatic after the shot, and grabbed another from the man in the doorway.

He made the house in a half dozen jumps, felt something tug at his clothes, then felt the whiff of a bullet by his face, the reports sounding in his ears, flat and ugly. A big man with a scarred face was standing in the door of the bungalow firing at him. Dropping to one knee, Turk fired steadily and methodically, three shots hitting the man, another taking a stocky-built blond fellow who came around the corner.

Then Turk scrambled through the door over the fallen man's body and rushed inside. There was no one in sight, but on the table was a tommy gun, a Luger automatic, and several other weapons. Turk sprang past them, and seeing a closed door, tried it. It was locked. He shot the lock away and stepped inside, gun ready.

Angela Yorke was tied in a chair in the center of the room. Tony Yorke, his face white and battered around the eyes, was lying on his back against the wall. Hurriedly, he cut the girl loose, handing her the gun.

"You two watch your step. I think I made a cleanup, but if any more show up, shoot—and shoot to kill!"

Angela caught his arm, her face white. He brushed something away from his eyes, and was startled to see blood on his hand. He must have been shot.

"What are you going to do?" the girl exclaimed.

"I'm taking the Grumman. She's got guns that came with the ship, and I never bothered to dismantle them. I've got to stop those guys before they get to the *Erradaka*!"

"But you'll be killed!" she protested.

He grinned. "Anything's possible, but I doubt it."

The Grumman took off after a short run, and Turk Madden swung the ship out to sea. The gunmen would land somewhere and wait there for the psychological moment. Their best chance was when the crew and passengers were at breakfast. And the first thing would be to get the radio room. Then sweep the decks with machine-gun fire, board the ship from the yacht, and kill the passengers.

Turk climbed to six thousand feet and opened her up. The Grumman responded perfectly, her twin motors roaring along in perfect time, fairly eating up the miles. The other ships were well ahead of him, he knew, but they would be in no hurry, for the yacht had to come up before they could attack.

Switching to the robot controls, he carefully checked the tommy gun and the other weapons he'd brought along. His ship carried two guns anyway, and with the additional armament he wouldn't lack for fighting equipment. He left Tanna off to the east, then swung the ship a bit and laid a course for Erronan.

Erronan! His eyes narrowed. Why hadn't he thought of that before? It was the perfect base for an attack on the shipping lane. There was a good landing on Tabletop, the flat mountain that was the island's highest point, nearly two thousand feet above the sea. From there it would not be much of a jump to the course of the *Erradaka*. No doubt the attacking ships had settled there to await the proper hour of attack. Well, he grinned wryly, it wouldn't be long now.

He cursed himself again for letting the sending apparatus on his radio get out of whack. He slipped on the earphones and could hear the *Erradaka* talking to another ship near the coast of New Caledonia. He turned his head, watching the blue expanse of sea beneath him and searching for the yacht. Then, suddenly, he picked it up, and a moment later, the *Erradaka*.

The yacht was taking a course that would bring her up with the *Erradaka,* and he heard the passenger liner calling her, but the yacht did not reply. Suddenly, a flicker of motion caught his eyes, and he turned to see two ships closing in on the liner. They were flying fast, one slightly above and behind the other.

Then, even as he watched, the first ship dipped a wing, and glancing down, he saw a tarp suddenly jerked from a gun on the yacht's fo'c'sle-head. The *Erradaka*'s radio began to chatter fiercely, and then the gun roared and the shell crashed into the radio room, exploding with a terrific concussion. Fired rapidly, the second shell exploded at the base of the fo'm'st, dropping it in wreckage across the deck.

Then the first ship dove, and he saw the mass of people who had rushed out on deck suddenly scatter as the plane's machine guns began chattering. He had time to notice the ship was an older Fiat. Not so bad. At best they'd do about two hundred miles per hour, which would give him a little margin. The other ship was a Boeing P-26, somewhat faster than his own ship.

He swung her over hard and put the Grumman into a steep dive. He came down on the tail of the Boeing, both guns firing. The Boeing, seeming to realize he was an enemy for the first time, pulled into a left chandelle.

Madden let it go and swung after the Fiat. For just an instant, he caught the outlaw ship full in his sights and saw a stream of tracers streak into his tail. Then Madden swung up in a tight loop, missing a stream of fire from the Boeing by a split second. He wheeled the Grumman around in a skid, but the Boeing was out of range, and the Fiat was climbing toward him.

He reached for altitude, saw pinkish tracers zip across his port wingtip, and went into a steep dive. Suddenly, he realized the yacht was right below him, her deck scattered with figures and a cluster of them around the gun. He pressed the trips on his guns and saw a man stagger and plunge over on his face.

The others scattered for shelter, and his guns swept the yacht's deck with a flaming blast of machine-gun fire. Three more of the fleeing gunmen fell headlong. One of them threw up his pistol and fired, then his body jerked, fairly lifted from the deck by the burst of bullets. Madden banked steeply and saw the topmasts of the yacht miss him by inches.

His stomach felt tight and hard. He was in a spot, and knew it. Only a few feet above the water and the Boeing above and slightly behind, closing in fast. There was no chance or room to maneuver. He saw a stream of tracers cross his wing, missing by inches, then he glimpsed the looming hull of the *Erradaka* dead ahead. He clamped his jaw and flew straight at the huge liner.

His twin motors roaring, he swept down on the

big ship, the Boeing right behind him. Then, just as it seemed he must hit, he jerked the Grumman into a quick, climbing turn, saw the starboard davits of the ship slip away beneath him, and he was climbing like a streak.

He glanced around, but the Boeing pilot had lost his nerve and swung off. Now he was desperately trying to close on the Grumman before Madden could get too much altitude. The Fiat suddenly loomed before Turk's sights and he pressed the trips, and saw a stream of tracers pound into the fuselage of the plane. He saw the Fiat's pilot jerk his head back, saw the man's mouth open as from a mighty shout, and then the Fiat swung around and plunged toward the sea, a stream of orange fire behind it!

Turk Madden swung the Grumman around, driving toward the Boeing with all he had. The Boeing held, guns flaming, and steel-jacketed bullets punched holes in the Grumman's wing, cracked the canopy and tore at the rudder. Then the other plane pulled up abruptly. In that split second the Boeing's belly was exposed. Turk fired a burst past the undercarriage and into the body of the ship. Yet still the Boeing seemed unharmed.

Turk did a chandelle, brought himself alongside her even as he saw the pilot jerk off his goggles and hurl them from him. The ship was wavering drunkenly, and the pilot fell over the edge of the seat, arms dangling. With a long whine that cut across the nerves like a tight board shrieking in an electric saw, the Boeing spun and dropped, a huge pear-shaped flame stretching out and out as the plane fell into the sea.

Turk Madden swung the Grumman and headed toward the yacht. If only he had a bomb now. He shrugged—no use thinking of that. He saw the yacht's gun was ready for another shot at the liner, and even as he went into a shrieking dive, he saw the flame leap from the muzzle of the gun and saw the gunners grab for another round. Then, he was spraying the deck with bullets, and he saw two men fall. Then something happened to the Grumman, or to him, and he jerked back on the stick and lifted the ship into a steep climb. But he felt sick now, and dizzy.

The ship wobbled badly, and he circled, let the ship glide in for a landing. It hit the waves, bucked a little. He cut the motor and tried to get up. The plane pitched in the sea and he slid to the floor.

He forced himself to his knees, startled to see the deck was red where he had rested. But he held himself there and pulled the tommy gun toward him. Even as he waited, he saw he was a little astern of the two ships, and about halfway between them.

Wissler wouldn't sink him. He would need the plane now. His eyes wavered to the liner, and he saw she had a hole through her forepeak and another on the waterline. He wondered why she wasn't moving, then looked aft and could see the steam steering-engine room was blasted. The splutter of a motor drew his attention and as the hull of the Grumman pitched up in the mild swell he saw a motorboat speeding toward him from the yacht.

He let the door swing open in case he fell and couldn't lift himself to see, and then leaned against the edge. Below him the water was stained with a little red. He didn't know where he was shot, and didn't even believe he was. Yet there was blood.

This was going to be close. If Wissler wasn't in that boat—but he would be. Leave it to Wissler to be there to kill the man who had hit so hard and fast. If he could cook Wissler, and maybe Karchel, there wouldn't be any raiding of peaceful ships, nor any attacking of plantations. The others would scatter without leadership.

The speedboat swung in alongside and cut the motor. Just beyond the plane. They'd ease her in slowly now. Maybe.

Turk Madden grinned. Puccini tried to get tough with him back in the States, and Puccini was a big shot. All right. Now let Wissler see what it meant to cut himself a piece of this cake. He felt sick, but he lifted the machine gun. Then Steve Karchel saw him and yelled, his face dead white and his gun coming up. As the body of the plane slid upwards and the boat sank a foot or two into the trough of a wave, Turk grinned.

There was the roar of the gun, and suddenly Steve Karchel's chest blossomed with crimson. The man sagged at the knees and sat down, his chest half shot away. Madden turned the gun and swept the boat. Flame leaped from somewhere, and there was a shocking explosion. Madden felt himself getting sicker, and he clung to the door. When he opened his eyes, the motorboat was drifting just beyond the Grumman's wing, and all aflame.

Then he saw Harry Wissler. He was standing in the stern, and his face was white and horribly red on one side from the scorching of the flames that were so close. The man's lips were bared in a snarl of hatred, and he was lifting his six-gun carefully.

Funny, what a fellow remembered at a time like this. That Wissler always stuck with a revolver. No automatics for him. Well, okay. Maybe he'd like this one.

The tommy gun was gone somewhere. Slipped out the door, maybe. But not the Luger. Turk lifted it. The gun felt terribly heavy.

He heard a report, and something smashed into the doorjamb. Then he began firing. From somewhere another boat was approaching, but he kept shooting until the gun was empty.

Slowly, the hulk of the speedboat tipped, and with it all that was left of Harry Wissler slid into the sea.

When Turk opened his eyes, he was lying in a clean white bunk and a couple of men were standing over him.

"Live?" one man was saying. "Sure, he'll live. He was shot, but it was mostly loss of blood from these glass cuts in his head." The doctor shook his head admiringly. "He certainly made a grand cleanup on that bunch of would-be pirates."

Turk smiled.

" 'Has-been' pirates, now," he murmured as he passed out again.

THE SUCKER
SWITCH

W hen Jake Brusa got out of the car, he spotted me waiting for him and his eyes went
hard. Jake and I never cared for each other.

"Hi, Copper!" he said. "Loafing again, or are you
here on business?"

"Would I come to see you for fun?" I asked. "It's
a question or two; like where were you last night?"

"At the Roadside Club. In fact," he said, grinning
at me, "I ran into your boss out there. Even talked
with him for a while."

"Just asking," I told him. "But you'll need an alibi.
Somebody knocked off the Moffit Storage and Transit
Company for fifty grand in furs."

"Nice haul. Luck to 'em!" Jake grinned again
and, sided by Al Huber and Frank Lincoff, went on
into the Sporting Center.

The place was a combination bowling alley and
billiard parlor. It was Jake Brusa's front for a lot of
illegal activities. Jake had been operating, ever since

his release from Joliet, but nobody was able to put a finger on him.

If James Briggs, my boss, had been with him the night before, then Jake might be in the clear, but in my own mind, I was positive this had been a Brusa job.

Old Man Moffit had been plenty sore when I'd showed up at his office earlier that morning. His little blue eyes glinted angrily in his fat red face.

"About time you got here!" he snapped at me. "What does Briggs think he's running, anyway? We pay your firm for security and this is the third time in five months we've taken a loss from thieves or holdup men."

"Take it easy," I said. "Let me have a look around first." I dug into my pocket for chewing gum and peeled three sticks. He had reason to complain. The robberies were covered by insurance, but his contracts to handle merchandise would never be renewed if he couldn't deliver the goods. Not that he was the only one suffering from burglary or stick-ups. The two rival firms in town had suffered a couple of losses each, and the police had failed to pin anything on anybody. All three of the companies had been clients of my boss's detective agency.

Moffit's face purpled. "I lose fifty thousand dollars' worth of furs and you tell me to take it easy!" he shouted. "I've got a good mind to call—"

"It wouldn't do you any good," I said. "Briggs only told me somebody knocked over the joint. Suppose you give me the details."

Moffit toned down, but his jaw jutted, and it was obvious that Briggs stood to lose a valuable client unless we recovered those furs or pinned this on somebody.

"My night watchman, a man investigated by your firm and pronounced reliable, is missing," Moffit told me. "With him went one of our armored trucks and the furs."

That watchman was Pete Burgeson and I'd investigated him myself. "And then what?" I asked. "Give me the whole setup."

"The furs were stored in the vault last night," he continued a little more mildly, "but when we opened it this morning, it was empty. The burglar alarm on the vault door failed to go off. The vault door and the door to the outer room were both locked this morning. So was the warehouse door.

"Our schedule called for the furs to be delivered to Pentecost and Martin the first thing this morning. The furs are gone and the truck is gone and Burgeson is gone too!"

Naturally, after I'd heard Moffit's story, I thought of Brusa and went down to see him. In his youth there had been no tougher mobster; he had a record as long as your arm in the Midwest and East. After his release from Joliet, he had come west to Lucaston and opened the Sporting Center.

Supposedly, he had been following a straight path since then, but I had my own ideas about that. Years ago, he had been a highly skilled loft burglar. Huber

had been arrested several times on the same charge.
Lincoff had been up for armed robbery and assault.
The Sporting Center was the hangout for at least
three other men with records.

Lucaston, while not a great metropolis, was a
thriving and busy city near the coast and we had several select residential areas loaded with money. Such
a place is sure to be a target for crooks, and I don't
believe it was any accident that Jake Brusa had located there.

Well, I had seen Brusa and heard his alibi, and
when I called my boss, Briggs told me that Brusa was
right. He had talked with Briggs at the Roadside
Club, and not only he but Huber and Lincoff had
been there all evening. Their alibi was rockbound.
But if they hadn't done it, who had? . . .

The warehouse itself offered little. It was a concrete structure, built like a blockhouse and almost as
impregnable. A glance at it would defeat an amateur
burglar, and the place was fairly loaded with alarms
that we had installed ourselves and checked regu-
larly. The fact that they hadn't gone off seemed to
imply an inside job, but I knew that a skillful burglar
can always manage to locate such alarms and put
them out of action. Two doors and the vault had
been opened, however, and there was no evidence of
violence and no unidentified fingerprints.

During the war, an annex of sheet metal had been
added to the warehouse. In this annex was the loading platform and the garage for the ten trucks em-
ployed by Moffit's firm. Two of these trucks were
armored. This annex also housed the small office

used by the night watchman. In one corner of the annex a window had been found broken, a window that opened on the alley.

Glass lay on the floor below the window, and a few fragments lay on a workbench that was partly under the window. The dust on the sill was disturbed, indicating that someone had entered by that means, and the glass on the floor implied the window had been broken from the outside. On the head of a nail on the edge of the window, I found a few threads of material resembling sharkskin. I put them in an envelope in my pocket.

Under the bench were a couple of folded tarps and some sacks. I flashed my light over them. At one end, those at the bottom of the pile were somewhat damp, yet there was no way for rain to have reached them despite the heavy fall the previous night. The outer door through which the truck would have to be driven was undamaged. It was then I started to get mad. Nobody goes through three doors, one with a combination lock, unless they are opened for him.

Moffit looked up, glaring, when I returned from my examination. "Well?" he demanded.

"Ghosts," I told him solemnly. "Spirits who walk through walls, or maybe Mandrake the Magician waved those furs out of the vault with a wand."

Hudspeth, Moffit's chief clerk, looked up at me as I came out of Moffit's office. "He's pretty worked up," he said, "he had a lot of faith in Burgeson."

I walked over to the water cooler. "Didn't you?"

"You can't be sure. I never trusted him too much. He was always asking questions that didn't concern him."

"Like what?"

"Oh, where we got our furs, what different coats cost, and such things." Hudspeth seemed nervous, like he was worried that I might not suspect the watchman.

When I got in my car, I sat there a few minutes, then started it up and swung out on the main drag, heading for the center of town. Then I heard a police siren, and the car slowed and swung over to me. Briggs was with them. He stuck his head out.

"Found that armored car," he called. "Come along."

There was a farmer standing alongside the road when we got there, and he flagged us down. It was on the Mill Road, outside of town. The car was sitting among some trees and the door had been pried off with a chisel and crowbar. It was empty.

They had picked a good place. Only lovers or hikers ever stopped in this place. About a hundred yards back from the road was the old mill that gave the road its name. It was one of the first flour mills built west of the Sierras.

While Briggs and the cops were looking the car over, I walked around. There had been another car here and several men. The grass had been pressed down and had that gray look grass has when it's been walked through after a heavy dew. The trail looked interesting, and I followed it. It headed for the old mill. Skirting the mill, I walked out on the stone dock along the millpond. Even before I looked, I had a hunch what I'd find and I knew it wouldn't be nice. He was there, all right, floating facedown in the water, and even before I called the cops, I knew who it was.

When Pete Burgeson was hauled out of the water, we saw his head was smashed in. There was wire around him and you could see that somebody had bungled the job of anchoring him to whatever weight had been used.

"Burgeson was no crook," I said unnecessarily. "I knew the guy was straight."

For a private dick, I am very touchy about bodies. I don't like to hold hands with dead men, or women, for that matter. I walked away from this one and went back to the car. The cops would be busy so it gave me a chance to look around.

Backtracking the car to the road, I found the place where it had left the pavement. There was a deep imprint of the tire, and I saw a place where the tread had picked up mud. Putting my hand down, I felt what looked like dry earth. It was dirt, just dry dirt. That brought me standing, for that car had been run in here after the rain ended!

Squatting down again, looking at that tread, I could see how it had picked up the thin surfacing of mud and left dry earth behind. If it had rained after the car turned off the road, that track would not be dry! Things began to click into place . . . at least a few things.

Without waiting for Briggs, I got into my car and drove away. As I rounded the curve, I glanced back and saw Briggs staring after me. He knew I had something.

My first stop was Pete Burgeson's rooming house. Then I went on, mulling things over as I drove. It was just a hunch I had after all, a hunch based on three things: a broken window, dampness on a tarp, and a dry track on the edge of a wet road. At least, I knew how the job had been done. All I needed was to fill in a couple of blank spaces and tie it all together with a ribbon of evidence.

A stop at a phone booth got me Moffit. "What's the name of the driver of the armored truck that was stolen?"

"Mat Bryan. One of my best men. Why do you ask?"

"Just want to talk to him. Put him on the phone, will you?"

"I can't," Moffit explained. "He's getting married . . . he's got the day off but promised to make some morning deliveries for me. When his truck was missing we told him not to bother coming in."

It took me a half hour in that phone booth to get what I wanted, but by that time I was feeling sharper than a razor. Two things I had to do at once, but I dialed the chief. He was back in the office, and sounded skeptical.

"Why not take a chance?" I said finally. "If I'm right, we've got these crooks where we want them. I don't know what this bird looks like, how tall or short, but he's wearing a gray sharkskin suit, and it's been rained on. Try the parks, the cheap poolrooms, and the bars."

When I hung up, I hit the street and piled into my

car. As I got into it, I got a glimpse of Huber coming down the sidewalk. He stopped to stare at me, and it was a long look that gave me cold chills.

When I reached the warehouse, I headed right for the night watchman's office. Hudspeth was standing on the loading platform when I came in.

"Anyone been in Burgeson's office?" I asked him.

"No." He looked puzzled. "He always locked it when he came out, even for a few minutes, and it's still locked. I have the key here. Mr. Moffit wanted me to see if there was anything there that would help you."

"Let's look," I suggested, and then as he was bending over the lock, I gave it to him. "They found Burgeson's body. He was murdered."

The key jerked sharply, rattling on the lock. Finally, Hudspeth got it into the keyhole and opened the door. When he straightened up his face was gray.

Burgeson's leather-topped chair was where it always had been. The windows in the office allowed him to see all over the annex. His lunch box was open on the desk, and there was nothing in it but crumbs.

My eyes went over every inch of the desk, and at last I found what I had been looking for. On the side of the desk, across from where Burgeson always sat, were a few cake crumbs. I looked at them, then squatted down and studied the floor. In front of the chair at that end of the desk was a spot of dampness. I got up. Hudspeth must have seen me grinning.

"You—you found something?"

"Uh huh." I looked right at him. "You can tell Moffit I'll be breaking this case in a few hours. Funny thing about crooks," I told him. "All of them suffer from overconfidence. This bunch had been pretty smart, but we've got them now. For burglary, and"—I looked right into his eyes—"murder!"

Then I went out of there on a run because when I'd said the last word, I had a hunch that scared me. I hit the door and got into my car, wheeled it around, and headed for the church. If I was right, and I knew I was, the phone from Moffit and Company would be busy right now, or some phone nearby.

There were a lot of cars at the church when I got there, and a bunch of people standing around as they always do for a funeral or a wedding.

"Where's Mat Bryan?" I demanded.

"We're waiting for him!" the nearest man told me. "He's late for his wedding!"

"Better break it to the bride that he probably won't make it today," I advised. "I'll go look for him." Without explanation, I swung my car into traffic and took off.

When I pulled up in front of his rooming house, I could see an old lady answering the telephone in the hallway.

As I walked up to her I heard her saying, "He should be there now! Some men drove up ten or fifteen minutes ago and took him away in a car!"

Taking the phone from her, I hung it up. "What did those men look like?" I demanded. "Tell me quick!"

She was neither bothered nor confused. "Who are you?" she demanded.

"The police," I lied. "Those men will kill Mat if I don't prevent them."

"They were in a blue car," she told me. "There were three of them—a big man in a plaid suit, and—"

"You call the police now," I interrupted. "Tell them what happened and that I was here. My name is Neil Shannon."

Racing back to my car, I knew it was all a gamble from here on. Bryan was an important witness, and unless I got to him he would go the way Pete Burgeson had gone. Mat Bryan was the one guy who could tip the police on what had actually taken place, and once they knew, they would have the killers in a matter of minutes.

Yet there was an even more important witness, and finding him was a bigger gamble than saving Mat Bryan.

All this trouble had developed because Jake Brusa had come out of Joliet determined to play it smart. This time he was going to be on the winning side, but now the sweetest deal he had ever had in his life was blowing up in his face, and when he was caught there he wouldn't have a chance if I could push this through.

If I'd expected to find him with Bryan, I was disappointed. He was just going in with Huber and Lincoff when I came in sight of the Sporting Center. I took a gander at my watch, then made a couple of calls to Briggs and the Roadside. They weren't necessary, for Jake Brusa had built his alibi the wrong way and for the wrong time.

Then I walked up to the Sporting Center and pushed the door open. Inside there was a cigar stand and a long lunch counter. You could bowl, play billiards or pool, and it was said that crap games ran there occasionally. You could also make bets on baseball, races, fights, anything you wanted.

Jake Brusa had a sweet setup there without going any further, but a crook never seems to know when he's got enough.

Huber was sitting at the counter with a cup of coffee. He turned when I started past him and grabbed at my wrist. I knocked the hand down so quick he spilled his coffee and jumped off the stool swearing.

"Where are you going?" he demanded.

"To talk to Jake," I told him. "So what?"

"He doesn't want to see anybody!"

"He'll see me, and like it."

"Tough guy, huh?" he said with a nasty smirk.

"That's right. You tell him I've come to get Mat Bryan!"

When I said that name, Huber's face went yellow-white, and he looked sick. I grinned at him.

"Don't like it, do you?" I threw it at him. "That was kidnapping, Huber. You'll get a chance to inhale some gas for this one!"

"Shut up!" he snarled. "Come on!"

I motioned him ahead of me, and after an instant's hesitation, he went. We went past a couple of bowling lanes, through a door, and up a stairway. The sound of the busy alley was only a vague whisper here. Soundproofed. That meant nobody would hear a shot, either. Nor a pushing around if it came to that. When he got to the door, he rapped and then stepped aside. "Think I'm a dope?" I said. "You first!"

His face went sour, but my right hand was in my coat pocket, and he didn't know I always carried my rod in a shoulder holster. He went in first.

Jake was behind a big desk, and Lincoff was seated in a chair at the opposite end. Brusa's face was like iron when he saw me.

"What do you want?" he growled.

"He said he wanted to see Mat Bryan!" Huber warned.

"He ain't here. I don't know him."

I leaned forward with both hands on the back of a chair. "Which one, Jake? Don't make me call you a liar," I told him. "Get him out here quick. I haven't much time."

Brusa's eyes were pools of hate. "No, you haven't!" he agreed. "What made you think Bryan was here?"

I laughed at him. I was in this up to my ears, and if I didn't come out of it, I might as well have fun.

"It was simple," I said. "You thought you had a good deal here. So what was it that gave you the idea you're smarter than everybody else? This time you thought you were going to be in the clear, and all you did was mess it up.

"You had a finger man point these jobs for you. You had a perfect alibi last night, and all the good it did you was to help you pull a fast switch. A sucker switch. You switched your chances at a cell for a chance at the gas chamber.

"When you drove that armored car off the road, Jake, you left a track, a track that was dry. That proved it was made this morning, after the rain had stopped. The rain stopped about seven A.M., and your alibi isn't worth a hoot. You took that truck out after the place opened up this morning!"

Brusa was sitting in his chair. He didn't like this. He didn't like it a bit. A crook can stand almost anything but being shown up as a fool.

"Smart lad!" he sneered. "Very smart! Until you walked in here!"

That one I shrugged off. Right now I wasn't too sure I had any more brains than he did, but I'd gambled that Bryan was here and alive. If I couldn't get him out, I could at least keep them thinking and keep them busy until the police followed up.

"You thought," I told him slowly, stalling for time, "you'd have the cops going around in circles over those locked doors. They'd all think the watchman had done it. But whoever sank that body did a messy job. It was already floating this morning."

Brusa's eyes swung around to Huber.

"He's lyin', boss!" Huber exclaimed in a panic. "He's lyin'!"

"He said the body was *floatin'*," Brusa replied brutally. "Why would he say that unless they'd found it?"

"You didn't go through those doors at all, Brusa," I broke in. "You didn't have to. The furs were all ready for you in the armored car, waiting to be driven away. Only two men knew how they got there, and one of them was honest, so you decided you had to kill him. Mat Bryan!"

Right then, I was praying for Briggs or the cops to

get to me before the lid blew off. It was going to come off very soon and I was afraid I was expecting too much.

I kept on talking. "Bryan wanted to get off early because of the wedding, so your finger man hinted that he might leave the furs in the truck and have them all set to go in the morning, that would save time. All you had to do was wait until the plant opened in the morning, then go in and drive the truck away. Burgeson butted in, so you killed him.

"That was a mistake. According to the watchman's time schedule, he should have been inside the plant by then. Only something happened to throw him off, and he was there in the loading dock and tried to stop you.

"Murder changes everything, doesn't it, Jake? You weren't planning on killing, but you got it, anyway. If Burgeson and the furs disappeared, well, he would get credit for stealing them, only Huber here did a bum job of sinking the body.

"You picked the right man for the finger job, too. A smart man, and in a position where he could get all the inside information, not only from his own firm, but from others. But now I've got a feeling you've killed one man too many!"

"Then one more won't matter!" Brusa said harshly. "I'm going to kill Mat Bryan, but first I'm going to kill you!" His hand went to the drawer in front of him.

"Look out, boss!" Huber screamed. "He's got a rod!" He dove at me, clawing at that coat pocket. But my right hand slid into my jacket and it hit the butt of my .38, which came out of the armpit holster, spitting fire.

My first shot missed Brusa as Huber knocked me off balance. My second clipped Lincoff, and he cried out and grabbed at his side. Then I swung the barrel down Huber's ear and floored him.

Grabbing at the doorknob, I jerked it open and even as a slug ripped into the doorjamb over my head, I lunged out of the door with a gun exploding again behind me.

The stairs offered themselves, but I wanted Mat Bryan. There was another door down the hall, and I hit it hard and went through just as Brusa filled the doorway of the room behind me. I tripped on the rug and sprawled at full length on the floor, my gun sliding from my hand and under the desk across the room.

There was no time to get it because Jake Brusa was lunging through the door. I shoved myself up and hit him with a flying tackle that smashed him against the wall, but he took it and chopped down at my ear with his gun. I slammed him in the ribs, then clipped his wrist with the edge of my hand and made him drop the gun.

I smashed him with a left as he came into me, but he kept coming and belted me with a right that brought smoke into my brain and made my knees sag. I staggered back, trying to cover up, and the guy was all over me, throwing them with both hands.

I nailed him with a right and left as he came on in, then stood him on his toes with an uppercut. He staggered and went to the wall. I followed him in and knocked him sprawling into a chair. It went to pieces under him, and he came up with a leg, taking a cut at my head that would have splattered my brains all over the wall had it connected. I went under it throwing a right into his solar plexus that jolted his mouth open. Then I lifted one from my knees that had the works and a prayer on it.

That wallop caught him on the jaw and lifted him right off his Number Elevens. The wall shivered as if an earthquake had struck and Brusa was out, but I was already leaving. I made a dive for my gun, shoved it into my belt, and went out the door and down the carpeted hall. My breath was coming in great gasps as I grabbed the knob and jerked the door open.

Lincoff had beat me to it, only I came in faster than he expected and hit him with my shoulder before he got his gun up. He hit the floor in a heap, and I grabbed up a paring knife lying beside some apples on the table and slashed the ropes at Bryan's wrists.

I got in that one slash, then dropped the knife and grabbed at the gun in my waistband. Lincoff had got to his feet and had his gun on me by that time. I knew once that big cluck started to shoot, he'd never stop until the gun was empty, so I squeezed mine and felt it buck in my hand.

His gun muzzle pointed down as he raised on his tiptoes, and then it bellowed and the shot ripped into the floor. Lincoff dropped on his face and lay still. Thrusting the gun back in my pants, I wheeled to help Mat. He was almost free now, and it was only a minute's work to complete the job.

Down the hall there was a yell, then quiet, and then the pounding of feet. Briggs loomed in the door, a plainclothesman and a couple of harness cops with him.

"You!" Briggs's face broke into a relieved grin. "I might have known it. I was afraid they'd killed you!"

There wasn't much talking done until we got them down to Moffit's office. When we marched them in, he got up, scowling. Hudspeth was there, and I've never seen a man more frightened.

Jake Brusa and Huber, handcuffed, looked anything but the smart crooks they believed themselves to be. Brusa stood there glowering, and Huber was scared silly. But they were only the small fry in this crime. We wanted the man behind the scenes.

"All right," Briggs said, "it's your show." Most of the story he'd heard from me on the way over from the Sporting Center, and Bryan had admitted to the furs left in the truck.

"There's only one left," I said, watching one of our men come in beside a tall young fellow in a decrepit sharkskin suit, "and that's nailing the inside man, and we've got him. Dead to rights!"

Moffit sat up straight. "See here! If one of my men had been—" His eyes shifted to Hudspeth. "You, Warren?"

"No, Moffit," I said, leaning over the desk, "not the man you hired to be your scapegoat! You!"

His face went white as he sprang to his feet. "Why, of all the preposterous nonsense! Young man, I'll have—"

"Shut up, and sit down!" I barked at him. "It was

you, Moffit. You were the man who informed these crooks when a valuable haul could be made! You were the man who cased the jobs for them! You knew the inside of every warehouse in town, and could come and go as you liked.

"We've got the evidence that will send you to prison if not to the gas chamber where you rightly should go! I'll confess I suspected Hudspeth. I know he had done time, but—"

"What?" Briggs interrupted. "Why, you investigated this man. You passed him for this job."

"Sure, and if I was wrong, we'd have to make the best of it. Hudspeth was in trouble as a kid, but after looking over his record, I decided he'd learned his lesson. I checked him carefully and found he had been bending over backwards to go straight.

"Nevertheless, knowing what I did and knowing it was my responsibility if anything went wrong, I kept a check on his spending and bank account. That day in the office when I first came in, he acted strangely because he knew something was going on and he was scared, afraid he'd be implicated.

"Another reason I originally let him stay was that I found that Moffit had hired him while knowing all about that prison stretch. I figured that if he would take a chance, we could, too. Now it seems Moffit was going to use him if anything went haywire."

"That's a lie!" Moffit bellowed. "I'll not be a party to this sort of talk anymore!"

Briggs looked at me. "I hope you've got the evidence." I looked at the man in the gray sharkskin suit and he stepped forward. "It was him, all right," he said, motioning toward Moffit. "He opened the doors this morning and he was standing by when the crooks knocked Pete out and took him away. He talked with this man," he added, pointing at Brusa.

"That's a lie!" Moffit protested weakly. "How would you know?"

"Tell us about it," I suggested to the man in gray.

He shifted his feet. "Pete Burgeson and me were in the same outfit overseas. But I got wounded and I've been in and out of the hospital for the last two years. He told me to come around and he'd give me money for a bed and chow. When I got here, the rain was pouring down and I couldn't make him hear. I tried to push up that back window and it busted, so I opened it and crawled in. Pete was some upset but said he'd take the blame. There weren't any burglar alarms on the annex.

"I was out of the hospital just a few days, and I got the shakes, so I laid down on those tarps under the bench after sharing Pete's lunch with him. Pete came along and put his coat over me.

"When I woke up, I saw them slug Pete. Moffit was standing right alongside. Every morning, I have to rub my legs before I can walk much and knew if I tried to get up they'd kill me, so I laid still until they left, then got away from there. One of the detectives found me this morning in the park."

"All right, boys," Briggs said, turning to the plain-clothesman and the cops. "They're yours. All of them."

Jerking my head at Hudspeth, I said to one of the cops, "We represent the insurance company as well as this firm, so Hudspeth might as well stay in charge. The lawyers will probably want a reliable person here."

"Sure," Briggs said. "Sure thing."

We walked outside and the air smelled good. "Chief," I suggested, nodding at the man in the gray suit, "why not put this guy to work with us? He used to be an insurance investigator."

The man stopped and stared at me. Briggs did likewise. "How, how the devil did you know that?" he demanded. "You told me about the gray threads, the dampness on the tarp, the crumbs on the table, all the evidence that somebody was with Pete! But this—next thing you'll be telling me what his name is!"

"Sure," I agreed cheerfully. "It's Patrick Donahey!"

"Well, how in—" Donahey stared.

"Purely elementary, my dear Watson." I brushed my fingernails on my lapel. "You ate with your left hand, and insurance investigators always—"

"Don't give me that!" Briggs broke in.

"Okay, then," I said. "It did help a little that I found his billfold." I drew it out and handed it to Donahey. "It fell back of that tarp. But nevertheless, I—"

"Oh, shut up," Briggs said.

GLOVES
FOR A TIGER

The radio announcer's voice sounded clearly in the silent room, and "Deke" Hayes scowled as he listened.

"Boyoboy, what a crowd! Almost fifty thousand, folks! Think of that! It's the biggest crowd on record, and it should be a great battle.

"This is the acid test for the 'Tiger Man,' the jungle killer who blasted his way up from nowhere to become the leading contender for the world's heavyweight boxing championship in only six months!

"Tonight he faces Battling Bronski, the Scranton Coal Miner. You all know Bronski. He went nine rounds with the champ in a terrific battle, and he is the only white fighter among the top contenders who has dared to meet the great Tom Noble.

"It'll be a grand battle either way it goes, and Bronski will be in there fighting until the last bell. But the Tiger has twenty-six straight knockouts, he's dynamite in both hands, with a chin like a chunk of granite! Here he comes now, folks! The Tiger Man!"

Deke Hayes, champion of the world, leaned back in the chair in his hotel room and glanced over at his manager. "Toronto Tom" McKeown was one of the shrewdest fight managers in the country. Now he sat frowning at the radio and his eyes were hard.

"Don't take it so hard, Tom," Deke laughed. "Think of the gate he'll draw. It's all ballyhoo, and one of the best jobs ever done. I didn't think old Ryan had it in him. I believe you're actually worried yourself!"

"You ain't never seen this mug go," McKeown insisted. "Well, I have! I'm telling you, Deke, he's the damnedest fighter you ever saw. Talk about killer instinct!

"There ain't a man who ever saw him fight who would be surprised if he jumped onto some guy and started tearing with his teeth. This Tiger Man stuff may sound like ballyhoo but he's good, I tell you!"

"As good as me?" Deke Hayes put in slyly.

"No, I guess not," his manager admitted judiciously. "They rate you one of the best heavyweights the game ever saw, Deke. But we know, a damned sight better than the sportswriters, that you've really never had a battle yet, not with a fighter who was your equal.

"That Bronski thing looked good because you let it. But don't kid yourself, this guy isn't any sap. He's different. Sometimes I doubt if this guy's even human."

Toronto Tom McKeown tried to speak casually. "I talked to Joe Howard, Deke, Joe was his sparrin' partner for this brawl. That Tiger guy never says anything to anybody! He just eats and sleeps, and he walks around at night a lot, just . . . well just like a cat! When he ain't workin' out, he stays by himself, and nobody ever gets near him."

"Say, what the devil's the matter with you? Got the willies? You're not buyin' this hype?" Deke Hayes demanded.

But the voice from the radio interrupted just then, and they fell silent, listening.

"They're in the center of the ring now, folks, getting their instructions," the excited announcer said. "The Tiger Man in his tiger-skin robe, and Bronski in the old red sweater he always wears. The Tiger is younger, but Bronski has the experience, and—man, this is going to be a battle!" the announcer exclaimed.

The bell clanged. "There they go, folks! Bronski jabs a left and the Tiger slips it! Bronski jabs again, and again, and again! The Tiger isn't doing anything now, just circling around. Bronski jabs again, crosses a right to the jaw.

"He's getting confident now, folks, and—there, he's stepping in with a volley of punches! Left, right, left, right—but the Tiger is standing his ground, just slipping them!

"Wow!" the radio voice hit the ceiling.

"Bronski's down! The Battler led a left, and quick as a flash the Tiger dropped into a crouch, snapped a terrific, jolting right to the heart, and hooked a bone-crushing left to the jaw! Bronski went down like he was shot, and hasn't even wiggled!

"There's the count, folks!—eight—nine—ten! He's

out, and the Tiger wins again! Boyoboy, a first-round knockout!

"Wait a minute, folks, maybe I can get the Tiger to say something for you! He never talks, but we might be lucky this time. Here, say something to the radio fans, Tiger!" the announcer begged.

"He won't do it," McKeown said confidently. "He never talks to nobody!"

Suddenly, a cold, harsh voice spoke from the radio, a voice bitter and incisive, but then dropping almost to a growl at the end.

"I'm ready now. I want to fight the champion. Come on, Deke Hayes! I'll kill you!"

In a cold sweat Hayes snapped erect, face deathly pale. His mouth hung slack; his eyes were ghastly, staring.

"My God . . . that voice!" he mumbled, really scared for the first time in his life.

McKeown stared strangely at Hayes, his own face white. "Who's punchy now? You look like you've seen a ghost!"

Hayes sagged back in his chair, his eyes narrowed. "No. I ain't seen one. I heard one!" he declared enigmatically.

Ruby Ryan, veteran trainer and handler of fighters, looked across the hotel room. The Tiger was sitting silent, as always, staring out the window.

For six months Ryan had been with the Tiger, day in and day out, and yet he knew almost nothing about him. Sometimes he wondered, as others did, if the Tiger was quite human. Definitely he was an odd duck, and Ruby Ryan, so-called because of his flaming hair, had known them all.

Jeffries, Fitzsimmons, Ketchell, Dempsey. But he had seen nothing to compare with the animal-like ferocity of the Tiger. Through all the months that had passed since Ryan received that strange wire from Calcutta, India, he had wondered about this man. . . .

Who sent the cablegram Ruby Ryan didn't know. Who was the Tiger? Where had he come from? Where had he learned his skill? He didn't know that, either. He only knew that one night some six months before, he had been loafing in Doc Hanley's place with some of the boys, when a messenger had hurried to him with a cablegram. It had been short, to the point—and unsigned.

WOULD YOU LIKE TO HANDLE NEXT HEAVY-WEIGHT CHAMPION STOP READ CALCUTTA AND BOMBAY NEWS REPORTS FOR VERIFICATION STOP EXPENSES GUARANTEED STOP COME AT ONCE.

Ryan had hurried out and bought the papers. The notes were strange, yet they fascinated the fight manager with their possibilities. Ever alert for promising material, this had been almost too good to be true.

The news reports told of a strange heavyweight—a white man with skin burnt to a deep bronze. A slim, broad-shouldered giant, with a robe of tiger-skins and the scars of many claws upon his body, who fought with the cold fury of a jungle beast.

The *China Clipper* carried Ruby Ryan to the Far

East. He found his man in Bombay, India. In Calcutta, the Tiger Man had knocked out Kid Balotti in the first round, and in Bombay, Guardsman Dirk had lasted until the third by getting on his bicycle.

Balotti was a former top-notcher, now on the downgrade, but still a capable workman with his fists. He had been unconscious four hours after the knockout administered by the Tiger.

In Bombay, the Tiger, a Hercules done in bronze, had floored Guardsman Dirk in the first round, and it had required all the latter's skill to last through the second heat and one minute of the third. Then, he, too, had gone down to crushing defeat.

Ruby Ryan found the Tiger sitting in a darkened hotel room, waiting. The big man wore faded khakis and around his neck was the necklace of tiger claws Ryan had heard of.

The Tiger stood up. He was well over six feet tall and well muscled but he had a startling leanness and coiled intensity to his body. Looking at him, Ryan thought of Tarzan come to life. There *was* something catlike about the man, something jungle-bred. One felt the terrific strength that was in him, and knew instantly why he was billed as "The Tiger."

"We go to Capetown, South Africa. We fight Danny Kilgart there," the man said bluntly. "In Johannesburg, we fight somebody—anybody. If you want to come on you get forty percent of the take. I want the championship within a year. You do the talking, you sign the papers; I'll fight."

That was all. The man knew what he wanted and had a good idea of how to get it.

Danny Kilgart, a good, tough heavyweight with a

wallop, went down in the second under the most blistering, two-fisted attack Ruby Ryan had ever seen. The next victim, the Boer Bomber, weighing two hundred and fifty pounds, lasted just forty-three seconds . . . that had been in Johannesburg.

The Tiger didn't speak three words to Ruby Ryan in three weeks. But Ryan knew what he was looking at—that potentially, the Tiger was a coming champion. Of course it was unlikely that he was good enough to beat Deke Hayes. Hayes was the greatest heavyweight of all time, a master boxer with a brain-jolting wallop. And Hayes trained scientifically and thoroughly for every fight; Ryan's Tiger Man was, to push the allusion too far, an animal. Brutally strong, unbelievably aggressive, but he hadn't been in the ring daily with the best fighters in the world. . . . The Tiger wasn't just a slugger, he was better than that, but it was unlikely that he had the skill of the champ.

In Port Said, Egypt, accompanied by an internationally famous newspaper correspondent, Ryan and the Tiger had been set upon by bandits. The Tiger killed two of them with his bare hands and maimed another before they fled.

The news stories that followed set the world agog with amazement, and brought an offer from Berlin, Germany, to go fifteen rounds with Karl Schaumberg, the Blond Giant of Bavaria.

Schaumberg, considered by many a fit opponent

for the champion himself, lasted three and a half rounds. Fearfully battered, he was carried from the arena, while the Tiger Man, mad with killing fury, paced the ring like a wild beast.

Paris, France, had seen François Chandel go down in two minutes and fifteen seconds, and in London the Tiger had duplicated Jeffries' feat of whipping the three best heavyweights in England in one night.

Offered a fight in Madison Square Garden, the Tiger Man had refused the battle unless given three successive opponents, as in England. They agreed—and he whipped them all! One of them was unfortunate—he had lasted into the second round, and took a terrific pounding.

Then had followed a tour across the country. The best heavyweights that could be brought against the mystery fighter were carried from the ring, one after the other.

Delighted and intoxicated by the Tiger Man's color and copy value, sportswriters filled their papers with glowing stories of his prowess, of his ferocity, and of the tiger-skin robe he wore. The story was that the skins were reputed to have been taken with his bare hands.

Ruby Ryan, after the Bronski fight, was as puzzled as ever. He had his hands on the gimmick fighter of the century, a boxer who made his own press, packed stadiums, and had launched himself into the imagination of the public like a character from the movies. The Tiger Man had created a public relations machine beyond anything Ryan had ever seen but what bothered the old trainer to no end was that he wasn't in on the joke. His fighter played the part every hour of the day. He was good at it, so good that you'd swear the vague stories were real. Ryan, however, knew no more about his man than the average kid on the street—and sometimes thought he knew less.

Ryan drank the last of his coffee and turned to the man seated in the window.

"Well, Tiger, we've come a long way. If we get the breaks, the next fight will be for the title. It's a big if, though; Hayes is good, and he knows it. But McKeown won't let him fight you yet, if he can help it. I think we've got McKeown scared. I know that guy!"

"He'll fight. When he does I'll beat him so badly he'll never come back to the game . . . maybe I'll kill him."

The Tiger got up then, squeezed Ryan's shoulder with a powerful hand, and walked into the bedroom.

Ruby Ryan stared after him. His red face was puzzled and his eyes narrowed as he shook his head in wonderment. Finally, he got up and called Beck, his valet-handyman, to clear the table.

"I got an idea," Ryan told himself, "that that Tiger is a damned good egg underneath. I wonder what he's got it in for the champ for?"

Ruby Ryan shook himself with the thought. "Holy mackerel! I'd hate to be the champ when my Tiger comes out of his corner!"

Beck came in and handed the manager a telegram. Ryan ripped it open, glanced at it briefly, and swore. He stepped into the Tiger's room and handed him the message.

COMMISSION RULES TIGER MUST FIGHT TOM
NOBLE STOP WINNER TO MEET CHAMPION.

"Now that's some of Tom McKeown's work!"
Ruby exclaimed, eyes narrow. "They've ducked that
guy for five years and now they shove him off on us!"

"Okay," the Tiger said harshly. "We'll fight him.
If Hayes is afraid of him, I want him! I want him
right away!"

Ruby Ryan started to speak, then shrugged. Tiger
walked out, and in a few minutes the pounding of
the fast bag could be heard from the hotel gym.

The canvas glared under the white light overhead. In
his corner, Tom Noble rubbed his feet in the resin.
Under the lights, his black body glistened like polished ebony. This was his night, he was certain.

For years the best heavyweights had dodged him.
They had drawn the "color line" to keep from fighting big, courageous Tom Noble. His record was an
unbroken string of victories and yet even the fearless
Deke Hayes had never met him.

A fast, clever boxer, Noble was a pile-driving
puncher with either hand, and most dangerous when
hurt. He weighed two hundred and forty pounds;
forty pounds heavier than the slim, hard-bodied Tiger.

The Tiger Man crawled through the ropes, throwing his black and orange robe over the top rope, and
crouched in his corner like an animal, shifting uneasily, as if restless for the kill.

If he won tonight, he would meet the champion.

Meet Deke Hayes! Even the thought made his muscles tense with eagerness. It had been a long time. A lifetime . . . in some ways it had almost been a lifetime.

The Tiger stirred restlessly, staring at the canvas. He remembered every detail of that last day of his old life. How Deke and himself, on an around-the-world athletic tour nine years before, had decided to visit Tiger Island.

Rumor had it there were more tigers on the island than in all Sumatra, perhaps in all the Dutch East Indies. The hunting was the best in the world but they had been warned; the big cats were fierce, and they were hungry. The greatest of care had to be taken on Tiger Island . . . more than one hunter had died.

Deke Hayes, however, had insisted. And Bart Malone—who was later to become the feared Tiger Man—had gone willingly enough.

For years the two had been friends. They had often trained together, and had boxed on the same card together. The two were evenly, perfectly matched in both skill and stamina. Toward the end, as they had risen in the rankings, Bart Malone had seemed to get a little better. Then two things happened: both men were booked on an exhibition tour that was to take them around the world, and Margot had come into the picture. From the beginning she had seemed to favor Bart.

They had been in a tree stand, waiting fifty yards

from the body of a pig they had killed to bait the tigers. Suddenly, Hayes discovered the ammunition he was to have brought had been forgotten.

Despite Bart Malone's protests, he had gone back to the boat after it. A tiger had come along, and Malone had killed it. But as the sound of the shot died away, he heard the distant roar of a motor.

At first Malone wouldn't believe it. In the morning, when he could leave the tree with safety, he had gone down to the beach. The motorboat that had brought them over from Batavia was gone. On the beach was a little food, a hunting knife, and an axe.

Deke Hayes had never expected him to live, but he had reckoned without the strength, the adaptability, the sheer energy of Bart Malone. With but six cartridges remaining, Malone had made a spear, built a shelter, and declared war on the tigers.

It had been a war of extermination, a case of survival of the fittest. And Bart Malone had survived. He had used deadfalls and pits, spring traps, and traps that shot arrows.

He had learned to kill tigers as hunters in Brazil kill jaguars—with a lance. For nearly eight years he had lived on the remote island, then he had been rescued—and returned to the world as the "Tiger Man."

The Tiger Man shook himself from his reverie, and rubbed his feet in the resin.

And in the champion's apartment, Tom McKeown toyed with the dials, seeking the right spot on the radio.

"You should see him fight, champ. Might get a

line on him. This will be his big test. And if Noble beats him, as he probably will, we'll have to fight a Negro."

Hayes snorted. "I don't care. Noble is a sucker for a left uppercut. I can take him. I'd have fought him two years ago if you'd let me!"

"There's plenty of time, if you have to. He ain't getting any younger. You got seven years on him, champ," McKeown said smoothly. Deke Hayes grinned.

"That was neat work, McKeown, steering the Tiger into Noble. No matter who wins, we got a drawing card. And no matter who wins, if we move fast, he'll be softened by this fight. So the goose hangs high!"

The bell clanged. Tom Noble was easy, confident. He came out fast, jabbed a light left to the head, feinted, and hooked a solid right to the body. The Tiger circled warily, intent.

Noble put both hands to the head, and then tried a left. The Tiger slipped inside, but made no attempt to hit. As they broke the crowd booed, and the Negro looked puzzled.

The Tiger circled again, still wary. Noble landed a left, tried to feint the Tiger in, but it didn't work. The Tiger circled, feinted, and suddenly sprang to close quarters, striking with lightning-like speed.

A swift left, followed by a hard right cross that caught the Negro high on the side of the head. Tom Noble was stepping back, and that took the snap out of the punch; but it shook him, nevertheless.

Noble stepped in, jabbed a left three times to the head, and crossed with a right. The Tiger slipped inside Noble's extended left and threw two jarring hooks to the body.

The fans were silent as the round ended. The usual killing rush of the Tiger hadn't been there. Noble looked puzzled. The Tiger glanced up at Ruby Ryan, then bared his teeth in sort of a smile.

Noble boxed carefully through the second and third rounds, winning both by an easy margin. The Tiger seemed content to circle, to feint, and to spar at long range. The killing rush failed to come, and the Negro, who carefully studied each man he fought, was puzzled. The longer the Tiger waited, the more bothered Noble became.

The giant Negro could sense the repressed power in the steel of the Tiger's muscles. When they clinched, Noble could feel his great strength; but still the Tiger waited. He stalled, and Noble began to feel like a mouse before the cat.

In the fourth round, Tom Noble opened hostilities with a hard left to the head, and then crossed a terrific right to the jaw that snapped the Tiger's head back and split his lip.

Noble, eager, whipped over another right, but the Tiger slid under it and drove a powerful left hook to the body that jarred the Negro to his heels.

Before Noble could recover from his surprise, a hard right uppercut snapped his head back, and a steaming left hook slammed him to the floor in a cloud of resin dust!

Wild with pain and rage, the Negro scrambled to

his feet and rushed. Toe-to-toe, they stood in the center of the ring and swapped punches until every man in the house was wild with excitement.

Bronze against black, Negro from the Baltimore rail yards against the mysterious Tiger Man, they fought bitterly, desperately, their faces streaked with blood and sweat, their breath coming in great gasps.

The crowd, shouting and eager, saw the great Negro boxer, the man whom all white fighters were purported to fear, slugging it out with this jungle killer—the strange white man, bronzed by sun and wind, who had come out of the tropics to batter all his competition into fistic oblivion!

When the bell rang for the fifth round, the Tiger came out like a streak. His wild left hook missed. Overanxious, he stumbled into a torrid right uppercut that slammed into his jaw with crashing force. The Bronze Behemoth slid forward on his face, to all intents and purposes out cold!

For a moment the crowd was aghast. The Tiger Man was down! For the first time in his career, the Tiger Man was down! Roaring with excitement, the crowd jumped up on their chairs, shrieking their heads off.

Then suddenly, the Tiger Man was up! All the stillness, the watching, the waiting was gone from him now. Like a beast from the jungle, he leaped to the fray and with a torrent of smashing, bone-crushing blows, he battered the giant black man across the ring!

Twice the Negro slipped to one knee, and both times came up without a count. Like a fiend out of hell he battled, cornered, fierce as a wounded lion.

But with all his ferocity, all his great strength, it was useless for Tom Noble to stand up against that whirlwind of blows that drove him back, back, and back!

The Tiger was upon him now, fighting like a madman! Suddenly, a steaming right cross snapped the Negro's head back, and he came down with a crash! Like an animal, the Tiger whirled and leaped to his corner.

Tom Noble was up at nine. A great gash streaked his black face. One eye was closed tight, and his lips had been reduced to bloody shreds of flesh. His mouthpiece, lost in the titanic struggle, had failed him when most needed.

Noble was up, and bravely he staggered forward. But the Tiger dropped into a crouch. Grimly, surely, he stalked his opponent.

Seeing him coming, Tom Noble backed off, suddenly seeming to realize that no human effort could stem that tide of blows he knew would be coming.

He backed away, and the Tiger followed him, slowly herding him toward the corner, set for the kill. Not a whisper stirred the crowd. They were breathless with suspense, realizing they were seeing the perfect replica of a jungle kill. A live tiger from Sumatra couldn't have been more fierce, or more deadly!

Then, suddenly, Noble was cornered. Vainly, desperately, he tried to sidestep. But the Tiger was before him and a short, jolting left set Noble's chin for the right cross that flickered over with the speed of a serpent's tongue. The great legs tottered, and Tom Noble, once invincible, crashed to the canvas, a vanquished gladiator.

In Hayes's apartment, there was silence. McKeown wiped the sweat from his forehead, although he suddenly felt cold. He looked at the champion, but Hayes's face was a mask that told nothing.

"Well," Tom McKeown said at last. "I guess we overrated Noble. It looks now like he was a setup!" But in his heart there was a chill as he thought of those crashing fists.

"Setup, hell! That guy could fight!"

Hayes whirled.

"Listen, McKeown: you find out who this Tiger is; where he came from—and why! He started in Calcutta. Okay! I want to know where he was before then! I think I know that guy, and if I do—"

Toronto Tom McKeown walked out into the street. He stood still, looking at nothing. The Tiger had the champ's goat. What was behind it all? One thing he knew: if there was any way to prevent it, the Tiger would never meet Deke Hayes.

Ruby Ryan walked into the hotel room and threw his hat on the table. His eyes were bright with satisfaction.

"Well, that settles that! I guess McKeown has tossed every monkey wrench into the machinery that he can think of—but nevertheless, the fight goes on, and no postponements. The commission accepted my arguments, and agreed that Hayes has got to meet the Tiger—and no more dodging."

Beck looked up from the sport sheet he was reading. He seemed worried.

"Maybe it's okay, but you and me know Tom McKeown, and he's nobody's fool. There'll be trouble yet!" Beck opined.

"It'll have to be soon, then. Tomorrow night's the night," the manager said grimly.

Suddenly the door burst open and the Tiger staggered in. He was carrying "Pug" Doman, one of his sparring partners. Over the Tiger's eye was a deep cut from which a trickle of blood was still flowing.

"What th'—" Ryan's face was white, strained. "For cryin' out loud, man, what's happened?"

"Five men jumped us. I heard them slipping up from behind. We fought. Four of them are out there"—he jerked a thumb toward the door—"in the road, Doman got in the way of a knife."

"Well, that's more of McKeown's work!" Ryan said angrily. "I'll get that dirty so-and-so if it's the last thing I ever do! Look at that cut over your eye. And I just put up the same amount McKeown did— to guarantee appearance, and no postponements!"

The Tiger Man crawled through the ropes, stood rubbing his feet in the resin. Ruby Ryan, his face hard, was staring up the aisle for Hayes to appear. Beck arranged the water bottle and stood silent, waiting. Behind them the excited crowd continued to swell. The arena was fairly alive with tension.

Now Deke Hayes was in the ring. The two men stepped to the center for instructions. Hayes's eyes were fastened on the Tiger with a queer intensity. The Tiger looked up, and there was such a light in his eyes as made even the referee wince.

"It's been a long time, Deke Hayes!" the Tiger growled. "A long time! But tonight, you can't run off and leave me.

"You gypped me out of my girl. You tried to gyp me out of the title, too. Now I'm going to thrash you until you can't move! After tonight, Hayes, you're through!"

"I don't know what you're talkin' about!" Hayes sneered. Then they were back in their corners, and the bell clanged.

Hayes was fast. The Tiger, circling to the center, realized that. He was even faster than Tom Noble. Probably as good a boxer, too. Hayes feinted a left, then hurled a vicious right that spun the Tiger halfway around and made him give way. Deke Hayes bored in promptly, punching fast, accurately.

But the Tiger danced away, boxing carefully for the first time. Hayes's left flicked at the wounded eye, but was just short, and the Tiger slipped under it, and whipped both hands to the body as the round ended.

Deke Hayes came out fast for the second heat, and a right opened the cut over Tiger's eye. Hayes sprang in and, punching like a demon, drove the Tiger across the ring, where he hung him on the ropes with a wicked right uppercut that jerked his head back and slammed him off balance into the hemp.

The Tiger staggered, and almost went down. He

straightened and by a great effort of will, tried to clinch, but Deke Hayes shook him loose, floored him with a wicked left hook.

The crowd was on its feet now, in a yelling frenzy. Ryan sat in the corner, twisting the towel in his hands, chewing on the stump of a dead cigar. But even as the referee counted nine, the Tiger was up!

He tried to clinch, but Hayes shook him off. Confident now, he jabbed three fast lefts to the bad eye, then drove the Tiger to a corner with a volley of hooks, swings, and uppercuts. A short right hook put the Tiger down a second time—and then the bell rang!

The arena was a madhouse as the Tiger came out for the third round, his brain still buzzing. He couldn't seem to get started. Hayes's left flicked out again, resuming the torture. Hayes stepped in and the Tiger evaded a left, then clinched. He caught Hayes's hands, hung on until the referee broke them, warning him for holding.

Through the fourth, fifth, and sixth rounds, Hayes boxed like the marvel he was, but the Tiger kept on. In the clinches he hung on until the referee broke them; he slipped, ducked, and rode punches. He tried every trick he knew.

Only the terrific stamina of those long jungle years carried the Tiger through now; only the running, the diving, the swimming he had done, the fighting in the jungle, the bitter struggle to live, sustained him, kept him on his feet.

Strangely, as the seventh round opened, the Tiger

felt better. His natural strength was asserting itself. Hayes came out, cocky, confident. The Tiger stepped in, but his feet were lighter. Some of the confusion seemed to have gone from his mind. Between rounds the blood from his cut eye had been stopped. He was getting his second wind.

Deke Hayes rushed into the fray, throwing both hands to the head, but the Tiger was ready this time. Dropping into a crouch, he whipped out a snapping left hook and dug a right into the solar plexus.

But the champion fired a left to the head that shook the Tiger to his heels, then threw a right that cracked against his jaw with the force of a thunderbolt. The Tiger went to one knee; but came up, fighting like a demon!

He ripped into the champion with the fury of an unleashed cyclone, battering him halfway across the ring. But when the champion caught himself, he drove the Tiger back onto his heels with a straight left, crossed a right, and then threw both hands to the body.

The Tiger took it. He stepped in, swapping blow for blow, taking the champion's hardest punches with scarcely a wince. Deke Hayes backed off, jabbed a left, but was short, and then the Tiger was inside, tearing away at the other's body with the fury of a Gatling gun. He ripped a mad tattoo of punches against Deke Hayes's ribs; then, stepping back suddenly, he blocked Hayes's left and hooked his own solid left to the head.

The champion staggered, and as the crowd roared like a typhoon in the China Sea, the Tiger tore in, punching furiously. There was no stopping now. Science was cast to the winds, it was the berserk brawling of two killers gone mad!

Round after round passed, and they slugged it out, two fighting fools filled with a deadly hatred of each other, fighting not to win but to kill!

Hayes, panic-stricken, was fighting the fight of his life, backed into a corner by Fate and the enemy he thought he had left behind for good—the man he had cheated and left to die.

Now that man was here, fighting him for the world's title, and Hayes battled like a demon. Staggering, almost ready to go down, the champion whipped up a desperate right uppercut that blasted the Tiger's mind into a flame of white-hot pain! But the Tiger set his teeth, and bored in.

Shifting quickly, he brought down a short over-hand punch, and then deliberately stepped back. As the champion lunged forward instinctively, the Tiger Man knocked him flat with a straight right.

Then the champion was up again at the count of seven. Suddenly, with every ounce of strength at his command, he whipped up a mighty left to the Tiger's groin—a deliberately foul blow! The crowd leaped to its feet, roaring with anger; cries of rage came from officials at the ringside.

The Tiger, tottering, collapsed to his face in the center of the ring—just as the bell rang. The referee angrily motioned the champion to his corner amid a thunder of boos, and the Tiger was helped up.

Even Tom McKeown looked in disgust at his fighter

as he worked over him. The angry referee strode to the Tiger's corner, and asked whether he could continue. The official, thoroughly enraged at the foul blow, was all for declaring the Tiger the winner, then and there.

But the Tiger, through his daze of pain, shook his head. "Not that way!" he gritted. "We fight . . . to the finish!" and the referee, cursing the champion, let the challenger have his way.

Then the bell rang. But now it was different; and even the maddened crowd sensed that. Deke Hayes looked over at the slowly rising Tiger with real fear in his eyes. Why, the man wasn't human! No one could take a blow like that and keep coming!

Eyes red with hatred, the Tiger came out in a steel-coiled crouch. Hayes, wary now, had come to the end, and he knew it. He advanced slowly to the center of the ring, and the Tiger met him—met him with a sudden, berserk rush that drove the now frightened champion to the ropes.

There he hung, while the Tiger ripped punch after vicious punch to his body, pounded his ears until they were swollen and torn, cut his eyebrows with lightning-like twists of hard, smashing gloves.

A bloody, beaten mess, marked for life, the champion slipped frantically away along the ropes. Trembling with fright, he set himself desperately, shot a steaming right for the Tiger's chin.

But the Tiger beat him to the punch with an inside right cross that jerked Hayes back on his heels! Before the blood-covered champion could weave away, the Tiger—Bart Malone—whipped up a lethal left hook that started at his heels. Spinning completely around, the champion toppled to the canvas, out like a log, his jaw broken in three places!

The referee dismissed the formality of a count as the crowd went wild. Without a word, the referee raised the Tiger's hand in victory, as the rafters shook with the roaring of thousands of frenzied voices.

Ruby Ryan was beside himself with joy. "You made it, kid!" he yelled. "You made it! I never saw such nerve in my life! The greatest fight I ever seen! Damn, how did you do it?"

The Tiger looked down at him, grinned, though his body was a throbbing pain from the punishment he had absorbed.

"Somethin' I learned in the jungle," he growled.

POLICE
BAND

. . . C ar 134 . . . 134 . . . cancel your last call, 135 will handle. . . ."

Tom Sixte stopped turning the dial and listened. He was far over on the right side of his radio and was for the first time aware that it could pick up police calls. The book he was reading had failed to hold his interest. He put it down and lit a cigarette.

"42, station call . . . 1047 South Kashmir . . . 218, MT, Clear . . ." The signal faded in and out.

Sixte leaned back in his chair, listening with only half his attention. He had been in town to study a plan for moving an industrial plant to San Bernardino and the study was complete, his report written. At thirty-two he was successful, single, and vaguely discontented.

With only hours remaining of his stay in town, he

was profoundly bored. His work had given him no time to make friends, and he had seen too many movies. Waiting got on his nerves, and he was leaving in just forty-eight hours for Bolivia.

"All units . . . stolen truck . . . commercial . . . Charles . . . Henry. . . ." The voice trailed off again and Sixte turned in his chair and poured his glass half full of Madeira, then relaxed.

The dispatcher's voice came in suddenly. "179 . . . Redondo and San Vincente, neighbor reports a man hurt, a woman screaming. . . ."

Tom Sixte sat up abruptly. That was only two blocks away! He sat still for a moment but boredom pulled him to his feet. He shrugged into his coat and, hat in hand, stepped out the door.

Upon reaching the street, he hesitated. What was he rushing for? Like a ten-year-old kid after a fire truck!

But, why not? He was doing nothing and the walk might do him good. He went to the corner. He could hear no screaming, although far off he heard the wail of a siren approaching.

He turned the corner and started for Redondo, but just before he reached it, he saw a girl cutting across a lawn, coming toward him. Her coat was open, hair flying, and she was running.

She was in the middle of the street when she saw him. She slid to a stop and in the light reflected from the corner her face seemed set and strained. Her right hand was in her pocket.

"What's the trouble?" he asked. "Do you need help?"

"No!" She spat the word. But a glance over her

shoulder and her manner changed. She came up to him quickly. "Sorry, I do need help, but you frightened me. I just got away from a man."

"The police are coming. There's nothing to worry about now."

She paused, listening to the siren. "Oh, but I *can't* meet the police! I simply can't! They'd . . . my parents would hear . . ." She caught his arm impulsively. "Help me, won't you? Daddy and Mother didn't know I was out. . . ."

They were walking back toward the corner he had turned. A siren shrilled to a stop somewhere behind them. She clutched his arm. "Do you live close by? Can't we go there? Just until the police are gone? I . . . I fought him off, and he fell. He may be hurt. Take me to your place . . . oh, *please*!"

Tom Sixte shrugged. No use letting the kid get into trouble, and it would be only for a few minutes. He could not see her face well, but her voice and her figure indicated youth.

He led the way upstairs and unlocked the door. The room was small and simple. Aside from the clothes and his bags the only things in it that belonged to him were a half dozen books.

When he saw her face under the light, he felt his first touch of doubt. She must be . . . well, over thirty.

She saw the bottle. "Can I have a drink?" Without waiting for his reply, she picked up his own empty glass and poured wine into it. She tossed it off, then looked startled. "What was that?"

"It's wine. It's called Malmsey."

"It's good." She picked up the bottle and looked

at it. "Imported, isn't it?" She glanced swiftly around the room, and saw the telephone. "May I make a call?"

She moved the phone and dialed. He heard the phone ringing, then a hard male voice. "Yeah?"

"Kurt? This is Phyllis. . . . Can you come and get me?" Sixte heard a male voice asking questions. "What d'you think?" Her voice became strident with impatience. "Rhubarb? I'll say! The place is lousy with cops.

"No, I'm all right . . . some guy invited me up to his place." The male voice lowered a little. "How do I know who he is?" Phyllis grew more impatient. "Look, you're in this as deep as I am! You come an' get me! . . . Sure, I'll stay here, but hurry!"

Worried now, Sixte turned on her as she hung up the phone. "I didn't bargain for this," he said, "you'll have to go. I had no idea you were running from the police."

"Sit down." There was a small automatic in her hand. "I'm not fooling. That man out there is dead."

"*Dead?*" Sixte was incredulous. "You killed him?"

Her laugh was not pleasant. "He was a drunken fool. It was that woman spoiled it all."

"Woman?"

"Some dame who came up while I was going over him. She started to scream so I hit her."

Tom Sixte sat down, trying to focus his thoughts. Fifteen minutes ago, he had been reading, faintly bored. Now, he was mixed up in a murder and robbery. Kurt was coming to take her away, and then . . . his good sense intervened. That would not, could not be the end. They could not afford to let him go. And if she had killed a man . . .

She poured another glass of the Madeira. Steps sounded outside the door. There was a careful knock. Keeping her eyes on Sixte, the gun out of sight, Phyllis opened the door.

The man who stepped in was cadaverous, but handsome. He could have been no more than thirty, and he wore a dark suit. The eyes that measured Sixte were cruel.

Phyllis pulled him to one side and whispered rapidly. Kurt listened, then shook out a cigarette. "Who are you?" he said then. "What are you?"

"My name is Sixte. I'm an architect."

"Get up and turn around."

Sixte felt practiced hands go through his pockets, remove his wallet, some letters.

He was told to be seated and Kurt went through his billfold. There was seventy dollars in cash, some traveler's checks—and the tickets were with his passport.

"Bolivia, huh? Whatya know about that? I got a guy wants to leave town. He'd pay plenty for this passport and these tickets."

Sixte tried to sort out his thoughts. For the first time he began to appreciate his true danger.

Kurt smiled, and it was not a nice smile. "This is sweet, Phyl, real sweet. This joker has stuff here I can sell for a grand, easy. Maybe two. Rubio has to get out of town and this is it. Rubio pays, takes the ticket—this guy is gone and nobody even looks for him."

Tom Sixte sat very still. His mind seemed icy cold. He was not going to get out of this . . . he was not going to . . . he reached over to his radio and adjusted the hands of the clock, then the volume. . . .

Detective Lieutenant Mike Frost walked back to the lab truck. "Roll it, Joe," he said, "nothing more you can do here."

Suddenly the radio lit up. "179 . . . you up the block from the coroner's van? If so turn your radio down. We're getting complaints."

Frost picked up the microphone. "Dispatch . . . ? What's this about my radio?"

After a brief conversation Mike Frost got out of the car, spoke to Joe, and walked up the block. The sound was rolling from the hallway of a rooming house and Frost went up the steps two at a time. The door was open, and as people were emerging from the rooms and staring, Frost shoved through the door and went in. The blasting sound filled an empty room, with the light switch off.

Turning the lights on, he stepped to the radio and turned it off with a snap. Joe had come into the door behind him. "What is it, Lieutenant?"

"Oh, some crazy fool went off and left his radio turned on." He scowled. "No, it's one of those clock radios. Must have just switched on."

"Who'd want that volume?" Joe wondered. "And on a police band, too."

Mike Frost looked at Joe thoughtfully, then turned

slowly and began to look around the room. It was strangely bare.

No clothes, no personal possessions. The bathroom shelves were empty, no razor, shaving cream, or powder. No toothbrush.

The simple furniture of a furnished room, towels, soap . . . a clock radio and some books. The clock radio was brand spanking new . . . so were the books.

Frost stepped back into the bathroom. The sink was still damp. Whoever had been here had left within a very few minutes. But why leave a new radio and the books? The only other thing remaining was an almost empty bottle of Madeira. The glass on the table was still wet . . . and there was lipstick on the rim. In two places . . . some woman had taken at least two drinks here.

And not twenty minutes ago, a woman had fled the scene of a killing just two blocks away.

Somebody had left this room fast . . . and why was that radio set for a time when no one would want to get up and tuned for a police band with the volume control on full power?

"Get your stuff, Joe. Give it a going-over."

Joe was incredulous. "This place? What's the idea?"

"Call it a hunch, Joe. But work fast. I think we'd better work fast."

The landlady was visiting somebody in Santa Monica. Yes, she had a new roomer. A man. Nobody knew anything about him except that he was rarely in, and very quiet. Oh, yes! A neighbor remembered, Mrs. Brady had said he was leaving in a couple of days . . . this room would be vacant on the fifth. This was the third.

Frost walked back up to the room and stared around him. Was he wasting time, making a fool of himself? But why would a man leave a perfectly new clock radio behind him? And why leave the books?

There were six of them, all new. They represented a value of more than thirty dollars and given the condition of the spines three of them had not even been opened. Two were on South America. On Bolivia. One was a book on conversational Spanish.

Frost picked up the telephone and rang the airlines. In a matter of minutes he had his information. Three men were scheduled for La Paz, Bolivia, on the fifth . . . another check . . . at that address. Thomas Sixte. Frost put the phone back on the cradle.

He was no closer to an answer but he did have more of a puzzle and some reason behind his hunch. Why would a man, leaving within forty-eight hours, anyway, suddenly leave a comfortable room?

Where did he expect to spend the next forty-eight hours? Why did he leave his books and radio? He glanced at the dial on the radio. The man had his clock radio set to start blasting police calls within a matter of minutes after he had left his room.

Why?

Frost picked up the Madeira bottle . . . forty-eight years old. Good stuff, not too easily had . . . he checked the telephone book and began ringing. Absently, he watched Joe going over the room. His helper was in the bathroom.

The liquor store he called replied after a minute.

Just closing up. "Yes, I knew Mr. Sixte. Very excellent taste, Lieutenant. Knows wines as few men do. When he first talked to me about them, I believed him to be a champagne salesman.

"That brand of Madeira? Very few stores, Lieutenant. It would be easy to . . . yes? All right."

He glanced at his watch. He had been in the vicinity so had gone to Redondo and San Vincente. That had been at 9:42 . . . twenty minutes later he heard the blasting of the radio . . . it was now 10:35.

"Only three sets of prints," Joe told him. "One of them a man's. Two are women. One of them is probably the maid or the landlady, judging by where I found 'em."

"The others?"

"Only a couple . . . some more, but smudged. Got a clear print off the wine bottle, one off the glass."

"Anything else?"

"Soap in the shower is still wet. He probably took a shower about seven or eight o'clock. Some cigarettes, all his . . . and he'd been reading that book."

Joe rubbed his jaw. "What gives, Lieutenant? What you tryin' to prove?"

Mike Frost shrugged. He was not quite sure himself. "A man is killed and a girl is slugged by a woman. We know that much. Two blocks away a man suddenly leaves his room, with no reason that figures, and minutes later his clock radio starts blasting police calls.

"A woman has been in this room within the last hour. My hunch is it was the woman who killed that guy on Redondo. I'm guessing that she got in here somehow to duck the police, and when she went away, she took him with her."

"And he turned on the radio to warn us? How does he know we're near?"

"Maybe the girl told him. Maybe he saw the murder. Maybe she followed him. It's all maybe."

"Maybe he was in cahoots with her."

"Could be . . . but why the radio?"

"Accident . . . twisted the wrong dial, maybe."

Frost nodded wearily. "All right. Check those prints. All three sets . . . or whatever you got."

Had the girl taken the man away from here by herself? They had a call out, the area blanketed. Any girl alone would have been stopped. But if she had been with him? She might have been stopped, anyway. She was a blonde, about thirty, someone had said, slight figure . . . in a suede coat.

When Joe was gone Mike Frost sat down in the empty room and began to fiddle with the radio. After twenty minutes he had learned one thing. You just didn't turn this on to the police band. You had to hunt for it, adjust it carefully.

Heavy steps on the stairs . . . "Got something for you, Lieutenant." It was an officer from a radio car. "A girl across the street. She was parked with her boyfriend . . . high school kids . . . they saw two men and a woman come out and go to a car. Dark sedan of some kind."

"Two men?"

"Yeah . . . the car drove up while they were sittin' there. The guy who went upstairs was tall. Big in the shoulders."

It was something, but not much. There was the

phone. Had the girl gotten in here she could have called her boyfriend, and he might have been waiting nearby. The murdered man had been drinking, that was obvious. Probably quite drunk . . . and probably in a bar not a dozen blocks away.

If they could find that bar they might get a description . . . beat officers were looking but it might not be fast enough . . . a man's life might be at stake.

Mike Frost stood quietly gnawing gently at his lower lip. He was a big man, wide in the shoulders, with a rather solemn, thick-boned face. His fingers dug at his reddish-brown hair and he tried to think.

This Tom Sixte . . . he was no fool. In a tight spot he had thought of the clock radio and the police calls. It had been a chance, but he had thought of it and taken it. He might think of something else but they could not depend on that.

The bank. They might try to get some money out of Sixte. Suddenly, Frost was hoping Sixte would think of that. If he did, if he could play on their greed . . .

The wine bottle . . . he had liquor stores alerted for possible purchase of the Madeira. It was a wild chance, but the girl had tried a glass of it, and to get money they might humor Sixte. "Boy," Frost said, half aloud, "I hope you're thinking, and I hope you're thinking like I am."

Forty-eight hours. They would have the flight covered long before takeoff time.

Mike Frost went back to his office and sat down at the battered, scarred old desk. He ran his fingers through his rusty hair and tried to think . . . to think. . . .

• • •

Tom Sixte sat on the divan in a quaint, old-fashioned room. The sort of furnishings that were good middle-class in 1910. It gave him a queer feeling to be sitting there like that, the room was so much like his Aunt Eunice's.

Kurt was leafing through the paper and he was smoking. Phyllis was irritable. She kept looking over at Sixte. "You're a fool, Kurt. Get rid of him."

"Take it easy." Kurt leaned back in his chair, light-ing another cigarette with his left hand. With his coat off, his shoulders were not as wide and he was a lit-tle pigeon chested. "I've got a call out for Rubio. Let him do it."

Sixte's feet were tied, but his hands were free. There was no way he could move quickly, and nothing to use with his hands. He was trying to put himself in the position of the police and getting nowhere.

Suppose some neighbor had just turned off the radio? Suppose the police had become curious, that would make them look around? How smart were they?

All right. Suppose they had come, and suppose they had examined his room. Suppose they decided he had been kidnapped, all of which was a lot of supposing. But, if they had? What would they do?

Closing his eyes to shut out the room he was in, he tried to picture the situation. He knew something of police work, something of the routine. But there would be little to go on . . . the Madeira. It was the one thing that was different. That might help.

What else?

As long as they sat still, he had time. Yet as long as they sat still they could not make mistakes. He had to get them into the open, to start them moving. Sooner or later the nagging of Phyllis might irk Kurt into killing him.

But Kurt didn't want to kill, if he didn't have to . . . he wanted this Rubio to do it. Kurt didn't want to kill but Tom had no doubt that he would if pushed. Kurt might be the key, but what did he want?

He wanted money. Easy money, quick money.

Kurt hoped to sell the passport and tickets, for maybe a thousand dollars . . . a thousand dollars . . . who, if he could, would not buy his life for that sum? Or twice or three times as much? Or more?

Rubio had not called, so there was a chance. A faint, slim chance.

"Look," he said quietly, "I'm a reasonable guy. What you do is none of my business. Anyway, I'm supposed to go to South America. I don't know who either of you are, and I don't want to know, but I figure you're pretty smart."

All criminals, psychologists say, are both egotists and optimists. A good point. Flatter them—but not too much.

"Suppose you knock me off, and suppose you sell my papers to Rubio . . . will he pay a thousand bucks?"

Kurt smiled. "He does or he don't get them."

Sixte shrugged. "All right. You know him better than I do. But he knows you've got me on your hands. The only way you can make any dough is to sell those papers, otherwise you knock me off for nothing, am I right?"

"So what?"

"So he says, 'I'll give you five hundred, take it or leave it.' Then where are you?"

Kurt's smile was gone, he was studying Tom Sixte and he didn't like what he was thinking. Kurt was remembering Rubio, and he had a hunch that was just what Rubio would do—and where did that leave *him*?

"Now I want to live. I also want to go to South America. Rubio will give you a thousand bucks for my papers. All right," Sixte put his palms on his knees. "I'll boost the ante. You put me on that plane to Bolivia with my own tickets and I'll give you *five* thousand!"

"Don't listen to him, Kurt." Phyllis was uneasy. "I don't like it."

"Shut up." Kurt was thinking. Five thousand was good money. Five G's right in his mitt.

He shook his head. "You'd have them radio from the plane. What do you think I am, a dope?"

Sixte shrugged. "I know better than that. You're a sharp operator and that's what I'm banking on. Any dope can kill a man. Only a dope would take the chance at that price. Especially, when he can get more."

He took his time. "See it from where I sit. I want to live. If some drunk gets killed, that's no skin off my nose. I like women, good food, I like wine. I can't have any of them if I'm dead."

Tom Sixte lit a cigarette. "I haven't got a lot of money, but I could cash a check for five thousand dollars. If I tried to get more they'd make inquiries and you might get suspicious and shoot me. I'm going to play it smart.

"So I draw five thousand. You take it and put me on the plane. I don't know who you are . . . what exactly am I going to tell them? You could be out of town, in Las Vegas or Portland before they started looking—but that's not all. I wouldn't squawk because I'd be called back as a witness. If I wasn't here there'd be nothing to connect you with the job—and brother, I can make money in Bolivia. I've got a big deal down there."

There were plenty of fallacies in his argument, but Tom Sixte would point out nothing they could not see. He drew deep on his cigarette and ran his fingers through his dark hair. He was unshaved and felt dirty. If he got out of this, it would be by thinking his way out, and he was tired. He wanted a shower and sleep.

"I got to think about it." Kurt got up. "I don't like it much."

Sixte leaned back on the divan. "Think it over. If I was in your place, I would think a lot." Kurt leaned back and lit a cigarette. His face was expressionless but Sixte was remembering the padded shoulders in Kurt's jacket. "Your girlfriend, for instance. She'd look mighty pretty in a new outfit, and you two would make a pair, all dressed to the nines."

Kurt ignored him, looking around and speaking past his cigarette. "Phyl, fix some sandwiches, will you?"

"As long as I'm paying for this," Sixte grinned at them, "why not some steaks? The condemned man ate a hearty meal. . . ." He met Kurt's cold eye and added, "Maybe you'll soon have five thousand dollars, so why not enjoy yourself?" Keeping his voice casual, he added, "And while you're at it, why not a bottle of wine? Some of that Madeira?"

Detective Lieutenant Mike Frost sat behind the scarred desk. It was 10:00 A.M. and he had just checked with the morgue . . . nobody that could be Sixte had been brought in yet. But if he was dead they might never find him.

Joe stuck his head in the door. "Nothing on the prints. The man's were Sixte himself, a major in combat intelligence during the war. The woman was the landlady, who does her own cleaning up. And we drew a blank on the girl. Nothing on file."

There had been nothing on the bars, either. Nobody remembered any such couple. Frost was thinking . . . the other man had come at once, and it could not have taken him longer than ten minutes. It took time to get outside, get a car started and into the street . . . at most he would not be more than twenty blocks away. More likely within half that distance. Frost picked up the phone and started a check on bars and possible loafing places. Looking for a tall dark young man who answered a phone and left hurriedly.

Surprisingly, the break came quickly. Noonan called in. Frost remembered him as a boyish-looking officer who looked like a college halfback. A man answering the description took a call in a public booth at three minutes after ten. He paid for his drinks and went out.

Why so sure of the time? The bartender's girl was late. She usually came in at quarter to ten, so he was watching the clock and expecting a call.

"This guy didn't talk," Noonan said. "He nursed one drink for more than an hour, had just ordered the second. The bartender heard him say on the phone, 'Yes, this is Tommy Hart.' "

They ran a check on Hart . . . nothing. Noonan called back. "A guy in that bar, he says that guy Hart, if that was his name, used to hang out at a bar on Sixth Street. The Shadow Club."

It fit. A lot of hoods came and went around there. A lot of good people, too. Frost had Hart figured as small time—working through a woman—but even the small-time boys have big ideas, delusions of grandeur. And he might be afraid to turn Sixte loose.

At noon Frost went out for a sandwich. He drank two cups of coffee, taking a lot of time. He covered the ground again, step by step. The bank, the liquor stores, Hart, the airlines. The Shadow Club.

Shortly after one, he walked back to the desk. Sixte had been missing almost fifteen hours. By now he might be buried in the floor of a cellar or a vacant lot.

Tom Sixte . . . friendly, quiet, hard worker. Read a lot. Spoke French and German, studying Spanish. Expert in industrial planning . . . an unlikely man to be mixed up in anything. Mike Frost knew all about him now. Had reports on his desk from the government, from businessmen with whom he had talked . . . Sixte was top drawer. He was dark-haired, good-looking, smiled easily.

If the tickets were used, they would have their man. But Tom Sixte would be dead, a good man murdered.

Frost started thinking. Tickets to Bolivia were worth dough in the right place. So was a passport and visa . . . who wanted to get out of town? Who that they knew about? Who that was missing?

Tony Shapiro . . . from Brooklyn. A mobster. Big time. Wanted by the Feds. Something clicked in the brain of Mike Frost. Shapiro had been reported seen in Tucson . . . in Palm Springs.

Local connections? Vince Montesori, Rubio Turchi.

Frost picked up the phone. . . . Shapiro had connections in the Argentine. If he could get to South America, he might be safe.

Frost got up and put on his hat. He went down into the street, squinting his eyes against the sunlight. He walked west, then north. After a while he stopped for a shine.

The shine boy was a short, thickset man with a flat face and there was nobody around. He had never heard of Tommy Hart or anybody like him. Montesori was working his club, same as always. Rubio? The shine boy bent further over the detective's shoes. Nothing . . .

It all added up to nothing.

Back at the desk, Frost checked the file on Rubio. He had kept his nose clean since coming out of Q. He . . . Mike Frost picked up the telephone and began checking on Rubio and San Quentin . . . his cell mate had been in for larceny. Twenty-one years old, tall, dark hair, name . . . Kurt Eberhardt. He hung up the phone.

Kurt Eberhardt . . . Tommy Hart. It could be. It was close enough, and the description was right.

He had something to go on now. Check the Shadow Club on Eberhardt . . . check with the stoolies, his contacts on the criminal side. It might be a blind alley, but it could fit. There was nothing substantial, anywhere. A bottle of Madeira . . . he dropped in at a liquor store. Three principal varieties of Madeira sold here. Sercial, a dry wine, Boal was on the sweet side. Malmsey was a dessert wine, and sweeter. It was Malmsey that Sixte fancied.

At four o'clock, he was sitting at the scarred desk, thinking about Sixte. If the guy was alive, he was sweating about now. Time was drawing the strings into a tight knot around his throat.

All over town the wheels were meshing, the department was working . . . and they had nothing. Nothing at all.

Rubio Turchi could not be found. He had been around until shortly after midnight the previous night, and he dropped out of sight . . . the time tied in . . . which might be an accident. Mike Frost swore softly and irritably at the loose ends, the flimsy angles on which he must work. Nothing really . . .

A report from the Shadow Club. They remembered Eberhardt. A free spender when he had it. Some figured he had been rolling drunks for his pocket money. Always with a girl . . . a brunette. Her name was Lola, a Spanish girl, or Mexican.

Find Lola.

More wheels started to mesh. No rumble from the

bank. Nothing on the wine. Nothing on Turchi, nothing on anybody.

At ten o'clock, Mike Frost went home and crawled into bed. At 2:00 A.M., he awoke with a start. He sat up and lit a cigarette.

He called Headquarters. They had Lola. He swore, then got into his clothes. Sleepy, unshaven, and irritable, he walked into his office. Lola was there, with Noonan.

Frost lit a cigarette for her. "You're not in trouble," his tone was conversational, "you'll walk out of here in a few minutes and Noonan can drive you home.

"All we want to know is about a guy named Eberhardt, Kurt Eberhardt."

She turned on Frost and broke into a torrent of vindictive Spanish. Sorting it out, he learned she knew nothing about him, nor did she want to, he was a rat, a pig, a—she quieted down.

A few more questions elicited the information that she had not seen him in three months. He had left her . . . a blonde, a girl named Phyllis Edsall.

Lola talked and talked fast. Kurt Eberhardt thought he was a big shot, smart. That was because he had been in prison with Rubio Turchi. He had driven a car for Turchi a few times, but he bragged too much; Turchi dropped him. She had not seen him in three months.

Now they had another name, Phyllis Edsall. No record. A check on Edsalls in the telephone book brought nothing. They did not know her. Reports began to come in from contacts in the underworld. . . . Eberhardt probably had stuck up a few filling stations, but usually he had his girl get drunks out where he could roll them. Sometimes it was the badger game, sometimes plain muscle.

Nobody knew where he lived. Nobody knew where the girl lived.

Nothing more from the Shadow Club. Nothing from the bank. Nobody in the morgue that fitted. Rubio Turchi still missing.

Mike Frost and Noonan went out for coffee together. They stopped by the liquor store where Sixte had been buying his Madeira. The fat little proprietor looked up and smiled. "Say, you were asking about Madeira. I sold a bottle yesterday afternoon. I started to call, but the line was busy, and . . ."

Frost found his hands were shaking. Noonan looked white. "Who bought it? Who?" Frost's voice was hoarse.

"Oh," the little man waved his hand, "just some girl. A little blonde. I told her—"

"You told her what?"

The little man looked from Frost to Noonan. His face was flabby. "Why . . . why I just said that was good wine, even the police were interested, and—"

Mike Frost felt his fist knot and he restrained himself with an effort. "You damned fool!" he said hoarsely. "You simpleminded fool!"

"Here!" The little man was indignant. "You can't talk to me like—"

"That girl. Did she wear a suede coat?" Noonan asked.

The little man backed off. "Yes, yes, I think so. You can't—"

It had been there. They had had it right in their

grasp and then it was gone. The little man had not called. She looked, he said, like a nice girl. She was no criminal. He could tell. She was—"Oh, shut up!" Frost was coldly furious.

One fat, gabby little man had finished it. Now they knew. They knew the police were looking for Sixte, that they were watching the sales of Madeira, they knew. . . .

"S'pose he's still alive?" Noonan was worried. He had been really working on this case.

Frost shrugged. "Not now. They know they are hot, now. They probably won't go near a bank. That blew it up. Right in our faces."

"Yeah," Noonan agreed, "if he's alive, he's lucky."

Tom Sixte lay on the floor of the cellar of the old-fashioned house with his face bloody and his hands tied as well as his feet. Right at that moment he would not have agreed that it was better to be alive. When Phyllis came in with the wine, she was white and scared. She had babbled the story and Kurt had turned vicious.

"Smart guy, huh?" he had said, and then he hit Sixte. He had tried to rise, and Kurt, coldly brutal, had proceeded to knock him down and kick him in the kidneys, the belly, the head. Finally, he had bound his hands and rolled him down the cellar steps to where he lay. The door had been closed and locked.

Sixte lay very still, breathing painfully. His face was stiff with drying blood, his head throbbed with a dull, heavy ache, his body was sore, and his hands were bound with cruel tightness.

They dared not take him to the bank looking like this. They dared not put him on a plane now. Phyllis was sure she had not been followed. She had taken over an hour to come back, making sure. But there was no way out now. They would kill him. Unless he could somehow get free.

Desperation lent him strength. He began to struggle, to chafe the clothesline that bound him against the edge of the wooden step. It was a new board, and sharp-edged.

Upstairs, he heard a door slam and heavy feet went down the front steps. The floor creaked up above. Phyllis was still there . . . no use to ask her help, she was the one who killed the man on Redondo.

He began to sweat. Sweat and dust got into the cuts on his face. They smarted. His head throbbed. He worked, bitterly, desperately, his muscles aching.

Kurt Eberhardt was frightened. He got out of the house because he was scared. Despite what Phyl said, they might have followed her. He walked swiftly north, stopped there on a corner, and watched the house. Nobody around, no cars parked. After ten minutes, he decided she had not been followed and walked on, slower.

He had to see Rubio. Rubio would know what to do. He went to his car, got in, and drove downtown. He tried to call Rubio . . . no answer. He called two or three places, no luck. At the last one, he asked, "When is he leavin'?"

"You nuts?" The man's voice was scoffing. "He ain't goin' noplace. He can't. He's tied up here, wit' big dough."

Then, maybe Rubio would not use the tickets, either. He wouldn't want the visa and passport.

His stomach empty and sick, Kurt Eberhardt started up the street. On the corner, he stopped and looked back, seeing the sign. The Shadow Club . . . it was early yet. It might not be open. He stood there, trying to think, looking for an out.

He had never killed a man. He had bragged about it, but he never had. When Phyllis told him she had, he was scared, but he dared not show it. The fear had made him beat Sixte.

That had been foolish. With that beat-up face . . . still, the guy was scared now, bound to be. They could say he had been in an accident. Sixte wouldn't talk out of turn. He could draw out the money . . . not a bad deal. He could even take it and the tickets and scram. No, they would stop him . . . unless he killed Sixte.

It was better to play it straight with the guy.

Phyl . . . she made the trouble. She got him into this. Too rattle-brained. Lola now, she never made a wrong move. Killing that guy, Lola wouldn't have done it. Lola . . . no use thinking about that. It was over.

He would get Rubio. He would wait at his place until he came.

•   •   •

Mike Frost sat at his desk. It was 4:00 P.M. The plane for Bolivia left at 9:45. The banks were closed now, but there were a few places around town where a check might be cashed . . . they were covered.

No more chance on the liquor stores. The men checking up on those were pulled off. They were still worrying over the bone of Kurt Eberhardt and that of Phyllis Edsall. No luck on either of them. Nobody seemed to know either of them beyond what they had learned.

At 4:17 P.M., a call came in. Rubio Turchi's green sedan had been spotted coming out of the hills at Arroyo and the Coast Road. It would be picked up by an unmarked police car.

At 4:23 P.M. another call. A dark sedan with a dark-haired young man had been parked in front of Rubio's apartment for more than an hour. The fellow seemed to have fallen asleep in the car, apparently waiting. It was the first time the man covering Rubio's apartment had been able to get to a phone. He gave them the car's number.

The license had been issued to one Phyllis Hart, but she had moved from the old address, left no forwarding address.

Mike Frost rubbed the stubble on his face and swore softly. He walked to the door of an adjoining office and stuck his head in. "Joe? You got that electric razor here? I feel like hell."

He carried the razor back, loosened his tie, and took off his coat. He plugged in the razor and started to shave. Rubio would meet Eberhardt, if that was him in the car, and seven to ten it was. Then they would what . . . go back to the place where

Sixte was held . . . had been held? Or would it simply be a delivery of the tickets? If they split, they would be followed separately, if they went together, so much the better. He stopped shaving and called for another undercover car to be sent out to Rubio's place.

Mike Frost rubbed his smooth cheek and started on his upper lip.

Tom Sixte felt the first strand of the clothesline part, but nothing else came loose. He tugged, it was tight and strong. He waited, resting. It was getting late.

For some time now, there had been restless movements upstairs. Suddenly, the footsteps turned and started toward the cellar steps. Instantly, Sixte rolled over and over, then sat up, his face toward the steps.

Phyllis came down until she could see him, then stopped and stared. Her face was strained and white, her eyes seemed very bright.

She stared at him, and said nothing, so he took a chance. "Did he run out on you?"

Her lip curled and she came down onto the floor. For a minute, he thought she would hit him. Then she said, "He won't run out on me. He wouldn't dare."

Sixte shook his head a little. "Man, have I got a headache! My head got hit on the steps." She made no reply, chewing on her lip. "Look," he said, "can't we make a deal? You an' me?"

Her eyes were cold, but beyond it, he could see she was scared. "What kind of deal?"

"Get me on that plane and I'll give *you* the five thousand."

It got to her, all right. He could see it hit home. "You're in this deeper than he is. Why should he collect? Seems to me he's been gone a long time."

"The banks are closed now."

"You'd know somebody. My identification is good. We could tell them I got in a scrap with your boyfriend, and want to get out of town, that I have my tickets, but need cash."

She was thinking it over. No question about that. She had it in mind. "I know a guy who might have it."

"Then it's a deal?"

"I'll give him ten minutes more," she said. "It's almost five."

She went back up the stairs, and Sixte returned to his sawing at the ropes that bound him.

At 5:10 P.M., his cheeks smooth, his hair freshly combed, Mike Frost got a call. Rubio and Eberhardt had made contact. They had gone into the house and there was a man with them. He was a short, powerfully built man in a gray suit.

An unmarked police car slid into place alongside the curb under some low-hung branches. Nobody got out. A man sauntered up the street and struck a match, lighting a cigarette. It was a cloudy afternoon and there was a faint smell of rain in the air.

Mike Frost was sweating. He was guessing and guessing wild. The man in the gray suit could be

Tony Shapiro. He hesitated, then picked up the telephone and dialed the FBI.

When he hung up, his phone rang. Rubio, Eberhardt, and the other man had come out. They all got into Rubio's car and started away. They were being checked and followed.

At 5:22 P.M., the cellar door suddenly opened and Phyllis came down the steps sideways. She went over to Sixte and she had a gun in her hand. "You try anything, and I'll kill you," she said, and he believed her.

He had his hands loose and he brought them around in front of him. "See?" he said. "I'm playing fair. I could have let you come closer and jumped you." He began to untie the ropes on his ankles.

When he got up, he staggered. Barely able to walk, he got up the stairs. Then he brushed himself off, splashed water on his face, and combed his hair. As they reached the door, a taxi rolled up.

"Don't try anything."

The cabdriver looked around, his eyes hesitating on Sixte's bruised face.

"The Shadow Club," Phyllis said, and sat back in the seat. Her features were drawn and fine, her eyes wide open. She sat on Sixte's right and had her right hand in her pocket. "We'll get out by the alley."

They went up a set of stairs and stopped before a blank door. Phyllis knocked and after a minute a man answered. At her name, he opened the door, then wider. They walked in. When the man saw

Sixte's face, his eyes changed a little. They seemed to mask, to film. The man turned, went through another door, and walked to his desk.

He was a stocky man in a striped shirt. His neck was thick. "Whatya want, Phyl?" He dropped into his chair.

"Look," she said quickly, "this guy is a friend. He's got dough in the bank and he's got to get out of town. He wants to cash a check for five G's."

"That's a lot of cash." The man looked from one to the other. "What's it worth?"

"A hundred dollars."

The man chuckled. "You tell that to Vince Montesori? It's worth more."

Sixte produced his identification, and indicated the balance in his checking account. "The check's good," he said quietly, "and I'll boost the ante to five hundred extra if you cash it right away."

Montesori got to his feet. "I gotta check. There's a guy works for the bank. If he says you're okay, I'll cash it, okay?" He indicated a door. "You wait in there."

It was a small private sitting room, comfortably fixed up. There was a bar with glasses and several bottles of wine, one of bourbon. Tom Sixte stepped to the bar. "I could use a drink. How about you?"

Phyllis was watching him carefully. "All right."

He picked up the bourbon and then through the thin wall over the bar, he heard a faint voice, audible only by straining his ears.

"Yeah," it was Montesori, "they just came in. Tell Rubio. I'll stall 'em."

Sixte finished pouring the drinks, added ice and soda. He walked back and held the drink out to Phyllis. She stood back, very carefully. "Put it down on the table," she said, "I'll pick it up."

This was not going to work. Whatever happened, he had to get out of here . . . fast.

At 5:47, a call came in from a radio car. They had tailed Rubio and the other two men to a frame house, old place off Mission Road. They had all gone in, then had come rushing out and piled into the car.

After they had gone, followed by other cars, a check of the house revealed some cut clothesline in the cellar, an unopened bottle of Madeira, and clothes for a girl and a man. There was some blood on the cellar floor, and a few spots on the living room carpet.

Mike Frost got up and put on his coat. It looked like a double-cross. The babe had taken Sixte and lit out, for where?

The source of information at the Shadow Club would not talk . . . closed up like a clam. In itself, that meant something.

Frost motioned to Noonan and they walked out to the car. "The Shadow Club," he told Noonan. He sat back in the seat, closing his eyes. After a while all this waiting could get to a guy. It was time to squeeze someone and squeeze them hard. Patience got you only so far.

•   •   •

The girl was too cautious, Sixte could see that. He was on edge now. It had been a long time since he had played rough. Not since the Army days. But the events of the past hours had sharpened him up. He was bruised and stiff, but he was mad; he was both mad and desperate.

"It's a double-cross," he said, looking at Phyllis. "That guy out there, that Vince Montesori. He called Rubio."

Her eyes were level and cold. He could see how this girl could kill, and quickly. He explained what he had heard. "It's your neck, too," he said, "you were making a deal on your own, but our deal stands if we get out of here."

"We'll get out. Open the door."

It was locked. No answer came from the other side. Phyllis was frightened now. Sixte turned swiftly and picked up a stool that stood beside the little bar. He had heard voices through the wall, low voices, so—he swung the stool.

The crash of smashing wood filled the room and Sixte looked quickly through the hole in the cheap dividing wall. The room beyond was empty. He smashed again with the stool, then went through the hole, and opened the door. Phyllis came out, looking at him quickly—he had not tried to trap her.

The door to the alley was locked tight. The door to the club was locked.

The alley door was metal and tightly fitted, solid as the wall itself. The door to the club was not so tight, and breaking it down might attract help from the club itself. From the patrons . . . he heard foot-steps coming along the hall.

"Behind the door," he told her, "get them under the gun when they come in."

Her eyes were small and tight. There was an inner streak of viciousness in this girl. He was accepted as her ally at least momentarily. She looked at him and said, "Don't worry about Kurt. He's yellow."

A key sounded in the lock and Sixte dropped his right hand to the back of a chair. It was a heavy oak chair and he tilted it, ever so slightly.

Montesori stepped inside, behind him were Kurt and two other men. Startled, Montesori looked at him, then beyond him at the smashed panels of the wall. His face went white around the mouth.

"You busted my wall!"

Kurt stepped in, looking at Sixte like he had never seen him before. Rubio followed. "Where's she? Where's the girl?"

"Get over by the wall, Vince. You, too, Kurt. All of you." Phyllis stepped out with the gun.

Only the man in the gray suit remained in the door. Sixte gambled. He had the chair balanced and he shoved down hard on the corner of the back. The chair legs slid, shooting out from under his hand on the slick floor. The man tried to jump, but the heavy chair smashed him across the knees and he fell over it, into the room.

Tom Sixte went over him in a long dive and hit the floor sliding. Somebody yelled behind him and there was a shot, then another. Fists started pounding on the alley door, and Sixte scrambled to his feet only to be tackled from behind. Turning, with a chance to fight back for the first time, Sixte hooked a short, wicked left that caught Rubio as he scrambled to get up.

The blow smashed his nose and showered him with blood. He staggered, his eyes wide, his mouth flapping like a frightened chicken, and then Sixte was on him. Rubio tried to fight back, but Sixte was swinging with both hands. Rubio scuttled backwards into the chair and the gray-suited man who sat very still on the floor, clutching his shin, his face utterly calm.

Vince Montesori jumped through the door, scrambling over the chair, and tried to break past Sixte, but Tom Sixte was in the middle of the hall and he caught the running man coming in with a right that jolted him clear to the spine when it landed. Vince went back and down, and Sixte turned to run but suddenly the room was filled with officers in uniform.

Tom Sixte crouched over, his breath coming in gasps. Looking through the open hall door he could see Kurt lying on the floor inside. His throat had been torn by a bullet and there was a bigger hole behind his ear where it had come out.

Phyllis was handing her gun to an officer, and a big man in plainclothes walked up to Sixte. The man had rusty hair and a freckled face. He looked very tired. "You Sixte?"

"Yeah?"

Frost smiled wryly. "I'm Mike Frost. Glad to see you. . . . Heck, I'm glad to see you alive."

FLIGHT
TO ENBETU

Colonel Sharpe bent over the map as Turk Madden spoke. "Sure," he said, "I know the spot, I was there once. It's inland from Enbetu, the railroad from Hakodate to Wakkanai forks off here. Years back I was all over Hokkaido."

"Excellent. We bomb Wakkanai at dawn tomorrow. And naturally, before the attack, we want all communication with Hakodate and Japan proper destroyed. You will cut that railroad, also the telephone and telegraph lines that follow it."

"And Ryan takes care of the radio?"

"Right. The radio and power stations will be destroyed. Forty minutes later, which should allow time for any reasonable hitch in his plans, we attack. Everything must go on schedule."

He understood the situation perfectly. Wakkanai was a tough nut to crack but its defenders could also call on scores of Nipponese planes from Hakodate.

Should this happen the attack would meet with disaster.

The Kurile Isles had been attacked many times, and Wakkanai was the next step. But there was nothing in the Kuriles even remotely approaching Wakkanai.

The job of the saboteurs was essential. They had a fair chance of getting their mission done, but a very small chance of getting out with a whole skin, or even part of one.

Colonel Sharpe straightened.

"Well, that's the setup, Madden. You move out at two thousand hours, and you should be over your goal by midnight. Within a mile of your destination the Japs have an emergency landing strip. That field is unguarded at present.

"At ten minutes past midnight two lights will be shown to indicate the width of the field. These lights can be shown momentarily only. You will not see the men handling the lights. They are Ainu, white natives of the island. They will show their signals and leave. With your mission complete, you will take off and return here."

Madden studied the map thoughtfully. It wasn't as if he didn't know the country, or what he was going into. He did know all of that. But their success depended upon surprise, upon secrecy, and he knew something was wrong.

Two hours before he had opened his strongbox and found that a small, carefully drawn map of the northern tip of Hokkaido had been stolen. It could hardly be coincidence, on the eve of the attack.

The door opened suddenly, and two men came in.

Sparrow Ryan was a former stuntman and speed flyer. Like Madden he had been an itinerant soldier in many countries. He had the alert but battered look of a professional.

The other man was tall, good-looking Lieutenant Ken Martin. Martin had been a top-notch collegiate running back not long before. He was dark, sallow, and his eyes had a faint suggestion of the almond. This was one of the reasons he had been chosen.

With the exception of Madden, who knew the country and had made previous secret flights to Japan, all of them would pass for Japanese in dim light, it wasn't much but it was one of the few advantages they had.

"Hi, Turk!" Ryan grinned tightly. "Here we go again!"

"Yeah," Turk agreed, "don't let 'em get you! This has got to be good."

"Listen, honey-chile," Ryan said. "I've studied those charts until I know that country better than the natives. We'll hit them and get away before they know it."

Lieutenant Martin interrupted. "How about this fellow Sauten? I don't like the idea of taking him with us. He's a known criminal and not to be trusted."

Turk looked up from the map.

"Chiv Sauten is a tough baby. I want tough guys. This is no job for Milquetoasts."

"But the man's a gangster!" Martin insisted. "We've got to draw the line somewhere. He would sell out to anyone!"

"I don't think so," Turk said shortly. "And I'm

not going to marry the guy, I'm going to fight alongside him."

"If they'd known he was a criminal, he'd never have gotten into the Air Force," Martin persisted. His young good-looking face was hard. "For one, I don't like going into a tough spot with a man like that."

"He might not have gotten in," Turk agreed, "but he's in now. He volunteered for this job, and for my money, he goes."

Colonel Sharpe frowned a little.

"I didn't know about this man," he said, glancing accusingly at Madden. "Did you cover for him when he joined up?"

"Yes." Madden's voice was positive. "Frankly, sir, I'm a bit fed up on this lily-white stuff. We're fighting a war, not picking men acceptable to somebody's maiden aunt. That guy can handle a tommy gun.

"He's been kicked around and knocked down plenty. He got up. He's been shot at, and hit, and he kept shooting. I don't give a hoot in Hades if the man strangled his grandmother. If he's willing to go on this job, who are we to stop him."

Sauten came in then. He had a thin, hard face and looked as tough as his reputation.

"Ship's ready. Scofield and Gorman are standing by."

His eyes flickered over the room, resting momentarily on Martin, then moving on.

"Okay. We'll be right out," Madden said briefly. He picked up his 'chute. "See you later, Colonel."

Ryan and Martin had the toughest part of the job.

Turk was thinking of that as he climbed into the B-25 and got settled. They would be working in a populated area where discovery was almost a certainty. But the two Cantonese they had with them both looked more Japanese than Chinese, and Sparrow Ryan was small and wiry. Tucker, the navigator, was built along similar lines.

Chiv got in behind Turk.

"It's a good night for it," he said. He checked the magazine on the tommy gun. "Lieutenant Martin was in on that Morley job, wasn't he?"

"Right. The other two were killed. If it hadn't been for him, the whole mission would have been a washout. As it was, he got back with the necessary information, or most of it. He was a lucky stiff to make it out at all."

Turk Madden liked the feel of the ship in the air, despite the fact that it seemed odd not to be at the controls. But Scofield handled the medium bomber like a pursuit plane. Nick Gorman was navigator, and a good man. It would take a good man, for hitting the landing strip in the dark would be worse than finding one of those coral atolls far to the southeast.

The Morley job had been a mess. Vic Morley had gone out with Martin and Welldon. Their plane had been shot down, and Morley and Welldon had been captured. Martin had escaped, then, and only after great trials, got back to their base.

This time was going to be different. It had to be different.

They had been in the air three hours when Gorman touched his arm.

"This is it," he said, "two minutes!"

"Take her down," Madden told Scofield, "and put her on the ground in a hurry."

It was nine minutes past midnight.

Scofield glanced over his shoulder, indicating the altimeter with a finger. It was at a thousand feet. They dare not stay long at that low level. Yet no lights had appeared.

A minute passed, then another. Chiv Sauten shifted his tommy gun, waiting. Gorman glanced at Madden questioningly.

Had their man been captured? Should he play it safe and turn back? Madden set his jaw. To heck with it, he thought. They had come to do a job, and they were going to do it, come what might.

Directly below them was the landing field. Turk's memory for terrain was almost photographic.

He slid forward in the cockpit.

"Give her to me," he said. "I know this field. I might stand a shade better chance at bringing her in blind than you."

Madden leveled off and then nosed down for the field. Ahead, he knew, was a mountain. To the right and to the left were trees. He could see nothing but the loom of one great peak. He could only pray that he was bringing the big Mitchell in right. He let the ship down fast, pulling the nose up a trifle.

Sweat broke out on his brow as he felt the ship sideslip as it dropped away beneath him. It could crash any moment now, any . . .

Two lights flashed suddenly, ahead and to the right. He banked the ship, then flattened her out. A split second later the wheels touched, and the plane rolled forward on the level ground. The lights vanished.

Turk let the B-25 run as far as he dared, then braked her cautiously, his eyes straining against the dark, the big ship swung around, facing downfield.

Madden stepped down, and Chiv Sauten and Monte Jackson closed in beside him.

"Good luck, men," Scofield said softly, and the three of them moved away into the darkness. The last thing Turk saw was Nick Gorman standing by with his tommy gun at the ready.

With every sense alert, Madden led the way. Every moment now was fraught with danger. This was the heart of Japan's own territory. This was the first time American soldiers had set foot on Japan proper since the war began, except as prisoners. If successful, the Kurile Islands would be exposed to attack, along with the whole northern shore of Hokkaido.

He hesitated once, staring about him. There was something wrong about this setup, something very wrong. A subtle sense of danger was flowing through him. He felt as though his back were naked to a bullet-ridden draught.

It was no feeling of the danger ahead. That danger he had faced many times. This was something else . . . the missing map, he'd have to watch his own back on this one. He thought, then, of what Martin had said of Sauten—that the ex-gangster would sell out to anyone.

Certainly, the Capone bunch had been a gang of murderers. Yet Sauten was a silent, capable man. Common sense told him Chiv was not to be trusted.

His instincts made him less certain. The fellow felt right, whatever his past record had been.

He wasn't kidding himself about his chances on this mission, and he knew the others weren't. They weren't expected to come back alive. He knew that was what they thought at Headquarters. But Turk Madden had his own ideas.

You don't come through a lot of dangers without acquiring confidence. Turk knew just exactly what he faced, just exactly what chances he had. The odds were a thousand to one against them but experience with danger in many odd corners of the world had taught him that positive, determined action by men of quick wits and valor can do some strange things to the ordinary ratio of chances.

He moved forward, beside him, Sauten was like a ghost. Jackson was behind them both.

Madden's feet warned him when he reached the path. He could see nothing, but his soles found its hard smoothness, and his leg muscles felt the downward slope toward the roadbed.

The rail line showed abruptly, two glistening lines of steel. Accustomed to working alone as he always had, Sauten's nearness was disturbing. He kept his companions with him until their eyes were more accustomed to darkness, then at his signal, they vanished. He dropped to his knees and started digging under a tie.

When they had placed their mines, five under each rail, they armed them with detonators and drew back a short distance. Turk wiped his face with his sleeve and felt Jackson near him.

"The culvert's just below us," the man whispered, "the one on the map."

They moved on to the culvert. Sauten was already there, his explosives on the ground. Silently as possible, the three men went to work. This was to be the main, the vital part of the job. If the road were blasted here, it would take weeks to repair. Not only were they preparing the culvert for demolition, but the cliff above as well.

They worked swiftly, silently, with grim determination. There was a vague intimation of light now. Several times Turk looked up. Each time he saw Chiv Sauten peering around.

Finally, Turk Madden straightened up.

"Okay," he said, "now we go back."

"No! Somebody's coming," Sauten said. "And coming very quietly!"

Madden gave a hand signal, and the three of them dropped back into the rocks, on lower ground. From their new position, they could watch the skyline.

Suddenly they saw them—six Japanese soldiers moving slowly, carefully down the track. In the instant before the attack, Madden was grimly aware of one thing—these soldiers were looking for something. They knew!

His hand slid to his knife. It was a commando-style fighting knife, thin and deadly, an eight-inch, double-edged knife with a point so sharp an expert could almost sink it through a man. The last of the Japanese was passing when he moved. Some almost imperceptible sound must have warned the man. He turned his head suddenly.

Turk was close, but not close enough for a blow. He took a chance and let the knife go, throwing it underhand and hard.

He heard it thud as it hit, and he followed it in, slugging the man as he fell. Then he wrenched the knife from below the soldier's heart and went for the next one, hitting him low and hard.

He heard Sauten and Jackson close in. A blow caught him in the mouth, and he tasted blood. He stabbed quickly with the knife, felt it hang on some equipment, then slide off and into the man. He stifled the fellow's cry with a hand.

A soldier swung a rifle butt, and Turk dropped back onto his hands, kicking out viciously with both feet. The Japanese staggered, and Madden threw his body against the man's knees. He went down.

The knife slipped from Turk's hand, but he went in fast, reaching for the man's throat. It was a brutal, ugly bit of fighting. Someone kicked him in the head, and, desperately, he broke away from the man on the ground and rolled free. He came up fast, and a fist slugged him in the mouth, then a boot toe caught him in the stomach.

A sickening wave of pain and nausea went over him, and he was back on the ground. A soldier closed in, kicking at his face. Turk grabbed the man's ankle and hung on.

They both went down. Then he was up, and the Japanese lurched toward him. Turk had grabbed a rifle from the ground as he came to his feet, and before the imperial soldier could start another assault, Turk brought the rifle down, striking with an overhand butt stroke that crumpled the soldier's skull like an eggshell.

He turned then, swaying, gasping for breath. A shadow moved toward him, and he saw a gun leveled at his stomach, and for a moment he thought he was cold meat. It was Chiv Sauten.

"I thought you were a Jap," Chiv said.

"Where's Monte?" Madden demanded.

"Here," Jackson said, coming up the embankment. "I rolled down there with that guy. He nearly got me."

"You hurt?" Turk demanded.

"A scratch," Monte replied shortly. "Let's go!"

They moved off then. Surprise had done it, Turk knew, sheer darned fool luck and surprise.

Madden set a fast pace and as he moved, his mind worked swiftly. The Japanese could have taken the plane. If so, he and the men with him were grounded in Japan.

Turk halted suddenly. Ahead of them was the airfield, less than a dozen yards away.

Turning abruptly, he went off the path and across the brush- and tree-clad hill. Like ghosts, the two men followed him. Sauten remained at Madden's elbow, Monte, his breath coming hard, trailed a little behind.

It was warm and still. Turk eased down over a rock, feeling for the earth. He found it, and lowered himself gently. Then he turned. A bead of sweat trickled down his spine. He moved forward, stepping cautiously and placing each foot solidly before moving the next.

Suddenly, he stopped. A faint, sickening sweet smell. Perspiration dripped from his chin, and a slow drop slid past his ear. He knew that smell, could feel its aftertaste in his own mouth.

Blood!

Cautiously, he put out a foot. At the second step, his toes touched something. He leaned forward. He could see the body. It was a man, short, and very broad. Beside the man was something metallic. Turk reached for it. A flashlight.

He straightened uneasily. This was one of the men who had guided the plane to the field. He recognized the broad, powerful build, typical of the hairy Ainu. And the flashlight confirmed his suspicions.

The Japanese had known. Calmly, quietly, they had stood by and let the plane be guided in. Then they had killed the men who flashed the signals.

The feeling of unseen menace he'd had earlier possessed him again. The soldiers along the track had been no casual patrol. They had been searching for the flyers. They had known, as he had suspected.

If they knew, it could mean but one thing. The American plan of attack had been betrayed.

Sauten moved up beside him. The man's lips moved, and the whisper was ghostly. Turk had never believed a man could speak with so little sound, so little exhalation of breath.

"We're in a spot," the gangster said softly, "there's Japs south of us, and there's Japs across the field. I heard those nearest, saw the gleam on a rifle barrel."

What worried Madden was the plane. Had they taken the plane? He moved forward, touching Sauten.

Keeping the brush behind them, and the blackness of the looming cliff, they worked across the top of the field toward the Mitchell.

There was double danger now. If the plane were not taken, Gorman or Scofield might fire on them.

Crouching low, he saw the silhouette of the plane against the vague sky. Uneasily, he glanced downfield. Something was happening down there. There was no real sound, but a subdued whisper of movement, deadly, mysterious.

What had happened at Wakkanai? Had Ryan managed to wreck the radio? Or had he landed and walked into a trap—a trap that would soon engulf the whole American attack? For, Turk knew, if the enemy had known enough to prepare for this advance movement, they would be ready, multifold, for the attack to come.

Turk moved ahead, halted, then started on again. Suddenly, a figure shot up from the ground ahead of him, and he glimpsed a flicker of movement. Instinctively, he ducked, and just in time to let a rifle butt miss. Lunging, he let go with a wicked left hook for the body.

It landed, a glancing blow, partially blocked.

"Why you dirty—!" The voice was low and hoarse with anger. "I'll—!"

"Nick!" Madden gasped. "It's me! Madden!"

"We thought they'd got you," Nick whispered. "Let's get to the plane!" Lunging to his feet, he made a quick dash for the few remaining yards. Madden followed, then Sauten.

"Where's Monte?" Scofield demanded.

"Here."

Monte's voice was low with effort. He fell against Scofield, and the pilot felt blood on his hand. Jackson's whole side was soaked with it.

Hurriedly, yet gently, they got him into the ship. Scofield stared down the field. It was pitch dark.

"I don't like it," he said grimly, "but here goes!"

They climbed into the ship. Turk hesitated, remembering the subdued sounds. Then he shrugged, and crawled in.

The plane's motors broke into a roar of sound. Surprisingly, no one fired on them. The Japanese, and they must be all around, made no effort to stop them. Turk scowled. Suddenly, on the inspiration of the instant, he picked up the rocket pistol from the lifesaving equipment.

He stepped to the door, and even as the ship started to roll, he fired a shot into the air. There was a brief moment, then the flare burst.

The Mitchell was thundering down the narrow field, her twin motors roaring, and dead ahead, across the field, was a heavy barrier of logs!

Madden's face went white. He started to speak, then saw Scofield. The pilot's eyes were wide, his face grim. Turk saw him push the throttles wide, and at the same instant, he pulled back on the stick.

Turk grabbed his tommy gun. If she crashed, and he lived through it, he was going out fighting.

The Mitchell lifted, sagged, and headed straight at the barrier, her engines a thunder of impossible sound! Desperately, his face cold and stiff, Scofield held back on the wheel. Suddenly, her run seemingly not long enough, the B-25 lifted, a wheel touched the top log, and the ship shot over—they were free!

• • •

Below, a machine gun broke into a wicked chatter, bullets slamming into the fuselage, and in the fading light of the flare, they saw Japanese soldiers pour out upon the landing strip, weapons blossoming fire.

Steadily, the big ship climbed. Madden sank back, his face gray, and his mouth dry. He looked at Gorman and thought for a moment that the navigator was going to faint. Only Chiv Sauten showed no emotion, nothing but widened eyes.

"The torpedoes back in Chi thought they were hard guys," he said, just loud enough to be heard. "They thought they were tough! Boy!"

But Turk Madden was already thinking ahead. Their mission was complete. All of it had taken but a few minutes of actual time, a very little while. The bombers would be in the air now, they would be well on their way to Japan. What of Sparrow? Had he succeeded? Or did it matter?

Sauten looked at Turk.

"Well, we're out of that! And I ain't sorry!"

"No," Turk said, "we're not out of it . . . we're going on to Wakkanai!"

"What?" Scofield looked at Madden. "Are you nuts? If the Japs knew about us—" He scowled in concentration.

"Nick," he suggested, "if you knew what we know, and you were a Jap, what would you do?"

Gorman shrugged. "Run in a bunch of Zeros and park them out of sight until just before the attack began. Then knock down every Yank in the air."

Madden nodded.

"My guess, too. The ack-ack will be ready, of course, but unquestionably they'll have pursuit ships somewhere out of sight."

He bent over the chart, and pointing, said to Nick Gorman, "It will probably be here, but it might be here or over here. Try the first one."

Sauten made no sound, but his lips thinned to a queer, strained smile. Thoughtfully, he began to check the tommy gun.

Madden said no more. For an instant, he thought of San Francisco and the Top o' the Mark. He'd always liked the view from there, and it reminded him, somehow, of the view from the Peak in Hong Kong.

This was going to be tough. They might find the enemy field, and they might not. In either case, there was a good chance there'd be more trouble.

The whole area they had to cover was not large. Actually a few minutes of flying time would be enough. They could make it, and still have fuel to get safely back to base—if they were still able to fly.

Then he saw the planes. It was a small field, but a dozen ships were lined up to take off. Behind them, more planes were being wheeled from under camouflage nets. The vague lights were enough to show him that, and the Japanese seemed to be working with no thought of discovery.

Scofield had seen them too. He glanced around.

"How about it?" his lips framed the question, and Madden nodded.

The Mitchell wheeled around and down in a long, slanting dive. The Japanese airmen heard it, and he saw them suddenly scatter. Anti-aircraft guns flashed, but the B-25 was already too low for the shrapnel.

Scofield took the ship in fast, and the men in the Mitchell manned the guns. Madden opened up with the fifty in the nose. He saw a man run for a ship, let go with the gun, and watched the Jap stumble and fall on his face.

The angry teeth of the bullets gnawed the earth, then ripped at the sleeping plane. An explosion burst in the concealed hangars with a terrific concussion, and as the Mitchell lifted away from the field, Turk could see three of the parked ships were in flames.

"Again?" Scofield asked, but Madden shook his head.

He pointed north.

"Wakkanai," he said. He was worried about Ryan. It wasn't only the man, although the flyer was his friend. It was the job. The mission always came first and Ryan had been betrayed—Turk Madden knew he had.

Someone had stolen his map of Hokkaido before they began the flight. Someone had warned the enemy.

Sauten moved a little, and his black, slitted eyes turned toward Madden. He was cold. Turk thought, the man was like ice.

Then he remembered Martin. Lieutenant Ken Martin had been the hero of another flight over Japan. Martin had doubted Sauten. Turk looked again at the man.

True, he had been a gangster. The man had been a

criminal. Why should he believe in a man who had done nothing to warrant belief?

Wakkanai was still in the quiet night. As the Mitchell came in toward the great Japanese naval base, Turk's brow furrowed. If Sparrow had gone down there, he had done nothing. There were no fires, had been no explosions. Something was wrong, radically, bitterly wrong!

He got up, pulling on his 'chute. Gorman stared. Turk motioned down, then going nearer, gave it to him.

"I'm bailing out! You go on back!" Gorman's protest was lost as he turned. The port opened, and he spilled out into the night.

Over and over he tumbled through the blackness. Then he pulled the string, and after a moment, the 'chute jerked him up, hard.

Studying the dark ground below, he spilled air from the 'chute, trying to guide himself toward a black spot where there were no lights.

It was wildly reckless but Ryan had failed to succeed with his mission. The whole attack depended on their success and the planes would be over the town within the hour. Perhaps the surprise was gone, yet they could take no chances. The attack was going forward regardless.

He landed in soft earth among some bushes. Quickly, he bundled up the 'chute and checked his gun. He cleared the branches just as something dark slipped by him, and then a white cloud descended, enveloping him into its folds!

Desperate, he fought free, lunging to his feet. Another man staggered erect, and he saw the dark glimmer of light on a gun barrel.

"Skipper?" the voice was low, questioning.

Chiv Sauten!

"What the heck?" Madden demanded softly. "I left you in the ship!"

"Yeah," Sauten nodded agreement as he got himself free of the parachute, "but things looked kind of slow up there. I had this typewriter, so I thought I'd come down and see what was cookin'."

"Let's go!" Turk felt relieved. There was no denying the security he felt with Chiv at his elbow. Then, a cold chill went over him.

Why had Sauten joined him? Had the man come to help or to prevent Turk's effort from succeeding?

He could only drive ahead and take a chance on that.

He knew where the radio station was. The plan had been well studied. They had landed close together in a small park. Chiv, who had followed Madden by seconds only, had observed a tall building to their rear, a dwelling dead ahead of them. He spoke of this now.

Turk nodded.

"We'll skirt the smaller place, then head for the radio. It isn't over a thousand yards away."

Suddenly, the night was broken wide open by the whine of an air raid siren!

Turk broke into a run. Men were dashing about everywhere, and his running did not attract attention. Nearby, covering him, was Sauten.

Dodging past the dwelling, they rushed across a

street and down an alleyway. Lights were going out, and in a matter of seconds the town would be in total darkness.

Suddenly, from ahead of them, muffled by the screaming siren, there was a burst of small arms fire!

A soldier darted from a building and started up the street toward the sound. Then, under the scream of the siren he must have heard the running feet and spun around—too late!

Turk was running full tilt, and he jerked up his tommy gun and smashed the butt into the man's face with all the drive of his powerful shoulders. Behind him, as the man fell, he heard another thud, a heavier one. Chiv Sauten was always thorough.

The shooting had broken into a roar now, and it came from a building dead ahead where there still were lights.

There was no time to hesitate. Turk slid to a stop at the door, then turned the corner quickly and flattened against the wall inside the doorway.

Two Japanese policemen were dead on the steps. At the top of the steps was Lin, one of the Cantonese who had flown with Ryan. He was dead. Fairly riddled with bullets.

Turk started forward, working his way up the steps. Inside the shooting had slowed to an occasional shot. He stepped up, then stopped suddenly, his gaze riveted on the body of the Chinese!

Lin had been shot in the back!

Eyes narrow, Turk cleared the top step. Four Japanese soldiers were crouched by the switchboards, their eyes on something across the room.

"All right," Turk said loudly, "this is it!"

As one man, they wheeled, and, turning, they faced a blasting, hell of fire! Through a haze from his tommy gun, Turk saw one Japanese then another toppling to the floor. Beside him Sauten's weapon was hammering.

Across the room, Sparrow Ryan suddenly lunged to his feet and poured a battering chain of .45-caliber slugs into the switchboard.

Sauten jerked a handful of wires then, punching a hole in the wall near him he pulled the pin on an incendiary grenade and dropped it in.

A bullet clipped the door over Turk's head, and he wheeled, firing at a soldier in the side door. There was a dull thud and part of the wall blew out as the grenade sent a rush of hot flame toward the ceiling. The three men ran and, as they reached the door, Madden jerked the pin on another grenade, tossing it over the switchboard into the maze of wires. That would take care of the telephone exchange.

They made the street. Madden wheeled to run, and then something smashed across his forehead, and he felt himself falling. He hit the ground on his hands and knees, struggled to get up and then another blow landed on his skull from behind, and he slid facedown on the sidewalk, his head roaring with a gigantic blackness shot through with the lightning of pain.

It could only have been minutes later when he opened his eyes. His face, which had been lying on the floor, was stiff with blood from his cut scalp. He tried to move, and the attempt made his head throb horribly. He lay still, gathering strength.

"Who is it?"

The voice was scarcely a whisper.

"Are you a Yank?"

Turk's head jerked. "A Yank?" he gasped. "Yes. Who are you?"

"My name's Morley, I—"

"Vic!" Madden heaved himself to a sitting position. "It's Madden! We thought you were dead!"

"They kept me alive for interrogation," Morley replied bitterly. "But if I ever get out of this—" He hesitated, his voice queer and strained. "Turk, we were sold out. It was . . ."

The door opened, and a brilliant light flashed on. Two Japanese officers stepped in, and following them, were four soldiers, supporting the wreck of what had been Sparrow Ryan. They threw the little flyer to the concrete floor, and one of them kicked him brutally.

The stockier of the two looked at Madden. His eyes were malignant.

"You are a fool!" he snapped, his words clipped, but in excellent English. "You think you will surprise us? We have been ready for you for days!"

He stared at Madden, then stepped close.

"You tell me—how many planes come in the attacking force?"

Turk smiled. "Go to the devil," he said quietly.

The officer kicked him in the head. Once, twice, three times. Turk let his head roll with the kicks, and held himself inside against the burst of pain.

"You will tell." The man's voice was distinct. He kicked Turk again, breaking ribs.

"Sure," Turk gasped, "I'll tell."

The Jap's eyes gleamed.

"How many come?"

"Ten thousand," Turk said. "It won't end until Dai Nippon is a heap of smoldering ruins."

"Yes? I have seen your country. They are soft! They will tire of the war, then Japan will be left with all she needs!"

He looked down at Turk contemptuously.

"Bah! I know how many ships come! Their size, their bomb loads, their route!"

He turned on his heel and left the room. The guard loitered, his eyes ugly. He glanced over his shoulder at the door, then walked back to Madden. For a moment, he stood looking down, then slowly, he raised the rifle and pointed the bayonet at Turk's chest.

Madden's eyes were cold.

"Go ahead, yellow belly! Some Marine will feed you one of those soon enough!"

The soldier snarled, and the bayonet came down, and suddenly, with all his remaining strength, Turk Madden rolled over, thrusting himself hard into the soldier's legs!

The Japanese had started to shift his weight, and Turk caught him off balance. The guard toppled, and fell, his head striking the corner of the table as he dropped. He rolled over and, groggy, started to get up. Morley, lying almost beside him, fastened his teeth on the man's ear.

At that moment, the sky turned into a roar of

sound, and they heard the shrill scream of bombs, punctuated by explosions.

Madden heaved himself closer to the struggling guard and, drawing his knees back to his chest, kicked out hard with the heels of both bound feet. The man's head slammed back into the wall, and then Madden struggled nearer, and kicked again, kicked with all the strength in his powerful legs.

"Quick!" Madden snapped. "Get his rifle and work the bayonet under the ropes on my wrists!"

Outside, the world was an inferno of flame and the thunderous roar of bombs. There was a fight going on overhead, too, and amid the frightful explosions of anti-aircraft fire and the high, protesting yammer of machine guns, Turk could hear the scream of diving planes.

He could feel the blade of the bayonet working against the ropes. It was slow and hard, for Morley was working with bound hands. Suddenly, everything happened at once. A Japanese officer stepped into the doorway, and the ropes on Turk's wrists came free.

There was an instant of paralyzed astonishment, and then the officer reached for his pistol. The holster flap was buttoned and Turk had time to whip the Arisaka rifle to his shoulder and fire.

His hand still fumbling helplessly at the flap, the officer tumbled back through the door. Turk hastily freed his ankles, then turned to Morley.

Stopping only to grab up the officer's pistol, they dashed from the room and then down the steps.

A shadow loomed nearby, and Turk whirled, the rifle poised.

"Hold it, Skipper." Chiv Sauten stepped into view. "It's me."

There was no darkness now. Wakkanai was a roaring mass of flame, and the pound of exploding bombs roared on, unceasing.

"Sparrow got away, too," he said. "We'd better get out of here."

He led them at a fast walk. They carried their guns ready. Rounding a corner, they came face-to-face with a cluster of men fighting a fire. They ran toward the blaze, hoses at the ready, and showed no interest at all in Madden's armed group. Sauten led the way down an alley, picking up the pace. The roar of wind-captured flames was so great as almost to drown the sound of the nightmare overhead. Somewhere a munitions plant let go, and glass cascaded into the street. An arrow of fire shot across in front of them from a burning building, and then a huge wall fell in, and a great blast of flame gulped at the sky.

Moving through the destruction, Turk felt himself turn sick with horror at what was happening to the town. This was fury such as no man had seen short of Hamburg or Berlin.

Soon they were at the edge of town, and they turned into a small field to see Sparrow's B-25 waiting.

And then, Turk Madden saw the officer who had spoken to them.

The Japanese was standing across the field, with him were three soldiers, one behind a heavy-caliber machine gun. Even as Turk glimpsed them, he saw the officer lift a hand as a signal.

Turk's Arisaka went to his hip, and he fired. The shot missed, but knocked the gunner to a kneeling position. Sauten dropped into a crouch and opened up with the tommy gun, but on the third round the gun went dead.

Madden was halfway across the short intervening space before the gun had stopped pounding. The officer was the only man on his feet, and he cried shrilly and sprang from behind the gun, drawing his samurai sword.

Leaping back before the slashing arc of the great sword, Turk hurled the rifle. Its bayonet point was within four feet of the officer's chest, and Madden's throw drove the long knife deep into the man's body! Turning, Turk Madden ran stumbling toward the bomber. . . .

Behind him, the bullet-riddled body of the Mitchell once again stood on the Air Corps field. As dawn began to light the sky Turk Madden walked quickly toward the Headquarters office. At his side was Sauten, behind him Sparrow Ryan and Morley limped, trying to keep up. Beyond them planes returning from the raid of Wakkanai were beginning to fill the sky and drop toward the landing strip.

Stepping up, Turk stopped in the doorway. For an instant, there was complete silence.

Colonel Sharpe's eyes widened, then narrowed.

"You? Thank God you're back!"

"Yes," Turk said. "And I know who gave us away. I know who the traitor was who blew up the Morley job and who gave us away this time."

The Colonel's eyes were calculating.

"You do?"

Turk turned to face Martin, and his face was quiet. Then Morley stepped through the door, his face thin and pale, his eyes burning.

"Well Martin, I see you got back again. I supposed you had another story cooked up as good as the one you told after you betrayed us?"

"He landed in a radio-equipped Jap plane a few minutes ago," Colonel Sharpe said. "When the rest of you were shot up, he got away in a stolen plane."

"Did you come back, Martin," Morley said slowly, "to betray us again? Or were you afraid of what the Japs might do to you for failing?"

Turk turned to Sharpe. "The burning fighter planes gave away their airfield and the burning signal station ended up being a guide to the bombers."

Sharpe turned to Morley. "Are you claiming he sold us out?"

"He didn't sell anything, Colonel. He's a Japanese!"

"He's a what?"

Martin's lips twisted with contempt.

"You're right, Morley. My mother was, and I'm proud of it! You Americans forced us into this war but we'll . . ."

His hand lurched to the holster at his hip and the gun swung up, but he never made it, for Turk sprang, driving his shoulder hard into Martin's chest.

Martin staggered, tried to remain erect, but Turk stepped back and hooked a left, high and hard. Martin slammed into the wall, and then slid to the floor.

Madden turned.

"That was it," he said, "he sold us out as he did

Morley. He even might have succeeded again, except when they threw me in a cell it was with Morley and he'd figured some of it out.

"I should have guessed. Martin was the only one who lived in the building with me, and who might know where I kept the maps he stole from me. But Vic reminded me of something I had forgotten. Before the war there was an up-and-coming football player at USC. He went back to Japan but this kid was the nephew of Commander Ishimaru of the Japanese air force! It was Ken Martin!"

Chiv Sauten looked down at Martin.

"Yeah?" he said slowly. "What was that he was spoutin' about our starting the war? Didn't he ever hear of Pearl Harbor?"

Vic Morley collapsed into a chair. "I heard it a couple of times while I was locked up. You won't find too many in Japan who know the truth. They've all been told that Japan declared war on the U.S. before the attack and that we forced them into it by cutting off their supplies of steel and fuel oil."

"That's ridiculous!" Sharpe barked. "Our boycott was in protest to their invasion of China!"

"It makes it seem they're in the right, Colonel. That's important for motivating troops, especially with a people for whom honor is so important." Turk nudged the unconscious Martin with a toe. "It even works with men who have been around enough to know better."

"Come on, Morley," Sparrow Ryan said, "I think we'd better get to the infirmary."

Turk paused in the doorway of the building with

Chiv Sauten at his side. "When I go out again, buddy, I want you along. You'll do to ride the river with!"

"Me?" Sauten grinned. "You should see my brother Pete. He was fifteen years old before he learned you were supposed to take the cans off the beans before you ate 'em!"

DREAM
FIGHTER

He never even cracked a smile. Just walked in and said, "Mr. Sullivan, I want a fight with Dick Abro."

Now Dick Abro was one of the four or five best heavyweights in the racket and who this kid was I didn't know. What I did know was that if he rated a fight with anybody even half so good as Dick Abro, his name would have been in every news sheet in the country.

At first I thought the guy was a nut. Then I took another look, and whatever else you can say, the kid had all his buttons. He was a tall, broad-shouldered youngster with a shock of wavy brown hair and a nice smile. He looked fit, too, his weight was around one eighty. And Abro tipped the beam at a plenty tough two hundred.

"Listen, kid," I said, shoving my hat back on my head and pointing all four fingers at him. "I never saw you before. But if you were twice as good as you think you are, you still wouldn't want any part of Dick Abro."

"Mr. Sullivan," he said seriously, "I can beat him. I can beat him any day, and if you get me the fight, you can lay your money he will go out in the third round, flatter than ten pancakes."

What would you have said? I looked at this youngster, and then I got up. When I thought of that wide, brown face and flat nose of Abro's, and those two big fists ahead of his powerful shoulders, it made me sick to think what would happen to this kid.

"Don't be a sap!" I said, hard-boiled. "Abro would slap you dizzy in half a round! Whatever gave you the idea you could take that guy?"

"You'd laugh if I told you," he said quite matter-of-factly.

"I'm laughing now," I said. "You come in here asking for a fight with Abro. You're nuts!"

His face turned red, and I felt sorry for the kid. He was a nice-looking boy, and he did look like a fighter, at that.

"Okay," I said. "You tell me. What made you think you could lick Abro?"

"I dreamed it."

You could have knocked me down with an axe. He dreamed it! I backed up and sat down again. Then, I looked up to see if he was still there, and he was.

"It's like this, Mr. Sullivan," he said seriously. "I know it sounds goofy, but I dream about all my fights before I have them. Whenever I get a fight, I just train and never think about it. Then, a couple of nights before the fight, I dream it. Then I get in the ring and fight like I did in the dream, and I always win."

What would you do with a guy like that? If Dick Abro ever smacked this lad for a row of channel buoys, he'd do a lot of dreaming before he came to. Still, there's a lot of nuts around the fight game. At best, and it's the grandest game in the world, it's a screwy one. Funny things happen. So I tipped back in my chair and looked up at him, rolling a quid of chewing gum in my jaws.

"Yeah? Who'd you ever lick?"

"Con Patrick, in two rounds. Beetle Kelly in four, Tommy Keegan in three. Then I beat a half dozen fellows before I started to dream my fights."

I knew these boys he mentioned. At least, I knew one of them personally and two by their records. None of them were boys you could beat by shadow-boxing.

"When'd you have this pipe about Abro?" I asked.

"About a week ago. I went to see the pictures of his fight with the champ. Then, two weeks ago I saw him knock out Soapy Moore. Then I dreamed about fighting him. In the dream, I knocked him out with a right hook in the middle of the third."

I got up. "You got some gym stuff?" I asked.

He nodded.

"I thought maybe you'd want to see me box. Doc Harrigan down in Copper City told me to see you soon as I arrived."

"Harrigan, eh?" I rolled that around with my gum a few times. Whatever else Harrigan might be, and he was crooked enough so he couldn't even play a game of solitaire without trying to cheat without catching himself at it, he did know fighters.

We walked down to the gym, and I looked around. There were a couple of Filipinos in the ring, and I watched them. They were sure slinging leather. That man Sambo they tell about in the Bible who killed ten thousand Filipinos with the jawbone of an ass must have framed the deal. Those boys can battle. Then, I saw Pete McCloskey punching the heavy bag. I caught his eye and motioned him over. The kid was in the dressing room changing clothes.

"Listen, Pete," I said. "You want that six-round special with Gomez?"

"I sure do, Finny," he said. "I need it bad."

"Okay, I'll fix it up. But you got to do me a favor. I got a kid coming out on the floor in a couple of minutes, and I want to see is he any good. Watch your step with him, but feel him out, see?"

"I get it. You don't want him killed, just bruised a little, eh?" he said.

The kid came out and shadowboxed a couple of rounds to warm up. Pete was looking him over, and he wasn't seeing anything to feel happy about. The kid was fast, and he used both hands. Of course, many a bum looks pretty hot shadowboxing.

When they got in the ring, the kid, who told me his name was Kip Morgan, walked over and shook hands with Pete. Then he went back to his corner, and I rang the bell.

McCloskey came out in a shell, tried a left that the kid went away from, and then bored in suddenly and slammed a wicked right to the heart. I looked to see Morgan go down, but he didn't even draw a breath. He just stepped around, and then, all of a sudden, his left flashed out in four of the snappiest, shortest jabs I ever saw. Pete tried to slide under it, but that left followed him like the head of a snake. Then, suddenly, Pete and I saw that opening over the heart again. And when I saw what happened I was glad I was outside the ring.

McCloskey hadn't liked those lefts a bit, so when he saw those open ribs again, he uncorked his right with the works on it. The next thing I knew, Pete was flat on his shoulders with his feet still in the air. They fell with a thump, and I walked over to the edge of the ring. Pete McCloskey was out for the afternoon, his face resting against the canvas in a state of calm repose. I couldn't bear to disturb him.

That night I dropped in on Bid Kerney. Race Malone, the sportswriter, was sitting with him. We talked around a while, and then I put it up to him.

"What you doing with Abro?" I asked. "Got anybody for him?"

"Abro?" Bid shrugged. "Heck, no. McCall wants the champ, an' Blucher wants McCall. There ain't a kid in sight I could stick in there that could go long enough to make it look good. Even if I knew one, he wouldn't fight him."

"What's in it?" I asked. "You make it ten grand, and I got a guy for you."

Race looked up, grinning. "For ten grand I have too. Me! I'd go in there with him for ten grand. But how long would I last?"

"This kid'll beat Abro," I said coolly, peeling the

paper off a couple of sticks of gum casually as I could make it. "He'll stop him."

"You nuts?" Kerney sneered. "Who is he?"

"Name of Morgan, Kip Morgan. From over at Copper City. Stopped Patrick the other night. Got ten straight kayoes. Be fighting the champ in a year."

When I talked it up so offhand, they began wondering. I could see Malone smelling a story, and Bid was interested.

"But nobody knows him!" Bid protested. "Copper City's just a mill town. A good enough place, but too far away."

"Okay," I said, getting up. "Stick him in there with Charlie Gomez. But after he beats Gomez, it'll cost you more."

"If he beats him, it'll be worth it!" Bid snapped. "Okay, make it the last Friday this month. That gives you two weeks."

When I walked out of there, I was feeling good. There would be three grand in this, anyway, and forty percent of that was a nice cut these days. Secretly, I was wondering how I could work it to make the kid win. He had some stuff. I'd seen that when he was in there with Pete, and while Gomez was tough, there was a chance. Pete was fighting Tommy Gomez, Charlie's brother, so he would be training. That took care of the sparring partner angle.

Suddenly, I thought of Doc Van Schendel. He was an old Dutchman, from Amsterdam, and a few years before I'd done him a favor. We'd met here and there around town several times, and had a few bottles of beer together. He called himself a psychiatrist, and in his office one time, I noticed some books on dreams, on psychology, and stuff like that. Me, I don't know a thing about that dope, but it struck me as a good idea to see the Doc.

He was in, with several books on the table, and he was writing something down on a sheet of paper. He leaned back and took off his glasses.

"Hallo, hallo, mein Freund! Sit yourself down and talk mit an oldt man!"

"Listen, Doc, I want to ask you a question. Here's the lay." Then I went ahead and told him the whole story. He didn't say much, just leaned back with his fingertips together, nodding his head from time to time. Finally, when I'd finished, he leaned toward me.

"Interesting, very, very interesting! You see, it iss the subconscious at work! He boxes a lot, this young man. He sees these men fight. All the time, he iss asking, 'How would I fight him?' Then the subconscious takes what it knows of the fighter, and what it knows of boxing, undt solves the problem!"

He shrugged.

"Some man t'ink of gomplicated mathematical problem. They go to sleep, undt wake up mit the answer! It iss the subconscious! The subconscious mindt, always at vork vile ve sleep!"

Race Malone was short of copy, and he took a liking to Kip Morgan so we drove over together. When we got down to the arena, the night of the fight, it was jammed to the doors. Charlie Gomez was a rugged, hard-hitting heavy with a lot of stuff. If the kid could get over him, we were in the money. Race grabbed a seat behind our corner and the kid and I headed for the changing rooms.

"How is it, Kip?" I asked him. I was bandaging his hands, and he sat there watching me, absently.

"It's okay. I dreamed about the fight last night!"

"Yeah?" I said cautiously. I wasn't very sold on this dream stuff. "How'd you do?"

"Stopped him in the second."

We got our call then, and it wasn't until I was crawling through the ropes after him that it struck me what a sweet setup this was. It was too late to get to a bookie, but looking down I saw Race Malone looking up at us.

"Want a bet?" I asked him, grinning. "I'll name the round."

Race grinned.

"You must think the kid's a phenom," he said. "All right. You name the round, and I'll lay you three to one you're wrong!"

"Make it the second," I said. "I don't want it over too soon."

"Okay," Race grinned. "For two hundred? It's a cinch at any odds."

I gulped. I'd been figuring on a five spot, a fin, like I always bet. That's why they called me Finny Sullivan. But if I backed down, he'd kid me for crawfishing. "Sure," I said, trying to look cheerful, "two yards against your six."

. . .

The bell sounded, and Gomez came out fast. He snapped a short left hook to the kid's head, and it jerked back a good two inches. Then, before the kid could see, Charlie was inside, slamming away at Morgan's ribs with both hands. The kid pushed the Portugee off and ripped his eye with a left, hooked a short right to the head, and then Gomez caught him with a long overhand right, and the kid sailed halfway across the ring and hit the canvas on his tail!

I grabbed the edge of the ring and ground my teeth. I wasn't thinking of my two yards either, although I could afford to lose two yards as much as I could afford to lose an eye, but I was thinking of that shot at Abro and what a sap I was to get taken in on a dream fighter. Second round, eh? Phooey!

But the kid made it to one knee at seven and glanced at me. He needed rest, but there wasn't time, so I waved him up. He straightened up, and Gomez charged across the ring throwing a wild left that missed by a hairsbreadth, and then the kid was inside, hanging on for dear life!

Gomez shook him loose, ripped both hands into the kid's heaving belly, then jerked a wicked right chop to the chin. The kid toppled over on the canvas. I was sick enough to stop it, but the referee had to do that, so I just sat there, watching that game youngster crawl to his feet. Gomez rushed again, took a glancing left to the face that split his eye some more, and then whipped a nasty right to the body. They were in a clinch with the kid hanging on when the bell rang.

Race Malone looked over at me shaking his head. "I never thought I'd be smart enough to take you for two hundred, Finny," he said. "At that, I hate to see the kid lose."

So did I.

"Listen, Kip," I said. "You ain't got a chance. I'm going to call the referee over and stop it!"

He jerked up on the stool.

"No you won't!" he snapped. "I'm winning in the next round! I've been ready for this. I knew it was going to happen! Now watch!"

The bell rang, and the kid walked out fast. Charlie Gomez was serious. He was all set to win by a kayo this round, and he knew what it meant. It meant he'd be back in the big money again.

He snapped a vicious left hook, but it missed, and then that flashy left jab of the kid's spotted him in the mouth. I'm telling you, there never was one like it. Bang-bang-bang-bang! Just like a trip-hammer, and then a jolting right to the body that wrenched a gasp from Charlie, and had the fans yelling like crazy men.

Leaping in, Gomez swung a volley of punches with both hands so fast you could hardly see them travel, but the kid slid away, and then stepped back and nearly tore Charlie's head loose with a wicked left hook. Then came a crashing right that knocked Gomez into the ropes, and then a left that laid Charlie's cheek open like it had been cut with a knife!

With Gomez streaming blood, and the fans howling like madmen, the kid stepped in coolly, measured the Portugee with a nice straight left, and fired his right—right down the groove! The referee could have counted to five thousand.

I was trembling so I could hardly control myself, but I calmly turned around to Race.

"I'll take that six yards, son," I told him, in a bored voice. "And I'll treat you to a feed and beer."

Race paid me carefully. Then he looked up.

"Honest to Roosevelt, Finny," he said, "what kind of dope did you slip that kid? It sure snapped him out of it. He acted there for a while like he was in a dream!"

Maybe you don't think I grinned then.

"Maybe he was, Palsy, maybe he was!"

The next two months slipped by like another kind of dream. Morgan trained hard, and I spent a lot of time with him. If Doc Van Schendel was right, and I was betting he was, there wasn't any hocus-pocus about the kid's fighting. It was just that he had some stuff, a good fighting brain, and he thought fighting so much that his subconscious mind had got to planning his battles.

It isn't so wild as it sounds. You know how a guy scraps, and what to use against him. Dempsey was a rusher who liked to get in close and work there, so Tunney made him fight at long range and then tied him up in the clinches. Every fighter is a sucker for something, and a guy who learns the angles can usually work out a way to beat the other fellow.

The kid had a lot on the ball, and I wanted him to have more. In those two months while we were building up for Abro, I gave him plenty of schooling. I knew he had the old moxie. He was fast, and he could hit. This dream business was just so much gravy. I'll admit there was an angle that bothered me, but I didn't mention it to the kid. I was afraid he'd get to thinking about it, and it would ruin him.

What if he dreamed of losing?

Now wasn't that something? The day I first thought of that wasn't a happy one. But I kept my mouth shut. Race Malone was around a good deal. He liked the kid, and then there was a chance the promoter was slipping him a little geetus on the side for playing Morgan up for the Abro fight. With the sensational win over Gomez and the ten kayoes behind him, not much was needed. If it had been, his fight with Cob Bennett would have been enough.

Cob had rated among the first ten for six or seven years. He was a battle-scarred veteran, whose face was seamed with scar tissue and who knew his way around inside the ropes. A lot of fans liked him, and they all knew he could fight. About a month after the Gomez scrap, I took the kid over to Pittsburgh and stuck him in there with Bennett. It lasted a little over two minutes.

If I live to be a hundred, I'll never forget that Abro fight. The preliminaries had been a series of bitter, hard-fought scraps, and the way things shaped up, anything but a regular brannigan was going to be sort of an anticlimax.

Dick Abro crawled through the ropes, looking

tough as always. When he came over to our corner, I confess I got a sinking sensation in the pit of my stomach. Sometimes I think maybe I ain't cut out for this racket. There was going to be four grand in this fight for me, yet when I thought of this kid going out there with that gorilla, I got a qualm or two. I'll admit I didn't let them queer my chances for that four grand, because four grand will buy a lot of onions, but nevertheless, I was feeling plenty sorry for Kip.

Abro grinned.

"Howya, keed?"

He had a face like a stone wall, all heavy bones and skin like leather. "You lika da tough going, huh?"

He gripped Morgan's hand and then spun on his toe and walked back across the ring, easy on his feet as a ballet dancer, and him weighing in at two-oh-eight for this brawl.

When the bell sounded, the kid took his time. Abro wasn't in any hurry either. His big brown shoulders worked easily, his head lowered just enough. Most people figured Abro as a tough slugger, but a guy doesn't get as far as he did without knowing a thing or two. Abro feinted and landed a light left. Then he tried another left but the kid stepped away. Dick walked in, feinted again and jerked a short right hook to the ribs. He dug a hard left into the kid's belly, and then jerked it up to slam against his chin.

Abro was cool. He knew the kid was no bum and was watching his step. The kid's left shot out, twisting as it landed, and I saw Abro's head jerk. He stepped back then, and I could see that it jarred more than he'd expected. Abro shot a steaming left to the head, jerked a right to the chin, then pushed his head against Morgan's shoulder and started ripping punches into his body.

Morgan twisted away, flashed that left to Abro's face twice, making the big fellow blink. I could see his eyes sharpen, saw him move in. Then the kid dropped a short right on his chin, and Dick Abro sat down hard. The crowd came off their seats yelling, and Abro sprang up at the count of one, and slammed a vicious right to the kid's head.

Morgan staggered, and backed away, with Abro piling after him, both hands punching. Then Kip ripped up a short right uppercut, and Abro stopped dead in his tracks. Before he could recover, a sweeping left hook dropped him to the canvas. He was up at five, and working toward the kid cautiously.

But Morgan was ready and stepped in, his left ripping Abro's face like a spur, that short right beating a drumfire of punches into the bigger man's body. Abro staggered and seemed about to go down, but, as the kid stepped in, Dick fired a left at close quarters that set Morgan back on his heels.

Boring in, Abro knocked Morgan back into the ropes with a hard right. The kid was hurt. I could see him trying to cover up, trying to roll away from Abro, who was set for the kill. Always dangerous when hurt, the big fellow had caught Kip just right.

Morgan backed away, desperately trying to hold Abro off with a wavering left. Just as Dick got to the kid with two hard wallops to the body, the bell rang.

"Take it easy, kid," I told him. "Don't slug with this guy. Box him and keep moving this round."

Abro came out fast for the next round, but the kid jabbed and stepped around, jabbed again and stepped around further. He missed with his right and took a stiff left to the ribs. Then Abro leaped in, splitting the kid's lip with a snappy left hook, and as the kid tried to jab, rammed a right into his belly with such force it brought a gasp from his lips. The kid tried to clinch, but Abro shook him off and floored him with a short right.

The kid was hurt bad. He got to his knees at five, and when the referee said nine, swayed to his feet. Dick walked in, hitching up his trunks, looking the kid over. He was a little too sure, and Kip was desperate.

He let go with a wild right swing that fairly sizzled. Abro tried to duck, jumped back desperately, but the kid lunged, and the punch slammed against Abro's ear! The big fellow went down with a crash. Thoroughly angered, he leaped to his feet, groggy with pain and rage, and sprang at the kid, swinging with both hands.

Toe-to-toe they stood and swapped it out. Tough as they come, and a wicked puncher, Dick Abro was fighting the fight of his life. He had to.

Ducking and weaving, swaying his big shoulders with every punch, his face set in grim lines, Kip Morgan was fighting like a champion. They were standing in the center of the ring, fighting like madmen, when the bell sounded. It took the referee, the timekeeper, and all the seconds to pry them apart.

Race Malone was battering away at his typewriter between rounds, and the kid sat there on his stool, grim as death. When the bell sounded, Abro looked bad. One eye was completely closed, the other cut. His lips were puffed and broken. I think everyone in the crowd that night sensed what was going to happen.

Abro rushed in and swung a left, but the kid slid inside, hooked short and hard with his left, and whipped a jolting, rib-loosening punch into the big man's body. Abro staggered, and his legs went loose. He tried to clinch, but the kid shook him off, took a left without flinching, then chopped a right hook to the chin that didn't travel a bit over six inches. Abro turned half around and dropped on his face, dead to the world.

Maybe you think I was happy. Well, I wasn't. The kid was suddenly one of the ranking heavies in the game, but me, I had worries. The more I thought of what might happen if the kid dreamt of losing, the more I worried. We were matched with Hans Blucher, a guy who had beaten Abro, had fought a draw with Deady McCall and been decisioned by the champ. Blucher, in a lot of ways, was one of the toughest boys in the game.

So I went to see Doc Van Schendel.

"Listen, Doc," I said. "Supposing that kid dreams of losing?"

Doc shrugged.

"Vell? Maybe hiss psychology is spoiled by it, yes? Maybe he t'ink these dreams iss alvays true. Probably he vill lose."

"You're a big help!" I said, and walked out. Leaving, I saw Race Malone.

"Hello," he said. "What's the matter? You going to a psychiatrist now? Nuts, are you? I always suspected it."

"Aw, go lay an egg!" I said wittily, and walked away. If I'd looked back I'd have seen Race Malone going into the Doc's office. But I had enough worries.

When I walked into the gym the kid was walloping the bag. He was listless, and his heels were dragging. So I walked over.

"What's the matter?" I said. "Didn't you get any rest last night?"

"Yeah, sure I did," he growled. It wasn't like the kid to be anything but cheerful.

"Listen," I said. "Tell me the trouble. What's on your mind?"

He hesitated, glancing around. Then he stepped closer.

"Last night I dreamed a fight," he said slowly, "and I lost! I got knocked out . . . I think I'd been winning until then."

I knew it! Nothing lasts. Everything goes haywire. A guy can't get a good meal ticket but what he goes to dreaming bad fights.

"Yeah," I said. "Who were you fighting?"

"That's just the trouble," he said. "I couldn't see who it was! His face was all vague and bleary!"

I grinned, trying to pass it off, hoping he won't worry. "That sounds like Pete McCloskey," I said.

"He's got the only face I know of that's vague and bleary."

But the kid doesn't even crack a smile; as if it wasn't bad enough for him to dream of losing a fight, he has to go and dream of losing to somebody he can't see!

If I knew who it was he was going to lose to, we'd never go near the guy. But as it was, there I stood with a losing fighter who didn't know who he was going to lose to!

Blucher is the next guy we fight, and if we beat him, we get Deady McCall and then the champ. There's too much at stake to take any chances. And I can see that dreaming about that knockout has got the kid worried. Every time he fights he'll be in there under the handicap of knowing it's coming and not being able to get out of it.

At best, this dreaming business is logical enough. But there's a certain angle to it that runs into fatalism. The kid might just have found some weakness in his own defense, and thought about it until he got himself knocked out in his dreams.

Me, I don't know a lot about such things, but I got to thinking. What if he got knocked out when he wasn't fighting?

Pete McCloskey was punching the heavy bag, and when I looked at him, I got a flash of brains. Heck, what's a manager good for if he can't think?

"Listen, Pete . . ." I gave him the lowdown, and he nodded, grinning. After all, Morgan had knocked him so cold he'd have kept for years, and this was the only chance Pete would ever have to get even.

* * * *

When they crawled into the ring for their afternoon workout, I chased the usual gang out. I gave Kip some tips on some new angles I wanted him to try. That was the gag for having a secret workout, but I just didn't want them to see what's going to happen.

They were mixing it up in the third round of the workout, and like I told him, Pete was ready. I looked up at Kip and yelled. "Hey, Morgan!"

And when he turned to look at me, Pete let him have it. He took a full swing at the kid and caught him right on the button! Kip Morgan went out like a light.

But it was only for a half minute or so. He came out of it and sat up, shaking his head.

"What—what hit me?" he gasped.

"It was my fault, kid," I told him, and me feeling like a heel. "I yelled, an' Pete here had started a swing. He clouted you."

"Sure, I'm sorry, Kip," Pete broke in, and he looked it, too.

"That's okay." He got up, shaking his head to clear it of the effects of the punch. "No hard feelings."

"That's enough for today, anyway," I told him. "Let it go, and have a good workout tomorrow."

Morgan was crawling from the ring when suddenly he stopped, and his face brightened up.

"Hey, Finny!" he dropped to the floor and grabbed my arm. "I'm okay! You hear? I'm okay! That was the knockout. Now I'm in the clear."

"Yeah, sure. That's great," I told him.

But now, tell me a ghost story, I was still worried.

One way or another the kid had convinced me. There might still be that knockout to think about—if there was really anything to it—but he could go in the ring without it hanging over him, anyway. He was in the clear now.

He was in the clear, but I wasn't. You can't be around a big, clean-looking kid like this Kip Morgan without liking him. He was easygoing and good-natured, but in the ring, he packed a wallop and never lacked for killer instinct. And me, Finny Sullivan, I was worried. Sooner or later the kid was going to get it, and I didn't want to be there. Some guys are all the better for a kayo, and maybe he would be. But they are always hard to take.

Kip was climbing into the ring the night of the Blucher fight when Race Malone reached over and caught me by the coat. He pulled me back and spoke confidentially.

"What's this dope about Morgan dreaming his fights? Before he fights 'em, I mean?"

"Where'd you get that stuff?" I asked. "Whoever heard of such a thing?"

Race grinned.

"Don't give me that. Doc Van Schendel let the kitten out of the bag. Come on, pal, give. This is a story."

"Can't you see I got a fight on?" I jerked a thumb toward the ring. "See you later."

Morgan went out fast in the first round. He was confident, and looked it. Blucher feinted and started to throw a right, but the kid faded away like a shadow. It was just like he was reading Blucher's mind. The German tried again, boring in close, but for everything he tried, the kid had an answer. And Morgan kept that jarring, cutting left, making a mess of Blucher's features.

Honest to Roosevelt, it was just like he'd rehearsed it, and, of course, that's what he'd done. What the kid had, I was hoping, was a photographic memory. He'd see a guy fight a couple of times, and he'd remember how he got away from every punch, how he countered, and what he did under every condition. It was instinctive with him, like Young Griffo slipping punches. Tunney got the job done as thoroughly, only he did it by hard work and carefully studying an opponent.

There's only a certain number of ways of doing anything in the ring, and a fellow fighting all the time falls in habits of doing certain things at certain times. Morgan thought about that, remembered every move a man made, and knew what to do under any circumstance. It was a cinch. Or would be until he met some guy who crossed him up. Some of them you could never figure—like Harry Greb. He made up his own style each time and threw them from anywhere and everywhere.

Blucher stepped in, taking it cautiously and hooked a light one to the ribs. The kid stabbed a left to the mouth, then another one. Blucher threw a right, and the kid beat him to the punch with a hard right to the heart. Then Morgan put his left twice to the face, and sank a wicked one into the solar plexus. Blucher backed away, covering up. Kip followed him, taking his time. Just before the bell rang, Morgan tried a right to the body and took another left hook.

Glancing down between rounds, I saw Race Malone looking at the kid with a funny gleam in his eye . . . which I didn't like. Put that dream stuff in the papers, and it would ruin the kid. They'd laugh him out of the ring.

The second round started fast. Morgan went out, then dropped into a crouch and knocked Blucher into the ropes with a terrific left hook that nearly tore his head off. Blucher bounded back and tried to get in close, but the kid danced away. Then he came back with that flashy left jab to Blucher's mouth, feinted a right to the heart, and left his head wide open.

Blucher bit, hook, line, and sinker. Desperate, he saw that opening and threw everything he had in the world on a wide left hook aimed for the kid's chin!

It was murder. Morgan had set the German right up by taking those other left hooks, and when that one came he was set. He stepped inside with a short right to the chin, and I'm a sun-kissed scenery-bum if Blucher's feet didn't leave the floor by six inches! Then he hit the canvas like somebody had dropped him off a building, and the kid never even looked down. He just turned and walked to his corner and picked up his towel. He *knew* Blucher was out.

The payoff came in the morning. I crawled out of the hay rubbing my eyes and walked to the door.

When I picked up my paper, it opened my eyes quick enough.

DREAM FIGHTER KAYOES BLUCHER
Morgan Fights According to Dream Plan.
Blucher Completely Out-Classed.

I walked back inside and read the rest of it. Race had been getting around. He'd picked up a statement from Van Schendel, whom I'd not asked to keep still, and then had found two or three other guys who knew something about it. Here and there the kid had mentioned it before I took him over. Then Race went down the line of his fights and showed how the kid had won—and how I'd called the round on Charlie Gomez.

It made a swell yarn. There was no question about that. I could see papers all over the country eating it up. Good stuff, if you just wanted to make a couple of bucks, but the wrong kind of publicity for a champ.

Champ? Yes, that's what I figured. I'd been figuring on it ever since the kid took Gomez. This dream stuff didn't mean a thing to me. I was banking on the kid's boxing and his punch. And down in the corner of the sports sheet I saw something else . . .

DEADY McCALL TO RETIRE
Contender to Marry

That left Kip Morgan the leading contender for the world's heavyweight title. That put Kip in line for a fight for the world's championship, and it had to be within ninety days. I knew the champ, Steve Kendall, had signed with Bid Kerney to defend his title. And Bid had a contract that made the kid his for one more fight in that same period. We had the champ, and we had Bid, and there was no getting away from that.

That dream stuff built the fight up beautifully, and everything went fine until about four days before the battle. I dropped around to the dressing room after the kid's workout. He was sharp, ready to go. I'd never seen him look better. His body was hard as iron, and he'd browned to a beautiful golden tint that had all the girls in camp oohing and aahing around. But he looked worried.

"What's the matter, Kip?" I asked him. "Working too hard?"

He shook his head.

"No. I'm worried though. I slept like a log last night—and never dreamed a bit! I was just dead from the time I hit the bed until I woke up this morning."

"So what?" I said, shrugging. "You got four nights yet."

He nodded, gloomily. We talked awhile, and then I went outside. Stig Martin was a hanger-on around the fight game I'd picked up to rub the kid. Maybe he knew his way around too well. But he was an A-1 rubber. He grinned at me.

"How's the kid? Dreaming any?"

"Listen, Duck-Bill," I told him. "You lay off that

stuff, see? That dream business is a lot of hooey, get me? Now forget it."

I turned away, but when I got to the door, I glanced back. Stig was standing there with a sarcastic grin on his face that I didn't like. I was about to go back and fire him when Race Malone came up. So I postponed it. Which only goes to show what a sap I was.

Race took me back to town to get some publicity shots of me signing articles to guarantee that the kid would defend his title against Kendall if he beat him, and it was the next morning before I saw Morgan or Stig again. The minute I saw the kid, I knew something was haywire.

"What's eatin' you?" I asked him, gripping his arm. "You feel all right, don't you?"

"Yeah," he muttered. "Only I haven't dreamed about this fight. I dreamed last night, but it was all a confused mess where nothing got through. Only sometimes I'd think about punches, and I'd hear them saying how I was getting beat. That I was blood all over, that I couldn't take it. Over and over again."

I frowned, pushing my hat back on my head. Stig Martin was standing on the edge of the porch, smoking a cigarette. He was grinning. It made me sore.

"Listen, you," I said. "Take a walk. I'm sick of seeing your face around. Walk around someplace and keep out of the way."

He pouted, and walked off. Something didn't smell right about this deal.

"Listen, kid," I said. "You never mentioned hearing

voices before. Before it was all like a motion picture, you said."

He nodded.

"I know. But now I don't see anything. I just hear a lot of confused stuff about me getting whipped."

I could see he was worried. His eyes looked hollow, and his face was a little yellow. I decided to get hold of Doc Van Schendel.

When I drove back to the camp with Van Schendel the next day, I saw the kid sitting on the steps, twisting his hands and cracking his knuckles nervously. His face was drawn, and he looked bad. Just as we got out of the car, I heard Stig Martin speak to him.

"What of it, kid? Everybody has to lose sometime. You're young. You couldn't expect to take the belt the first time out."

"What's that?" I snapped at him. "Where'd you get that stuff, talking to my fighter like that? Listen, you tramp! Morgan's going to knock the champ loose from his buttons, an' don't forget it!"

Stig got up, sneering.

"Yeah? Maybe. But not if he doesn't have the right dream. He's got to be ready for that . . . got to be ready to lose. If he goes in without his dream, he's going to get beat to a pulp! Right, Kip? For your own good, I suggest you duck this one."

Well, I haven't hit a guy since I used to hustle pool around the waterfront, but I uncorked that one with the works on it. Stig Martin hit the ground all in one bunch. He wasn't out, but he had a lot of teeth that were. He got up and stumbled away, mumbling through mashed lips, and I walked over to the kid, rubbing my knuckles, and hustled him inside. I came out to get Doc and found him looking at Stig's retreating back.

"Who iss dese man?" he asked, curiously. "I see him talking mit Steve Kendall undt Mister Johnson."

"What?" I yelled. "You saw Stig—!" I backed up and sat down cussing myself for a sap. I should have known Martin was a plant. And here I was feeling so good about getting the champ, worrying about dreams and everything, that I let something like that happen. Why, if Doc hadn't seen—

"Hey, wait a minute!" I shouted, scrambling up again. "Where did you see Kendall and his pilot?"

Doc turned, looking at me over his glasses. "Vhy, they was oop to my office. They were asking me questions about zose articles in de newspaper. Vhy, iss it nodt all right?"

Then I just let go everything and sat down. I sat there with the Doc staring at me, kind of puzzled. Finally, I get up courage enough to take it.

"All right," I said. "Tell me. Tell me all about it. What did they ask you, and what did you tell them?"

"They asking me aboot dreams, undt vhat vould happen if he don't dream at all."

The Doc rambled on into a lot of words I didn't understand, and a lot of talk that was all a whistle in the wind to me, and if Race Malone hadn't come up I never would have got it figured out.

"It's simple enough," Race said. "They went to the Doc to find some way of getting your boy's goat.

They decided to keep him from dreaming, and they found out dope might do it. If you look into it, I'll bet you find Stig Martin has been slipping the kid something to make him sleep."

Then the Doc had told them some people were subject to suggestion when asleep or doped, so (I found this out later) Stig evidently gave the kid a riding all night a couple of times, telling him over and over that he'd lose, that he didn't have a chance. He kept it up even when the kid was awake, and they were together.

After listening to all of this Race shrugged his shoulders.

"It's a lousy stunt, and the nuttiest thing I ever heard of, but it'll make a swell story."

I got up.

"Listen," I said, trying to be calm. "If one word of this ever makes the paper I'll start packing a heater for you, and the first time I see you I'll cut you down to the curb, get me? Those stories of yours spilled the beans in the first place!"

Race promised to say nothing until after the fight, and I walked inside with Doc Van Schendel to look the kid over. We didn't let on about Stig, Kendall, or Johnson. I had a better idea in mind. I asked the Doc to stick around the camp with us, and, feeling guilty for his part in all this, he agreed to help.

When we went into town for the fight, I was feeling much happier. The kid was looking pretty good and rarin' to go, with a nervousness that's just right and natural.

I was still pretty nervous myself. This fight wasn't going to be a cinch, by no means. But when the kid crawled into the ring, I was in a much better frame of mind than I had been some days before. Stig Martin contributed his little share to my happiness, too. When I saw him in the hall near the dressing room, I licked my lips.

He didn't see me until I was within arm's length of him, and then it was too late to duck. I slammed him into the wall, then hit him again. He slid down the wall and sat there, blood streaming from his nose.

A big cop looked around the corner, came back, frowning.

"What's going on here?" he demanded.

"I am," I returned cheerfully, and went.

It will be a long time before they have a crowd like that again, and a long time before they see two heavyweights put on such a fight. When we walked down to the ring, the ballpark was ablaze with lights, and there was a huge crowd stretching back into the darkness, a sea of faces that made you feel lost. Then the lights went out, and there was only the intensely white light over the ring, and the low murmur of voices.

Kip Morgan was wearing a blue silk dressing gown, and he crawled into the ring, walking quickly over to the resin box. The champ took his time. I saw him take in the kid's nervousness with a sleepy smile. Then he rubbed his feet slowly in the resin and walked back to his corner.

Then I was talking to the kid, trying to quiet him down, trying to get him settled when I was so jittery that a tap on the shoulder would have set me screaming. I'd been handling scrappers a long time, but this was my first championship battle, and there, across the ring, was the Big Fellow, the world's heavyweight champion himself, the guy we'd been reading about, and seeing in the newsreels. And here was this kid that I'd brought up from the bottom, the kid who was going out there to fight that guy.

I'm telling you, it was something. I saw the champ slip off his robe and noticed that hard brown body, the thick, sloping shoulders, the slabs of muscle around his arms, watched him dancing lightly on his toes, moving his arms high. He was a fighter, every inch of him.

We got our instructions, and both men stared down at the canvas. I whispered a few last-minute instructions to the kid, tossed his robe and towel to a second, then dropped down beside the ring. Morgan was standing up there, all alone now. He had it all ahead of him in the loneliest place in the world. Across the ring the champ was sucking at his mouthpiece, and dancing lightly on his toes. When the bell sounded you could hear it ring out over the whole crowd, and then those guys were moving in on each other.

Did you ever notice how small those gloves look at a time like that? How that dull red leather seems barely to cover their big hands? I did, and I saw the kid moving out, his fists ready. They tried lefts, and both landed lightly. The kid tried another. He was still nervous. I could see that. The champ stepped away from it, looking him over. Then he feinted, but the kid stepped back. He wasn't fooled. The champ moved in, and the crowd watched like they were in a trance. They all knew something was going to happen. They had a hunch, but they weren't hurrying it.

Suddenly, the champ stepped in fast, and his left raked the kid's eye, and a short, wicked right drummed against the kid's ribs. The champ bored in, slamming both hands to the head, then drilled a right to the body. The kid jabbed and walked around him, taking a hard right. The champ landed another right. He was confident, but taking his time.

The kid jabbed twice, fast. One left flickered against the champ's eye, the other went into his mouth—hard. The champ slipped under another left and slammed a wicked right to the ribs and I saw the kid's mouth come open.

Then the champ was really working. He drilled both hands to the body, straightened up and let the kid have a left hook on the chin. The kid's head rolled with the punch and Morgan jarred the champ with a short right. They were sparring in mid-ring at the bell.

The second opened with the champ slipping a left and I could see the gleam of grease on his cheekbones as he came in close. A sharp left jab stabbed Morgan twice in the mouth, and he stepped away with a trickle of blood showing. The champ came in again, jabbed, and the kid crossed a right over the jab that knocked the champ back on his heels.

Like a tiger the kid tore in, hooking both hands to the body. A hard right drove the champ into a neutral corner, and the two of them swapped it out there, punching like demons, their faces set and bloody. When they broke, I saw both were bleeding, the champ from an eye, and the kid from the mouth.

They met in mid-ring for the third and started to swap it out, neither of them taking a back step. Then the champ straightened up, and his right came whistling down the groove. Instinctively, I ducked—but the kid didn't.

Then I was hanging on to the edge of the ring and praying or swearing or something and the kid was lying out there on the canvas, as still as the dead. I was wishing he never saw a ring when the referee said four, and the kid gathered his knees under him. Then the referee said five and the kid got one foot on the floor. At six he was trying to get up and couldn't make it. At eight, he did, and then the champ came out to wind it all up.

Behind me someone said, "There he goes!" and then Kip wavered somehow and managed to slip the left, and before the right cross landed he was in a clinch. The champ pounded the kid's ribs in close, but when they broke the kid came back fast with a hard left hook, then another, and another and another!

The champ was staggering! Kip walked in, slammed a hard right to the head and took a wicked one in return. I saw a bloody streak where the champ's mouth should be, and the kid jerked a short left hook to the chin, and whipped up a steaming right uppercut that snapped the champ's head back.

Morgan kept boring in, his lips drawn in a thin line. All the sleepiness was gone from the champ. Morgan stabbed a left and then crossed a right that caught the champ flush on the nose as he came in. Out behind me the crowd was a thundering roar, and the kid was weaving and hooking, slamming punch after punch to the champion's head and body, but taking a wicked battering in return.

Somewhere a bell rang, and they were still fighting when the seconds rushed in to drag them back to their corners.

The kid was hot. He wouldn't sit down. He stood there, shaking his seconds off, swaying on his feet from side to side, his hands working and his feet shuffling. I was seeing something I never saw before, for if ever fighting instinct had a man, it had Kip Morgan.

When the bell rang I saw the champ come off his stool and trot to the center of the ring, and then the kid cut loose with a sweeping right that sent him crashing into the ropes. Before he could get off them, the kid was in there pounding away with both hands in a blur of punches that no man could evade or hope to stem.

Kendall whipped a right to the kid's body, but he might as well have slugged the side of a boiler, for the kid never slowed up. The champion was whipped, and he knew it. You could see in his face there was only one thing he wanted, and that was out of there. But he clinched and hung on, his eyes glazed, his face a bloody mask, his mouth hanging open as he gasped for breath.

When the bell rang for the fifth, not a man in the house could speak above a whisper. Worn and battered by the fury of watching the fight, they sat numb and staring as the kid walked out there, his face set, his hands ready. There was nothing of the killing fury about him now, and he moved in like a machine, that left stabbing, stabbing, stabbing.

The champ gamely tried to fight back, throwing a hard right that lost itself on air. Then a left set him back on his heels, and as he reversed desperately to regain his balance, the kid stepped back, coolly letting him recover. Then his right shot out and the champion came facedown to the blood-smeared canvas— out cold!

Mister, that was a fight.

Race cornered me first thing.

"Give, Finny," he said, all excited. "What did you do to the kid?"

I smiled.

"Nothing much, Race. I only used the same method Stig Martin used. With Doc's help, we doped him that night, kept repeating over and over that he'd win the fight, that it was surefire for him! The next day he was all pepped up! The Doc and I worked on him after that, putting him into the right kind of physical shape. So how could you stop him in the ring tonight?"

"What a story!" breathed Race. "What a—"

"What a nothing!" I snapped. "No more stories from you, Race Malone. The dream fighter business is going to be all over, anyhow, Race. I'm going to tell Morgan just what happened to him! How long do you think he's going to believe in this dream business after that?

"I'll bet you ten to one it'll knock his dreams out of the ring!"

VOYAGE
TO TOBALAI

CHAPTER 1

Vivid lightning burst in a mass of piled-up cloud for an instant, revealing a black, boiling maelstrom of wind-lashed waves. The old freighter rolled heavily as she took a big one over the bows. Ponga Jim Mayo crouched behind the canvas dodger and swore under his breath.

Slug Brophy, his first mate, ran down the steep, momentary incline of the bridge.

"That lightning will give the show away," he shouted above the storm, "if there's a sub around she'll spot us quick as an Irishman spots a drink!"

"I'm glad we cleared Linta before we hit this," Ponga Jim yelled back at him. "Even if we're seen, we'll be safe until this blows itself out. There's no sub in the Pacific that could hit us in this mess."

He stared over the dodger into the storm, pelting rain and blown spray beating against his face like hail. The storm might keep the subs below, and that was good. Even if their batteries were low and they had to run on the surface, effectively firing a torpedo or deck gun in these wildly pitching seas would be next to impossible. Once the storm was over, however, they would be back to carefully scanning the sea in all directions.

Out of Capetown with a cargo of torpedo planes, she was running for Balikpapan, and there wasn't a man aboard ship who didn't know how desperately those planes were needed now, in February of 1942. They were American planes, taken aboard from a crippled freighter in the harbor at Capetown. The original ship had been damaged by a submarine attack.

The *Semiramis* wasn't one of your slim, brass-bound craft with mahogany panels, but a crusty old Barnacle Bill sort of tramp. She was rusty, wind-worried, wave-battered, and time-harried; in short, she had character.

Taking on the cargo for the East Indies, Ponga Jim pushed her blunt bows across the long, lonely reaches of the southern Indian Ocean, far from the steamer lanes where the submarines waited. Then, avoiding the well-traveled route through Sunda Strait, he held a course through the empty seas south of Mava and the Lesser Sunda Islands. Passing up Lombok, Alas, and Sapeh Straits one after the other, Mayo finally turned north through Linta Strait, a little-used route into the Java Sea.

Not merely content with using Linta Strait, he deliberately avoided the safe passage east of Komodo, and took the dangerously narrow opening between Padar and Rinja Islands.

When Brophy had come on deck and noticed Jim

was taking the freighter through the narrow passage, he looked over, his expression grim.

"Cap," he said, "you better get the boys over the side and have them grease up the hull, otherwise you're going to scratch her paint job."

But they got through, and back along the routes they could have taken, ships were sunk. Waiting subs scored three times in one day at Sunda, twice at Lombok. Even off Linta, a schooner had been shelled and sunk, but the *Semiramis,* hull down across the horizon by then, had slipped away into the oncoming storm. Now, headed north for Balikpapan, lightning might spoil it all.

Another wave broke across the bows and water ran two feet deep in the stern scuppers. Slug Brophy grinned, his hard, blue-jowled face dripping with rain.

"God have pity on the poor sailors on such a night as this!" he chanted, in a momentary lull. "That's what the fishwives would be saying tonight along the chalk cliffs of England. How is it, Cap? Will we make it?"

Mayo grimaced. "We've got a chance."

In a flash of lightning, Brophy could see rain beating against Jim's lean, sun-browned face.

"I'm not taking her through Makassar Strait," Ponga Jim said suddenly, "it smells like trouble to me. That's ugly water for submarines."

"How you going?" Brophy asked quizzically.

"I'm taking her north around the east end of Mangola Island, then through Bangka Strait an' down the west coast of Celebes. From there to Balikpapan, we'll have to be lucky."

Brophy nodded. "It's twice as far, but there haven't been any sinkings over that way. Funny, too, when you think about it."

"Nothing much over there right now. A few native craft, an' maybe a K.P.M. boat. But the Dutch ships are off schedule now."

Jim pulled his sou'wester down a little tighter. He stared into the storm, shifting uneasily. He was remembering what Major Arnold had told him in the room at the Belgrave Hotel in Capetown.

"Jim," the major had said, "I flew down here from Cairo just to see you. You're going right into the middle of this war, but if there's anyone in this world knows the East Indies, it's you. After you deliver your cargo at Balikpapan, you'll be going to Gorontalo.

"I'd like you to go on from there, go down through Greyhound Strait. If you see or hear of any ship or plane concentrations, let me know at Port Darwin."

On the rain-lashed bridge Ponga Jim voiced his thoughts. "Slug, you could hide all the fleets of the world in these islands. Anything could happen down here, and most everything has."

"I'd feel better if we didn't have that woman aboard," Brophy said suddenly. "A woman's got no place on a freight ship. You'd think we were a bloody tourist craft!"

"Don't tell me you're superstitious, Slug," Jim chuckled. "Anyway, this scow runs on fuel oil, and you don't skim it off a lagoon, you've got to buy it with cash. As long as that's the way it is, anybody who can pay can ride."

"Yeah," Brophy said cynically, "but that gal isn't ridin' for fun. Something's going on!"

Jim laughed. "Take over, pal," he said, slapping the mate's shoulder, "keep her on the same course, an' don't run over any submarines! I'll worry about the woman!"

"Huh!" Brophy grunted disgustedly. "If you'd worry I wouldn't be gripin'!"

Ponga Jim swung down the ladder and started to open the door into the cabin. Instead, he flattened against the deckhouse and stared aft. There had been a vague, shadowy movement on the boat deck!

Swiftly and soundlessly, Ponga Jim slipped down the ladder and across the intervening space. Then he went up the ladder to the boat deck like a shadow, moving close against the lifeboats. Carefully, he worked his way aft toward the .50-caliber anti-aircraft guns where he had seen the movement.

Lightning flared briefly, and he saw someone crouching over the machine gun. It was an uncertain, fleeting glimpse, but he lunged forward.

Some instinctive warning must have come to the crouching figure for even as Jim sprang, he saw the white blur of a face, then it melted into the darkness and was gone.

At the gun, nothing. In two steps, Jim was at the edge of the boat deck, his .45 poised and ready, but the afterdeck was empty. His eyes narrowed with thought, he retraced his steps to the cabin. Someone had been tampering with the guns, and that someone would not be satisfied with one attempt.

He stepped into the cabin, shedding his oilskins. He started to hang them up when a voice froze him immobile.

"I hope I'm not intruding . . . ?"

Rayna Courcel sat at his desk smoking a cigarette. In slacks, he reflected, she was as seductive as in anything else. But then, her figure would give sex appeal to a shroud.

"Up early, aren't you?" he suggested. "What's on your mind? Don't you know it's four o'clock in the morning?"

"Of course. I wanted to ask a favor, and didn't want anyone to know . . . I want to go ashore. I have to go ashore."

"Ashore?" Ponga Jim's face was bland. "Why?"

"Because," Rayna said quietly, "this ship is going to be blown up."

"That strikes me as reason enough," Jim said, unbuttoning his coat. "When does the big event come off?"

"Tomorrow or the following day . . . when you're somewhere in the Spermonde Archipelago."

"Is there a crystal ball in your cabin? Maybe you should read my palms. . . ." He gave her a moment to understand his question.

"Oh, I know what I'm talking about, Captain.

You have a spy on your ship. I was up on the lifeboat deck having a cigarette and I heard someone sending Morse code. I read Morse, learned it in the girl scouts. . . ."

Mayo arched an eyebrow, "I'll bet you did."

"Are you going to let me finish? Good. The message was being sent ahead to a submarine . . . that's all I got."

Ponga Jim leaned back in his chair. His dark blue woolen shirt was open at the neck, and just under the edge of his coat Rayna could see the butt of his .45.

"All right. You're a smart girl, aren't you?" Jim said. "If I put you ashore where will you go?"

"To Makassar. I have it all planned. I go to Makassar, and . . ."

"And we go ahead and be blown up," Jim chuckled. "Lady, you please me. The only thing wrong with the setup, besides the fact that I don't like being blown up, is that we're not going to be anywhere close to Makassar tomorrow. I'm not even going near Celebes."

Rayna Courcel's face turned a shade white.

"What do you mean?" she exclaimed sharply. "Your route takes you that way!"

"Honey," Ponga Jim stood up, running his fingers through his hair. "I'm tired. You may not need beauty sleep, but I do. And don't worry about being blown up. Your spy may be trying to communicate but, in all likelihood, he has no idea where he is."

She started to speak, then bit her lip. At the door, she turned to face him, her hands behind her on the doorknob.

"I can't figure you out," she said, "but I'm afraid you're headed for a big surprise."

"Maybe," Ponga Jim said. "And maybe I won't be the only one."

CHAPTER 2

Bright morning sunlight sparkled on the sea when Ponga Jim Mayo went on deck. Tam O'Neill and Ben Blue were leaning on the rail. Both were gunners taken on at Capetown.

"Better check those machine guns," Mayo said briefly.

"Beggin' your pardon, sir," Tam said, "but my guns are always ready."

"O'Neill," Ponga Jim said shortly, "I'm not doubting you. But I never give an order without adequate reason. Last night they were tampered with."

O'Neill's face flushed. "Thank you, Captain," he said. He wheeled and was up the ladder in two jumps.

It was barely eight o'clock, but his three passengers were already at the table when Jim sat down. Eric Frazer, his third mate, was also there. With Millan splitting his time as artillery officer, Jim had shipped an additional third mate.

Frazer had come aboard in Zanzibar. He was short, powerful, and without expression. He had been, he said, a mate on a Danish vessel running to Rio, Para, and up the Amazon until the war put him on the beach.

The two men who, with Rayna Courcel, made up

the passenger list were Brace Lamprey, an engineer, and Ross Mallory. Both were South Africans with interests in New Guinea. Now Jim was beginning to wonder if everyone was what they first seemed to be.

"When should we sight the Spermonde Islands?" Lamprey asked casually, as Jim seated himself. "If I remember my East Indies, they are off the southwest corner of Celebes."

Rayna's hand tightened on her fork, but she did not look up.

"We'd be seeing them now," Jim said, "if we were going that way."

Mallory started violently, and stopped eating. He seemed about to speak when Lamprey interrupted.

"What do you mean, Captain?" he inquired. "Where are we going? Isn't that the route to Borneo?"

"Too many submarines that way," Jim said. "We're going north around Celebes."

Jim looked over at Frazer but the man was eating steadily, apparently ignoring the conversation.

Mallory straightened up. "See here, Captain!" he began angrily, "I don't propose to be dragged all over the ocean during a war. They are bombing the north coast of Celebes. I demand to be set ashore at once!"

"At once?" Jim asked. "That would mean the closest possible point, wouldn't it. I expect we can manage without much trouble. We're not quite a mile from land now."

They all looked up, surprised. Rayna's eyes strayed to the porthole.

"Not quite a mile?" Mallory was startled. "Where!"

"Straight down," Jim said.

Lamprey laughed, but Mallory's face grew red and angry.

"That isn't funny, Captain!" he growled. "I demand you put me ashore immediately!"

"What's the matter," Jim asked innocently, "afraid you'll be blown up with the ship?"

In the sudden silence that followed, they could hear the sea against the hull. Only Frazer was undisturbed. He ate in silence. Ross Mallory's eyes were suddenly wary.

"What do you mean?" he demanded.

"Mean?" Jim shrugged. "Well, it's one of the things that happen when a Japanese sub fires a torpedo at you."

He got up and walked out on deck. Mallory knew something, he decided. He began to feel better. Ever since the trip began, he had the feeling of trouble brewing. It was getting on his nerves. Now, at least, the trouble was beginning to show itself.

The girl had heard someone sending Morse code, she thought that they were going to be torpedoed . . . a spy who wanted to be torpedoed . . . that was a new one. Ponga Jim had no doubt that there were men out there who would give their lives for their country or cause but he doubted that destroying the small shipment of planes aboard the *Semiramis* was worth the ultimate sacrifice. Whatever was going on was something else . . . something else entirely.

He was staring off over the sea, and had been watching a fleck in the sky for almost a minute before he realized it was a plane.

It was coming fast and low. The blunt arrows of bombs racked under its wings.

He yelled, and saw O'Neill swing his gun. The Mitsubishi swooped in but even as they saw it, the plane was turning. The nose lifted into a climb, and was still climbing when O'Neill followed it with a long burst from the double fifties. The range was extreme and the bullets had no effect. As men ran to the other guns the plane circled, just out of range. Then, climbing at a terrific rate, the aircraft seemed to disappear into the cloudless blue sky.

Red Hanlon, the chief engineer, stood by No. 3 hatch rubbing his cauliflower ear.

"Skipper," he said, "that guy wasn't shooting."

"Just getting a look at us," Jim said dryly, "after all, he has friends aboard."

"*What?*" Mallory stopped. "Spies aboard here? What kind of ship is this, anyway?"

Ponga Jim ignored him. If they wanted the ship blown up, why not bomb or torpedo it? That job would have been simple for the plane they had just seen.

The only reason there could be for sparing the ship would be if there were enemy agents aboard who planned to leave the ship, and probably blow it up on leaving. But what was going on that had caused an agent to board his ship . . . and what was so important that the Japanese had sent out a plane to be sure of their location?

The *Semiramis* was on a course that would take her by the usual route through Makassar Strait. But he was just as sure that he no longer had any intention of going that way.

· · ·

Jim turned and went up the ladder to the bridge. Frazer, immaculate in a white linen coat, turned to face him. He had been studying the horizon through his glasses.

"We're changing course," Jim said. He stepped into the wheelhouse where Tupa, an Alfur seaman, was at the wheel. "Put her over to fifty," Mayo said. "And hold her there."

Frazer joined him. "Then you aren't going through the strait?" he asked.

"After being spotted like that," Jim said. "Not a chance. We're going east. I may decide to put in at Buton."

Frazer hesitated, as though about to speak. Then he turned and walked back to the bridge.

Twice during the day, Ponga Jim changed course, but each time swung back to the neighborhood of fifty degrees. Once, standing on the bridge, he saw Lamprey looking at the sun's position with a thoughtful expression. Obviously, the man had noted the changes of course. Rayna was watching the sky, too, but with an altogether different expression.

Millan stopped beside him on the deck after dinner. His face was troubled.

"You reckon we've got a spy aboard, Skipper? Should I search their cabins?"

"No," Jim told him, "whoever it is wouldn't have anything incriminating around. But today, we've changed course, so the spy will make an attempt to communicate within the next twenty-four hours, and my bet is within the next six. Then maybe something will break."

Yet it was not until an hour later that he remembered his conversation with Rayna.

She had heard Morse code being sent . . . but why from the lifeboat deck? It was nowhere near the *Semiramis*'s radio room, which was occupied around the clock. Walking out to a spot on the bridge wing where he could see the spot where she stood, he realized she must have been standing just behind one of the ventilators!

Taking a flashlight from a drawer, Jim put on his faded khaki coat and picked up his cap. Silently, he stepped out on the lower bridge. There was no one in sight. He walked aft along the windward side of the main deck to avoid meeting anyone. His soft, woven-leather sandals made no noise on the steel deck. He halted in the shadows by the deckhouse. There was no sound but the rustle of water along the hull but somewhere out there were Japanese submarines, and the sleek, swift destroyers. North Borneo had fallen, Menado in Celebes had been shelled and bombed.

In a swift succession of raids, the Japanese had struck at Rabaul, in the Bismarcks, and at Sorong, a village on poles alongside the beach at Doom Island. Singapore had its back to the wall in a desperate, all-out battle for survival.

But closer another enemy waited, a more dangerous enemy because he was unknown. Yet an enemy who held in his hand not only the lives of those aboard, but the men for whom these planes and munitions were destined. And that enemy was here on this ship with them.

Ponga Jim moved past the crew's mess unseen, and entered the rope locker.

All was still, a haunting stillness that concealed some living presence. Yet he knew there was no one in the locker but himself, it was only that he was getting closer. There was a smell of new hemp and tarred lines, of canvas and of turpentine.

Crawling around a pile of heavy line, he softly loosened the dogs and opened the door concealed there. He felt with his foot for the steel ladder, and like a wraith, glided down into the abysmal blackness of the hold.

CHAPTER 3

There the dark was something one could feel, something almost tangible. Ponga Jim hesitated, listening with every nerve in his body.

Down below, he could hear the sea much more plainly and he was conscious again, as he always was, of its dark power separated from him by only a thin partition of steel. There was a faint smell of old cargoes, of copra, rubber, tea and coffee, of sago, nutmeg, and tobacco. He waited an instant in the darkness listening.

Then he heard it, the faint tinkle of metal on metal. He felt the hackles raise on the back of his neck, and he moved forward on cat feet, feeling his way by instinct through the racked torpedo bombers and cases of ammunition. In his mind he was trying to locate whoever was in the hold, to locate the man by putting himself in the man's place.

Suddenly, he remembered. What a fool he had been! The Grumman, of course! The amphibian, his own ship, had a two-way radio as well as a code sender!

Then he heard the clicking of the key. Crouching in the darkness just forward of the tail assembly, he tried to make out the words, but the echoes made it difficult. He made out the name of the ship, *Semiramis,* and some numbers. . . . A compass heading!

Jim stepped closer, putting his foot out carefully. But even as he moved the cabin door opened. He felt rather than saw the figure and instantly, he sprang!

Yet even as he leaped something rolled under his foot and he crashed to the deck.

He heard a smothered gasp, and reached out desperately, suddenly gripping an ankle. Then a heel kicked him viciously in the head. He let go and rolled over. A pistol barrel, aimed at his head, missed and smashed down upon his shoulder.

He fell back, grunting with the pain of it, and then the same pistol caught him a glancing blow on top of the head. Momentarily stunned, he struggled to climb to his feet, his head blazing with pain.

Staggering, he fell against a packing case, and froze, listening. Jim heard no sound of retreating footsteps. Whoever he was, the man was no fool. Jim could hear nothing, not even breathing. He crept along behind the cases. He put his hand out and was startled by the touch of human flesh. In a kind of instinctive panic, he rocked back on his knees and swung with everything he had. His fist smashed into a muscular shoulder, and the man grunted. An arrow of pain slithered down his arm from a knifepoint, and he lunged close.

A fist slammed against his jaw, and he twisted, trying to catch the man's knife-wrist. As in everything else, there is a knack to fighting in the dark, an instinctive gauging of position that comes with experience. But it was experience his opponent had as well.

He jammed a fist against a corded stomach, but took a jolting punch himself. He felt the man draw back his arm and shift balance to drive the knife home, but he fell away from the blade and hooking his toe behind his opponent's ankle, jerked the leg from under him.

They got up together, and he took a smashing blow to the mouth then hooked a hard one to the chin, feeling the man go down under the blow.

Instantly, he dropped, falling knees first at the spot where the man's stomach should have been, but the fellow rolled away quickly. Then there was a scuffle of feet. Sensing the spy was trying to get away, Ponga Jim grabbed for the flashlight, which had fallen from his pocket during the fray. He felt around, finding the light after a few moments. He snapped it on, his gun ready. The hold was empty. He shook his head to clear it. Was it one or two different people he had struggled with there in the dark?

Mayo swore under his breath and ran for the topside ladder. On deck, he came to a stop, groping for the rail as he waited for his eyes to adjust to the blinding sunlight. Squinting forward and aft he searched for the mysterious man from the hold. No one was nearby.

Ponga Jim stopped amidships, Brace Lamprey had come on deck and not far from him was Ross Mallory. Lamprey looked at Jim curiously.

"What happened to you, man?" he asked. "You look like you've been slugging it out with them!"

"I was," Jim said coolly. Lamprey's face was smooth, unmarked. Nor did Mallory show any signs of conflict. The two of them seemed all too cool to have participated in the fight below.

Ponga Jim went up the ladder to the bridge. Blore, one of the South Africans, came out of the wheelhouse.

"Are we changing course to go in to Buton?"

"No," Jim said shortly, "we're swinging wide. We're going east, through Kelang Strait."

Blore turned a little, his eyes intent. "That's a long way around, isn't it? What's in the wind, Skipper? Do you have some mission other than delivering these planes?"

Ponga Jim shoved his cap back on his head. "My only mission is minding my own business. These planes go where they were sent, and anything that gets in the way gets smashed, understand?"

Blore's eyes dropped a little, but his face was expressionless.

"Yes, sir," he said sullenly. "I understand you, Captain."

Ponga Jim Mayo walked back to the chart room. He was getting jumpy, he shouldn't have spoken so hard to the kid.

He glanced down at the chart. Due north from Kelang Strait would take him just west of the Ombi Islands. Something stopped him cold, and he stared down at the chart, caught by a sudden thought. As he stared down at the map, he felt himself chill through and through at the realization of what was about to happen.

It was no longer a vague premonition, no longer a few scattered acts and words fitting to the hint dropped by Arnold. He could see it all, and the realization struck him speechless for the moment.

In his mind, Jim was seeing an island, a high tableland near Obi Major. Thick, dank green jungle ran down to the sea. But Jim was not thinking of the jungle, he was thinking of that tableland.

He was remembering the day he had climbed the steplike mountain and stood looking out over the top, a flat, dead-level field, waving with long grass. Eight hundred feet above the sea, it was. "Tobalai," he muttered, "Tobalai Island!"

From outside there was the shriek of an incoming shell followed by the deep concussion of a heavy cannon. Then ship's alarms blasted the signal for general quarters.

The waiting, it seemed, was over.

CHAPTER 4

Ponga Jim dived for the bridge. He saw, ahead of them, the low, dark profile of a submarine. In front of its conning tower a crew rushed to reload the deck gun.

"Starboard fifteen degrees," he called out and reached for the forward fire-control phone. But something was wrong. The sub had fired a warning shot, it had not tried to sink them, and Eric Frazer was standing in the door of the chart room, one side of his face a dark and purple bruise.

Even though he was ready for it, the punch almost nailed him. Frazer threw his right hand fast and hard. But Jim's left hook was harder.

"Never lead a right hand," he said, and knocked the third mate down. Frazer was up like a cat, but Jim fished out his pistol and covered him. Suddenly, the ship's heading started to swing, and Jim turned instinctively to the wheel. He was just in time to see the blow start, but too late to block it. Blore slugged him across the head with a blackjack.

Jim started to fall, and Frazer slugged him from behind. Then the blackjack fell again and Ponga Jim went to his knees, blinded with a sickening pain. He went down. Even then, his consciousness a feeble spark lost in a sea of blackness, he struggled. Someone must have hit him once more because he felt his knees slide from under him and he faded out in a pounding surf of agony.

When he opened his eyes, he was alive to nothing but the throbbing pain in his head. It felt heavy and unwieldy when he made an effort to move. His hands were tied, and his ankles also. He struggled to sit up and the pain wrenched a groan from his swollen lips.

"Skipper?" It was Brophy's voice.

"What happened?" Ponga Jim asked. "What in blazes happened?"

"They took over the ship," Brophy said. "They took us like Dewey took Manila. I woke up with a gun in my face, an' they got the Gunner when he came on watch."

"They?" Mayo puckered his brow, trying to figure it out.

"Yeah. Frazer, Lamprey, and Mallory. They had six of the South African crew with them. I heard some of them talking. I guess they are actually Boers who sympathize with the Nazis . . . anyway, they're working with the Japs."

"Makes sense," Jim said, remembering. "I think we're headed for Tobalai."

"Why Tobalai?" Brophy asked.

"I'm guessing they've turned the top of the island into a landing field. From there they can cover any point in the East Indies, but particularly anywhere from where we are now to Mindanao."

"That's slick thinking . . . you're probably right!"

"I don't feel so smart," Jim said bitterly. "A lot of good we can do, all wrapped up like premium hams."

The door opened, and Li came in with a tray of food. The Chinese put it down carefully for two armed men stood in the door, guns ready. One was a Japanese, the other the seaman, Blore.

"Wait until I get out of here," Ponga Jim said. "I'll see you guys swing for this."

"You will, eh?" Blore sneered. "You won't be getting out and tomorrow morning what is left of the

United States fleet will come steaming up through Greyhound Strait from the Banda Sea."

Ponga Jim turned cold inside, but he kept up the sarcastic, skeptical manner.

"Yeah? So what?" he said.

A weasel-faced seaman leaned into the hatch. "Then a couple of cruisers will draw their fighters into a trap and these planes of yours attack the carriers . . . the crews will think it's their own men coming back. There's two battleships lying behind Obi Major, an' a dozen submarines are waiting to clean up the job."

"Ah?" the voice was gentle, polite. "Are you being entertained, Captain Mayo?"

Weasel-face stopped, his mouth half open to speak. Slowly he turned a sickly yellow. Captain Toya Tushima stepped into view. The trim little Nipponese held his features in an expression of calm benevolence but weasel-face turned as though fascinated with horror.

"I cannot say that it is good to see you again, Captain Mayo, but, in a war of strangers, I do feel a certain pleasure in an old acquaintance."

"It's been a long time since Manchuria, hasn't it?"

"Perhaps for you." The Japanese looked at him carefully, as he might at a piece of awkward furniture. Then indicating the weasely crewman he spoke to Frazer who had come up.

"Do we need this man?" he asked.

Eric shrugged. "He is one of the recruits from the Transvaal . . . I don't think so."

"Good," Tushima said pleasantly. "Stand aside."

He unbuttoned his holster carefully and drew out a gun. His face twisted in a grimace of fear, his eyes distended, the crewman drew away.

"No!" he begged hoarsely. "No! Please!"

The report of the gun was thunder within the steel walls. The seaman crumpled slowly, a round blue hole between his eyes.

Tushima looked at Blore.

"You really mustn't talk so much," he said. Without a backward glance, he walked away.

Blore, his hands shaking, picked up the dead man and carried him out. Brophy swallowed and looked at Li.

"I don't think I'm eating," he said. "I don't think I got the stomach for it."

"Go on," Jim said, "this isn't over yet."

After they had eaten and Li was gone, the two men remained in the half darkness of the rope locker. Millan and the others, they heard, were confined in the seaman's fo'c'sle. Remembering the door into No. 5 hold he had used before, Jim began to work at his bonds. The door was behind the stack of line and, apparently, unnoticed. If they could get free . . .

For a long time, he worked in the darkness, twisting, tugging, and straining, but without success. And all the time, he carried a picture in his thoughts of the long gray ships of war coming up from the Banda Sea, taking the back door to the Philippines from their bases in Samoa and Port Darwin. Once their air cover had been lured away, the torpedo planes, the same ones that the *Semiramis* carried, would approach and, appearing to be the American planes returning from the battle, would get close enough to the carriers to launch a crippling attack. It was a potentially devastating plan.

"We've got to get out of here!" Jim exclaimed suddenly. "If they get away with this, it will make Pearl Harbor look like a pink tea!"

He was thinking rapidly. If he could get his hands free, he could get down the ladder into the hold. Unless Lamprey had found it, or one of the others, there was a tommy gun in the Grumman. If he could get that gun and get on deck, he'd take his own chances.

Tugging at the ropes was a waste of time. Jim growled under his breath. Suddenly, an inspiration struck him.

"Slug?" he whispered. "Where did you put the gear from that smashed lifeboat? The one that was blasted in the Red Sea?"

"Over there, in the drawers," Slug said. "Why?"

"There's a couple of hatchets, an' all the other gear. What I'm thinking of is the matches."

Jim stretched out his legs and dug in his heels, dragging himself to the place where the smaller articles of gear were stowed. By getting his chin in the handhold on the drawer, he worked it open. Backing up to a pile of line, he worked himself up the pile until he was on his feet. He felt around carefully, and found the matches.

Their hands were tied behind them but Brophy struck a light and held the match so that Jim could slide back and hold his wrists over the flame. It burned his hand, burned his wrist, then went out. Brophy awkwardly struck another but dropped it trying to maneuver the match toward Jim's wrists. The third time, however, Jim used the heat from the flame as a guide and positioned the rope carefully. It charred slowly, caught fire and burned, then went out. Brophy tried again, but the match broke in striking. Finally they got the rope burning and with a surge of strength, the strands parted. In a matter of minutes, they were both free.

CHAPTER 5

Rubbing his wrists to restore circulation, Jim got to his feet. Then picking up a couple of steel battens for fastening hatches, he slid them under the door handle, driving a couple of wooden wedges in place to hold them securely. Slug watched him curiously.

"You figure out the wildest things," he said. "What's the idea?"

"Keep them guessing awhile. Suppose somebody came in before we got out of the hold? We'd be killed before we could get anywhere close to the deck. As it is, they'll think we're just trying to keep them out in case they get an idea to bump us off."

Climbing over the rope, he grabbed the handle of the door to the hold, and twisted sharply. Nothing happened. The dismay on Brophy's face mirrored his own.

"Locked!" Jim said. "They locked it!"

The mate hesitated, then doubling a big fist he grinned at Jim.

"We can always jump them when they come in to feed us," he said.

"Won't do. They'd cut us down before we'd taken three steps."

"Then I guess you better start kicking a hole in the deck," Slug said dryly. "That's the only way out I can see."

"Wait a minute." Jim crawled over the lines to the one porthole. The paint was stuck, but cutting around the edge with the hatchet, he managed to get it open. "We'll have to wait until dark," he whispered, "but we're going out that port."

"Into the ocean?" Brophy asked. "Not me!"

Jim chuckled. "What's the matter? Getting chilly around the arches? You know blamed well you'll do it if there was a chance of getting a crack at those mugs."

Slug grinned. "Maybe, but I haven't got the build you have. I'm thicker in the middle and might not go through so easy."

Twice attempts were made to open the door, but they sat silent, listening. The Japanese weren't worried. Both exits were closed tight, and if the prisoners wanted to do without food, they had only themselves to blame, and were much less trouble.

As they waited, Ponga Jim was recalling what weasel-face had said. Two battleships behind Obi Major. That would mean they would be inside the reef somewhere between Tanjongs Woko and Parigi, probably. More ships might be lying in the Roads at Laiwoei.

On the other side of Greyhound Strait, several ships could lie out of sight in Banggai Bay, and even more in the deeper, spacious waters of Bangkalang

Bay. Scouting planes could only see them when almost over the bays themselves, but it would already be too late.

He was no nearer a plan. If he had a plane, he could fly over and warn the fleet before they were in danger. Once warned they could handle the situation. He had no doubt about that.

Before he realized, it was dark. Slug Brophy had been lying on the piled-up lines looking out through the porthole.

"We're not far offshore now," he said. "I thought I glimpsed moonlight on the tin roof of the storage shed at Laiwoei and I thought I recognized Mala Mala a while back."

"Then it's time for us to go into action." Jim got up quickly, thrusting a hatchet in his belt.

Picking up a heaving line he crawled to the port. He tossed the tail end of the line to Slug.

"Take a turn around some of that inch line," he said. "This all depends on whether anybody is near enough or not. If they see or hear, we're out of luck."

Putting one arm and shoulder out the port, he worked his broad shoulders through. Then, sitting in the port with Slug holding his legs, he leaned back and threw the monkey's fist.

The edge of the deck was just about eight feet above his head, and the ball of knotted rope went over the edge and under the lowest part of the rail. It hit the deck, rolled down with the roll of the ship, then back. He had missed.

Gauging the distance again, he tried another toss. But that time too he failed to make it roll down on the opposite side of the stanchion. On the seventh attempt, he was successful. It rolled back hard enough to come over the edge. Then by paying out line the weight of the monkey's fist brought it back down to him. Passing it on to Slug, he began hauling down on the line until the inch line was around the stanchion.

Sliding back into the port, he cut off the inch line while Slug unbent the heaving line.

"I'm going to take the piece we use with us, or drop it over the side," Jim said. "Let them think we're locked up. They'll find out too soon, anyway."

Pulling himself back to a sitting position in the port, he grasped the two lines in his hands and went up, hand over hand. As soon as he was over the ship's side, he dropped the rope close in front of the port so Brophy would see it.

He glanced around and was just in time to see the descending marlinspike, and jerked his head aside. The power of the blow jerked the man off balance and he almost fell over the rail.

Before he could cry out, Jim struck him. A driving right to the chin, and then another short one in the wind. Gasping for breath, the man struck wildly, and Jim almost lost balance and fell into the sea.

Clinging precariously to the rail, the two fought desperately and in silence. Then Ponga Jim's superior strength gave him an advantage. The man was slipping, and he let go of Jim and grabbed desperately at the rail, but Jim knocked his hands loose and as the man fell forward, Jim grabbed the back of his neck and tipped him over the side.

Brophy jerked back out of the way just as the man

fell past, but there was no scream, only a splash, and no further sound. Brophy came up the rope and Jim helped him to the deck. Then he wiped the cold sweat from his brow.

"What do we do?" Slug said. "Turn the boys loose an' take over the ship?"

"It's too late," Jim said. "Look!"

The *Semiramis* was just coming into the Roads at Laiwoei. Ahead of them lay a long gray destroyer, beyond that a cruiser and another destroyer.

They drew back into the darkness between a cargo winch and the mainm'st. "Go below in the hold somewhere and watch your chance to turn the others loose. Then if you can slip out of the Roads somehow, do it."

"What about you?" Brophy demanded.

"I'm going ashore. Somehow I'm going to get word to the fleet, and somehow I'm going to get on Tobalai and see if I can throw a monkey wrench into this deal. Do what you can."

Silently, the two men gripped hands, then Ponga Jim dropped to his knees behind the hatch-coaming and worked his way forward. A dash to the walk along the lee rail got him to shelter. He climbed up on the rail, did a hand-over-hand up the stanchion, and crawled over the edge to the boat deck.

There he lay, catching a breath, and looking under the lifeboat to estimate the situation. If he ran for it and made a dive over the side, he would be seen and heard. Probably on the destroyer as well as his own ship. His only chance was to wait.

He lay still, studying the situation. The deck was

stirring with movement. He heard them let go the anchor forward, and saw a fast motor launch coming alongside from the nearest warship. That would be for Tushima, as they must have signaled.

Crawling aft to the machine gun, a glance told him there was no ammunition. That was as he had expected. They had removed any chance of its use by any of the crew that might escape. Swiftly, he dodged down the ladder and into the lighted passage. Footsteps approached, and he opened the nearest door and stepped in.

There was a startled gasp, and he wheeled to find himself facing Rayna Courcel. The girl's eyes were wide.

"You!" she exclaimed. "Where did you come from?"

"Me? Seemed like a nice night for a stroll, so I started out. Got a gun?"

She picked up her handbag, drew the gun, and pointed it at him.

"I'm glad you reminded me," she said. "You came in so quickly I forgot."

"Are you giving it to me?" he said. "Or am I taking it?"

"You won't try that, Captain Mayo," she said quietly. "If you do, I'll shoot, and I should very much dislike to do that."

"It will not be necessary, Miss Courcel," a voice interrupted.

Before Jim could turn he was seized from behind

by a pair of powerful arms that were thrown about his body. Instantly, Jim dropped to one knee, at the same time grabbing his attacker's wrist and elbow and giving a hard jerk.

With surprising ease the man flopped over Mayo's shoulder and hit the deck hard. It was Eric Frazer. Before he could move, Jim hooked a short one to his chin, and slipped the man's .45 from his holster.

Wheeling, he jumped into the passage, kicked a surprised guard in the stomach, and ran for the rail. The motor launch was alongside, and Jim made the ladder running, and was halfway down before the two surprised Japanese seamen in the boat could act. One of them grabbed for a gun, and Ponga Jim fired. The man dropped the gun and spilled over on his face.

There was a sudden movement behind him, and Jim fired again. Then he wheeled. Big London and Lyssy had been under guard but now they were right behind him, and even as they dropped into the boat, Big London cast off.

Jim leaped to the controls and the idling motor roared into life. On deck there was confusion, shouting, jostling men rushed toward the rail, and Big London, balancing himself easily, lifted the automatic rifle the sailor had been about to use, and sprayed the rail.

Ponga Jim spun the launch in a turn that almost capsized the boat and with the motors roaring wide open, raced for the destroyer. Missing the bow by inches, and the starb'rd anchor hawser by less, he spun the wheel again and raced the boat down close under the lee of the warship. It was too close for accurate firing from the deck and the rocky islet of Kadera was just a bit over a hundred yards astern.

"Down!" Jim yelled. "Get down!"

Lyssy and Big London both dropped, but both opened fire on the destroyer. A gun roared from the stern, and a shell hit the waves twenty yards ahead of them. Jim swung the boat hastily toward the spot where the shell had landed, and with the motor wide open, water lifting in a roaring fan on either side of the bow, raced for the shelter of Kadera. A machine gun rattled, and a bullet glanced from the engine cowling and whined past his ear. He skidded the boat around a rock, and for an instant was sheltered by the islet.

Dodging and turning, he raced the boat for the coast beyond Tanjong Parigi. What he wanted wasn't at Laiwoei, but at Tobalai off the east end of Obi Major. But there wasn't a chance of retaining the launch. It was slower than other boats they soon would have in pursuit, and was unarmed except for the weapons they had themselves.

Lyssy came up beside him. The Toradjas' eyes were bright.

"Both yellow man dead," he said. "You shoot plenty good, Captain. Where we go?"

"Ashore," Jim said briefly. "You and London go through this boat. Get all the guns and ammunition you can find. Anything else that looks good. We're going to have a fight of it. They don't dare let us get away."

Cutting the motor for an instant, he listened, and hearing the roar of motors behind him, opened up again. Tensely, he crouched over the wheel. The pursuit was getting under way faster than he had believed. It would be nip and tuck now, and if they got away it would be sheer luck, nothing less.

The motor wide open, he rounded the Tanjong and headed off down the coast, his wake a streak of white, boiling water. Spray beat against his face, and the two widening fans of water cut away from the knifelike bow.

The water was black and glistening, the night speckled with stars. Behind him, Big London and Lyssy crouched in the stern, rifles ready. Beyond the boat he saw at a glance, the sea was empty to the point, and along the coast down which they were running the jungle crowded to the very water's edge.

Ponga Jim spun the wheel suddenly, and with his motor wide open, roared for the blackness of an opening under the mangroves. The launch shot through the hole like some insane monster of the sea, and hit the muddy shingle with such force that it ran halfway up the low bank before it stopped. Instantly, Jim cut the motor and leaped out.

"Grab the guns and let's go!" he said. "They won't find the boat for a while!"

CHAPTER 6

The launch was at least ten feet under the mangrove roots and out of sight from sea. They would have a good start, and fortunately, no two men in his crew were better bushmen than these two, Big London, who had grown up on the banks of the Congo, and Lyssy, the wandering warrior from the Toradjas' highlands of Celebes.

Lyssy took the lead, and with almost instinctive skill, led them into a game trail. They started off at a fast trot. The trail led steadily upward toward the interior mountains. If it had only meant escape, Ponga Jim thought, he could have kept alive and safe for years in this jungle with these two companions. But there was no time to lose.

Rounding a shoulder of cliff several miles back from the coast, Ponga Jim saw a searchlight sweeping the jungle. It would only be a few minutes now until they found the launch, and then the Japanese would be back on their trail.

Steadily, they kept on, weaving up into the mountains, but tending steadily toward the east and south. Once, crossing a stream, they saw the huge coil of a snake on the bank, later they walked into a herd of wild pigs that fortunately did not charge, but just wandered away, grunting stupidly.

"They come," Lyssy said suddenly.

In the moment of silence they could hear a shout as their trail was seen.

The moon had come up, and the jungle lay ominous and shadowy beneath the brightening sky. Ponga Jim hesitated. The country was too rough for fast travel, and he could see that his idea of crossing the island and seizing a boat at one of the three or four small villages along that coast was going to be a near thing. Already his ship would be arriving at Tobalai and the Japanese would be unloading the planes.

Keeping to the jungle trails, they waded down a stream, then cut back on another trail toward the coast. Then, suddenly, in the first open place they found, they saw beneath them, and some distance away, the climbing Japanese marines. Instantly, Jim lifted his rifle and all three fired at once. Two of the Japanese fell, and another staggered against the brush, clawing at his chest.

Confused, and not knowing where the shots came from, the soldiers fired randomly. But their shots were aimed south, up the trail. Ponga Jim gave the signal, and they fired another volley, then faded into the jungle. They moved at a fast trot, occasionally stopping to listen.

The moonlight was lost in the high upper branches of the mangroves, and the three slipped down to the coast unseen. Ponga Jim hesitated an instant, looking out over the water. A destroyer lay out there but here, within a hundred and fifty feet, were two patrol boats. Four men waited beside them, on guard.

"All right, here's where we take them," Jim said.

Working along the edge of the jungle, he got within sixty feet of the boats. Here was a small, sandy beach. Lyssy drew his knife, waited an instant, and then threw it.

The man facing the jungle grunted, and fell over on the sand. Startled, the three Japanese crowded about him. None of them had seen the knife, and they bent over to turn the fallen man on his back.

Jim ran swiftly and soundlessly. The nearest marine started to turn and straighten, but Jim's right hand smashed him on the point of the chin, knocking him to the sand.

Big London rushed in close, and a soldier grabbed at his extended left arm, but Big London was too quick, and he kicked viciously, his heel striking the man on the kneecap. With a low cry the man fell, and then Big London clamped on a headlock, twisted sharply, and sat down hard on the sand.

He got up quietly. The job was finished, and Jim sent the two men to one boat and he took the other. They started the motors and headed out to sea. Jim glanced at the destroyer. If they were challenged . . .

They were. They were just sheering off to bear away from the destroyer when a command boomed out over a loudspeaker. Big London and Lyssy were in the boat behind him. They kept on their path and instantly a shot plunged across their bows.

Without an instant's hesitation, Jim acted. Turning onto a course toward the destroyer, he opened the motor wide. With a roar, the boat almost leaped from under him. He slammed the two arming levers on the console down and punched every button he could see. Whirling, he leaped to the rear deck and dove off into the churning water.

The other boat was alongside, and Lyssy grabbed him by the shoulders. He was not quite in the boat when the first patrol boat was shelled by the destroyer. The bow went to fragments and the boat was dead in the water and sinking. Then there was an appalling crash, and the thunder of a terrific explosion. A burst of fire momentarily appeared alongside the Japanese warship.

Ponga Jim grabbed the wheel from Big London

and sent the speedboat roaring out to sea, her bottom fairly skimming the waves.

"What was that explosion?" London asked, staring with wide eyes. "The destroyer, she all afire."

"The speedboat had two torpedoes in its tubes," Mayo said, "so has this one."

The black sea swept past underneath them, and in the distance a thin gray line began to grow above the horizon. Jim's face was set and hard as the boat roared down the coast heading for Tobalai. The patrol boat would do fifty miles an hour, and was doing it.

The fleet would be moving now, moving out across the sea toward the north. And on the tableland of Tobalai, his planes, the aircraft he had been entrusted with, would be warming up, waiting for the American aircraft of the carrier squadron to take the bait and fly to attack the Japanese battleships. The trap was set and the disguise was perfect.

Big London crouched low behind Jim, and Lyssy stared back at the glow where the destroyer burned. The sea raced by, and Jim's hands gripped the wheel. It was a long way, but they could make it, they might make it.

"What happen to our ship, I wonder?" Big London asked.

"I don't know," Jim said. "I just don't know."

He had been thinking of that, too. The *Semiramis,* all he owned in the world, and the crew, who were not only men who worked with and trusted him, but his friends.

· · ·

Day was just breaking when he ran into the cove on the shore of Tobalai. Dropping anchor in shallow water, the three went over the side and Mayo and Big London walked ashore.

"We're here," Ponga Jim grinned. "Now there's not much left to do."

"Excuse me, *Capitan* Mayo," a voice said politely, "I dislike to interrupt but I must . . ."

Ponga Jim turned, unbelieving. "How . . . ?"

Captain Tushima smiled. "I flew here. You see . . ." He gestured with one hand to a line of soldiers with machine guns. "You two are my prisoners!"

Two? Mayo did not turn his head, but in his heart there was a sudden burst of elation.

"You're always around at the wrong time, Captain," he said coolly, "and this is the worst."

He turned carelessly. Big London, his black face sober, stood about a dozen feet away. Lyssy was gone. Evidently he had sensed trouble and stayed underwater after diving out of the boat.

Brace Lamprey and Mallory came down from the jungle. Lamprey looked around.

"Where's the guy with the trick haircut?" he demanded sharply.

"Who?" Ponga Jim asked innocently. "You mean the Toradjas?"

"I don't know what he is," Lamprey returned. "The big fellow with the front half of his head shaved."

"That's him. The Toradjas warriors all wear their hair that way. He left us back in the jungle on Obi Major. We scattered out, and he didn't get back with us."

Mallory said nothing, but stared at Jim, a curious light in his eyes. Eric Frazer came down out of the jungle. He was wearing a gun and his cheekbone was badly cut, one eye black.

Ponga Jim grinned at him, and Frazer's eyes blazed.

"I owe you one, Mayo, and I'm going to give it to you now!" He walked up, and drawing his gun, drew back to hit Jim with the barrel.

Ponga Jim made believe to duck, but instead, lunged forward and hit Frazer with his shoulder, knocking the man into the sand. His face red with anger, Frazer swung up the gun to kill Mayo, but Tushima spoke sharply, and he stopped.

"I thought you wanted him killed," Frazer said sullenly. "Why keep him alive?"

"Because," Tushima said slowly, "I want one American to see with his own eyes the destruction of the rest of their most-powerful fleet."

Ponga Jim looked at him, but said nothing. Tushima turned, and motioning the guards to follow with him, started back up the steep path.

Jim thought rapidly. He was a prisoner, but there still was time if he could free himself, and Lyssy had escaped. There was no greater woodsman alive, and if anything could be done, he would do it.

Tushima dropped back to walk beside Jim.

"This war has long been coming, *Capitan* Mayo," he said gravely, "but we shall win now that it is here."

"Yeah?" Jim shook his head. "If you'd been smart

enough to see that getting bogged down in China proper wasn't a solution to getting bogged down in Manchuria you wouldn't be trying to take over more territory than you can ever hold. The situation gets worse with every island you take."

Tushima shrugged. "I am only responsible for delivering a victory here and now. Policy, I leave to others."

"Well, someone hasn't studied their history and someday they are very likely to stick you with the problem."

The mountain rose toward the plateau in steplike formation, and on the topmost step before reaching the tableland itself, several houses and barracks had been constructed in the jungle.

Rayna Courcel came from a bungalow as Ponga Jim approached. Her eyes widened a little, but she said nothing. Once she glanced at Mallory, but Ross was silent.

Ponga Jim and London were put into a cell behind a barred door. Jim sat down on the cot. Only a few hours remained, probably less than that, and the only factor in the whole mess that promised anything at all was the fact that Lyssy was outside in the jungle.

Beyond the barracks and in the jungle on the edge of the tableland above were the two huge gasoline storage tanks with fuel for the planes. Already there was a bustle of movement around them as the planes were being readied for their big fight. The American torpedo bombers were being armed and serviced, crewmen were even freshening the insignias on their sides and wings to be sure that they couldn't be missed.

Excitement was in the air now, for all knew what was coming, and not one but knew that on this flight might rest the future of the Japanese empire. At one fell stroke, they might wreck the remaining naval power of the United States, sending the last of the Pacific Fleet into the dark turmoil of oil-slicked waves.

Ponga Jim stared thoughtfully at the fuel tanks. They weren't so far away at that. If he could rid himself of that guard he might be able to handle the door. He turned to examine it again and was surprised to see Rayna.

"You here?" he said. "I should think you'd be aloft watching the preparations."

Her expression did not change. "How long will it take the planes to get there? To the strait, I mean?"

He shrugged. "A bit less than half an hour, I think. But not much. If you're sticking around, you'd better keep out of the way. You wouldn't look very nice all mussed up, and I may take a notion to crash out."

"Would you?" Rayna looked at him curiously. "Why?"

"A lot of the usual reasons. I'm patriotic, I suspect. Then I wouldn't want to see all those kids in fleet getting ambushed by planes that I brought out here."

"But what could you do?" Rayna asked. "One man, against so many."

"As much as possible." He looked at her carefully.

"I haven't got you placed, though, honey. Just where do you fit in?"

"Actually I'm assistant to the Canadian military attaché in Pretoria." She smiled, "We heard that something was up but I think I'm in over my head. . . ."

"Is there a radio around here?" Jim asked, keeping his eyes on her.

"Yes. It's in the barracks, on the upper floor."

"Then talk to the guard a minute." Jim had been looking at the door. It was a door of steel bars, but the hinges were set in a wooden frame. It had been hastily made, with a guard on duty, it didn't have to be that strong.

He turned to Big London. "Step up here, old fellow. This guard doesn't savvy American. I've been watching him. You and me are going out of this joint, and I mean now."

Big London grinned, showing his white teeth and flexing his muscles.

"What do we do, Cap?"

Ponga Jim walked up to the door and took hold of the bars. The guard was standing in the door explaining something to Rayna in Japanese.

He took hold of the bars, looked at Jim, and Mayo grabbed them too and smiled.

"Let's go!" he said, and heaved with all his strength.

The iron bars of the door broke away from the frame on the first heave, splintering the crudely hewn wood. The guard whirled, jerking up his gun, but as he started to take a step, Rayna tripped him.

The marine spilled over on his face, and as Big London gave another terrific heave, wrenching the door away from its flimsy, shanty framing, Jim lunged through. A blow with the rifle butt as the guard started to get up, and he was knocked completely cold.

"Come on!" Jim snapped.

CHAPTER 7

Ponga Jim picked up the rifle and started at a rapid walk for the barracks. They had made it almost halfway before someone noticed them. Then two Japanese soldiers stopped and stared at them.

Without a second's hesitation, Ponga Jim walked right up to the nearest one, smiling. Rayna said something he didn't follow in Japanese, and the man frowned, looking uncertainly from Jim's gun to the Negro. Jim was almost within arm's length of the man when the soldier made up his mind that something was wrong. He opened his mouth to yell, and Jim drove the barrel of the rifle into the soldier's solar plexus with terrific force.

Big London, who had been carrying a length of wood, sprang up and knocked the rifle from the second man's hand, then brought the club down over his head. Grabbing up the rifles they ran for the barracks.

Behind them was a startled yell, then a shot. Jim turned and fired three times, taking his own sweet time and dropping each man he shot at. Then they rushed into the empty barracks and slammed the door. London jerked a table in front of it, and they rushed on upstairs after Rayna.

A Japanese sat at the desk when they came in, and

he reached for a gun. Big London whirled, smashing him across the back of the neck with the rifle butt.

"Get at the window," Jim said quietly. "Rayna, if you can shoot, take one of those rifles, but don't waste any shots."

The switch was open and he sat down and slipping on the headphones began to call:

"Calling U.S. Pacific Fleet, any ship . . . calling Pacific Fleet . . . you are running into danger . . . you are running into danger!"

Almost instantly and so quickly it surprised him, a voice snapped in his ear, the tones sharp, incisive: "Come in, please . . . identify yourself?"

"Captain James Mayo, master of the freighter *Semiramis* . . . calling from Tobalai . . . the enemy has planes waiting to take off . . . battleships and submarines in vicinity of Greyhound Strait . . . some planes bear American markings . . ."

Big London's rifle was firing steadily now, and outside shouts of anger could be heard. Above on the tableland a plane's motor broke into a roar. A hail of lead swept the room, but most of it was too high. Rayna was firing now.

Jim stayed at the instrument. "Check with Major Arnold, British Military Intelligence . . . two battleships . . ."

"Hold it!"

Jim turned his head, gun in hand, to see Ross Mallory in the hall.

"They've been holding me here," Mallory said. "Let me in on this!"

"Is this a double-cross?" Jim demanded harshly. "Mallory, you start anything now and I'll kill you!"

"Nothing like that. They had me in a tight spot. I was supposed to do the broadcast that made them think the American planes were returning early." Mallory was sweating. "I can't do it, no matter what it costs me. Here . . ." He handed Mayo a notebook.

Jim glanced down at the notebook, open at the page. "Those are the forces here," Mallory said. "Tell them."

Ponga Jim snapped into the mouthpiece: "Are you there?"

"Waiting," the voice was cool.

"Two battleships, *Nagato* class . . . three cruisers of the *Myokos* class, one *Furutaka* . . . at least ten submarines."

The firing was a steady roar now, and leaving the switch open, Jim jumped from the radio and grabbed up a rifle. Down below the men were trying to mount the stairs with Mallory holding it with bursts from a light machine gun.

They tried a rush, but the machine gun and Jim's rifle stopped it. Then a single shot rang out and Mallory backed up, coughing. The long gun started to slip from his hands and Jim caught it, charging halfway down the stairs, the gun chattering.

The crowd of Japanese melted, and Jim raced back up the steps. He grabbed up more ammunition, stuffing it in his pockets. Then, he lifted the machine gun and fired a burst at the nearest gasoline storage tank.

The tracers hit the tank and there was a terrific blast of fire; a wave of heat struck them like a blow.

The barracks sagged with the power of it, and then yells and screams lifted and were lost in the roaring inferno of the burning gasoline.

Catching Rayna by the hand, Jim yelled at Big London. Mallory was dead. Evidently, something crooked he had done in the past had given the spies a hold over him, but he had died a brave death in the end. The three raced down the stairs, forgotten in the roaring flames outside. Running, they started up a back trail to the plateau above.

Suddenly, from behind them there was a gigantic explosion that almost knocked them to their knees. "The other tank," Jim said.

They ran on, gasping for breath. The jungle had been showered with gasoline and flame, and burning and blackened shreds of foliage were falling around them. They reached the plateau in a dense cloud of smoke. Several Japanese saw them and ran forward. Ponga Jim opened up, firing a burst, then dashed for a plane.

Suddenly, from nowhere, Lyssy was beside them.

"The ship!" he yelled. Flames danced on his brown face and his staring eyes. "The ship, she come!"

Turning, Ponga Jim looked down. True enough, the old *Semiramis* was below, lying a half mile off shore. Even as they watched, her guns belched fire. She was firing on a Japanese submarine.

Jim wheeled, passing the machine gun to Big London.

"Go to the ship!" he shouted. "Hurry!"

"What about you?" Rayna cried, catching his sleeve.

"I'm going up there," he said.

Then he was gone, running for an idling plane. It was a captured fighter, probably taken from another supply ship taking American planes to the East Indies.

A Japanese was just getting into the seat, and Jim grabbed him, jerking him back. The flyer fell awkwardly, and a mechanic started to run around the plane, but Jim was already in, and in a matter of seconds the plane went roaring down the plateau. Just in time, he eased back on the stick and the fighter shot aloft.

Only a few planes remained on the field, for most of them had taken off just before the explosion of the first tank. Jim leveled off and opened the throttle wide, heading for Greyhound Strait.

What was happening up ahead he could only guess. There was a silence that worried him. Still, he had far to go. He swung wide, turning to go south of Taliabu.

Like a bullet from a gun, his ship roared through the sky at three hundred miles an hour.

Easing back on the stick, he climbed, reaching for more and more altitude. Then, through a break in the clouds, he saw it, the splendid majesty of the fleet, moving up the sea in formation, but no longer headed for a deadly surprise, now for a battle. Almost automatically, he had slipped into his 'chute.

Then, lower down and ahead of him, already swinging toward the fleet, he saw the flight of false American planes. The decks of the carriers were partially empty, indicating that they had launched aircraft in pursuit of the Japanese warships that had been intended as bait. Jim prayed that they would stay away from the coming battle and not add to the confusion and slaughter.

Ponga Jim looked down at the formation of planes, then at the fleet below them and ahead. With a grin and a wave to the gods who watch over fools and flyers, he pushed the stick forward. The nose went down and he opened the throttle wide. He was behind them, and with the sun behind him. A perfect start.

The heavy plane went into the roaring crescendo of a power dive, and he saw the air-speed needle climbing up 300 . . . 350 . . . 400 . . . 450, and then he was opening up with all six machine guns and the cannon. A fighter below him swerved and suddenly burst into flame. It crashed into another plane, and the two whirled earthward in a tangled mass of twisting metal. His guns were spewing flame again and in an instant he was in the middle of a dogfight, alone against a dozen enemy planes.

He saw a torpedo plane pull up and go whirling out of sight, then a fighter was in his sights, then he was past and the aircraft was a plummeting mass of wreckage. Ack-ack from the ships opened up and anti-aircraft machine-gun fire laced the sky.

Now that the formation had broken, the Japanese pilots couldn't locate him as quickly in the confusion of the battle. Every plane in the sky had American markings. Yet he knew that anything flying was his enemy. Fighting like a demon, and using the ship as though it were part of him, he circled, spun, dove, and climbed, fighting the ships with everything it had. In the middle of it, he glanced upward and saw something that made his heart jolt with fear. High above he saw a fighter ship peel off of a new formation and come shooting down toward them, and after it a long string of others. The American planes! The returning planes from the carriers!

Down below he could see the belching guns, and hear the mighty thunder of crashing cannon as the Japanese ships opened fire. But then he was shooting upward, climbing out and praying that he wouldn't be shot down by his own countrymen.

They fell upon the Japanese-piloted aircraft and suddenly Jim could see the method to their madness. Every American pilot had his cockpit canopy slid back. They were taking a horrible buffeting but, at close range at least, they could identify each other. Jim ripped the Perspex windscreen back and wheeled back into the fray.

A ship showed in his sights and he opened up, ripping a long line of holes down the side, and the plane suddenly turned into flame, and fell from sight.

How long he fought he didn't know, or how many ships he downed, but then suddenly, he saw a torpedo bomber headed toward a battleship, and he did an Immelmann and whipped around on the bomber's tail. The rear gunner opened fire on him, but he roared on into the blazing guns, his own, one steady stream of fire.

He was coming in from slightly below and suddenly, a shell from his cannon hit the torpedo on the enemy plane. There was a terrific blast of fire, and a crash like thunder, and then his own plane, hit by a barrage of flying fragments, dove crazily.

For an instant he righted it, but one wing was vibrating wildly and he knew he was finished. He struggled with the crash belts, a plane dove toward him, its guns roaring, and something struck him a terrific blow on the head.

In a blaze of pain lighted by the burning bomber, and accompanied by the rising crescendo of exploding shells, he turned back to the controls. He dropped toward the water, using his flaps to kill his speed and skipping across the ocean, like a stone. He saw sky and water, his body was pounded by forces he couldn't identify, whirled and slapped and was finally drenched with salty water laced with gasoline. He slipped out of the belts, gave thanks that the canopy was already open, and then lost consciousness.

It was a long time later when he opened his eyes, and for an instant he could not remember what had happened. Around him were the familiar sights of his own cabin on the *Semiramis*. He tried to sit up, and pain struck him like a physical blow. For an instant everything was black, then he opened his eyes.

Major Arnold was standing over him, a look of concern on his face. Ponga Jim grinned, painfully.

"Always show up in time for the payoff, don't you?" he said.

Arnold smiled. "I showed up in time to fish you out of the water, and if I hadn't you would have been feeding the fish by now."

"What happened?" Jim asked.

Arnold shrugged. "What would happen? Once our boys knew what the score was they moved in and mopped up. Seven destroyers sunk, one battle-ship, and two cruisers. The fighting is over except for a few cleanup jobs.

"I was with your fleet, and they got planes off the carriers right away and hit the Jap ships from above before they were expecting it. They caught two of the cruisers inside the reef near Parigi and they never got out."

"How about this boat?" Ponga Jim asked.

Slug Brophy stepped up, grinning. He had a welt on his cheekbone and a long gash on his head.

"I got to the Gunner. Longboy had already got loose. They only left a few men aboard once they had the planes off. So we took over."

"Sounds like it was a swell scrap," Jim mumbled. He looked at Arnold. "I got a real crew, William. I got some good boys!"

"Right you are," Arnold agreed. "They handled it nicely."

"Did any of them get away?" Jim asked seriously.

"Only one," Brophy said. "But we got two sub-marines before they could dive, and laid a couple of shells aboard a battlewagon. The Gunner always wanted to shoot at a battlewagon," Brophy added.

"Here's somebody who wants to talk to you," Arnold said as the girl appeared. "I don't get it, Mayo. Here I am, handsome, with a smooth-looking white and gold uniform, romantic eyes and the figure of a Greek god, and yet you get all the women!"

"It's the poissonality, William!" Jim sighed, grinning. "It's the poissonality!"

AFTERWORD

By Beau L'Amour

Thanks for reading *With These Hands*. It is the final book in a series of four that we began with *Beyond the Great Snow Mountains*. *With These Hands* includes "Gloves for a Tiger," the second sale of a short story that Louis ever made—it came almost two years after his "Anything for a Pal" and was a turning point in his life. Unlike the disheartening dry spell following "Pal," "Gloves for a Tiger" was the first in a string of sales that lasted until he left for Europe during World War II. Louis was in his middle thirties and it was the first time in his life that he could say that he had a career.

With These Hands contains the final installments of several Louis L'Amour series. "Flight to Enbetu" and "Pirates of the Sky" wrap up the Turk Madden stories, and "Voyage to Tobalai" is the last of the Ponga Jim Mayo series. "Dream Fighter" is the first of the Kip Morgan stories, although instead of being a hard-boiled crime story it is an amusing boxing yarn. Kip also appears in "Corpse on the Carpet"; he's not quite a detective yet, but "Corpse" is definitely a thriller set on the streets of 1940s L.A. These two stories complete the Kip Morgan set, and "The Sucker Switch" wraps it up for P.I. Neil Shannon.

The Louis L'Amour Biography Project has turned a corner and is beginning to wind down the research machine. Materials are now being organized and with any luck my writing will begin in 2002 or 2003. I would like to thank everyone who has helped out so much and to remind anyone who knew Louis in the 1908 to 1961 time period that they can still contact the Biography via the Biography Project section of louislamour.com.

louislamour.com has finally got its Louis L'Amour's Lost Treasures web site up and running. It is a subscription service that gives you access to a rotating archive of Louis's papers: unfinished stories and novels, notes, articles by Louis on writing, research, travel, and history. Also included will be complete treatments on stories that were never written, personal and business correspondence, uncollected short stories, and much more. With luck we will be able to turn louislamour.com into a portal to anything and everything that you ever wanted to know about Louis L'Amour.

Thank you all again for coming to the well time after time.

ABOUT LOUIS L'AMOUR

> *"I think of myself in the oral tradition—as a troubadour, a village tale-teller, the man in the shadows of the campfire. That's the way I'd like to be remembered—as a storyteller. A good storyteller."*

It is doubtful that any author could be as at home in the world re-created in his novels as Louis Dearborn L'Amour. Not only could he physically fill the boots of the rugged characters he wrote about, but he literally "walked the land my characters walk." His personal experiences as well as his lifelong devotion to historical research combined to give Mr. L'Amour the unique knowledge and understanding of people, events, and the challenge of the American frontier that became the hallmarks of his popularity.

Of French-Irish descent, Mr. L'Amour could trace his own family in North America back to the early 1600s and follow their steady progression westward, "always on the frontier." As a boy growing up in Jamestown, North Dakota, he absorbed all he could about his family's frontier heritage, including the story of his great-grandfather who was scalped by Sioux warriors.

Spurred by an eager curiosity and desire to broaden

his horizons, Mr. L'Amour left home at the age of fifteen and enjoyed a wide variety of jobs, including seaman, lumberjack, elephant handler, skinner of dead cattle, and miner, and was an officer in the transportation corps during World War II. During his "yondering" days he also circled the world on a freighter, sailed a dhow on the Red Sea, was shipwrecked in the West Indies and stranded in the Mojave Desert. He won fifty-one of fifty-nine fights as a professional boxer and worked as a journalist and lecturer. He was a voracious reader and collector of rare books. His personal library contained 17,000 volumes.

Mr. L'Amour "wanted to write almost from the time I could talk." After developing a widespread following for his many frontier and adventure stories written for fiction magazines, Mr. L'Amour published his first full-length novel, *Hondo,* in the United States in 1953. Every one of his more than 120 books is in print; there are more than 270 million copies of his books in print worldwide, making him one of the bestselling authors in modern literary history. His books have been translated into twenty languages, and more than forty-five of his novels and stories have been made into feature films and television movies.

His hardcover bestsellers include *The Lonesome Gods, The Walking Drum* (his twelfth-century historical novel), *Jubal Sackett, Last of the Breed, and The Haunted Mesa.* His memoir, *Education of a Wandering Man,* was a leading bestseller in 1989. Audio dramatizations and adaptations of many

L'Amour stories are available on cassette tapes from Bantam Audio Publishing.

The recipient of many great honors and awards, in 1983 Mr. L'Amour became the first novelist ever to be awarded the Congressional Gold Medal by the United States Congress in honor of his life's work. In 1984 he was also awarded the Medal of Freedom by President Reagan.

Louis L'Amour died on June 10, 1988. His wife, Kathy, and their two children, Beau and Angelique, carry the L'Amour publishing tradition forward.